COTTONMOUTHS

COTTONMOUTHS

A NOVEL

KELLY J. FORD

Skyhorse Publishing

First Edition

This is a work of fiction. Names, places, characters, and incidents are either the products of the author's imagination or are used fictitiously.

Skyhorse Publishing books may be purchased in bulk at special discounts for sales promotion, corporate gifts, fund-raising, or educational purposes. Special editions can also be created to specifications. For details, contactthe Special Sales Department, Skyhorse Publishing, 307 West 36th Street, 11th Floor, New York, NY 10018 or info@skyhorsepublishing.com.

Skyhorse® and Skyhorse Publishing® are registered trademarks of Skyhorse Publishing, Inc.®, a Delaware corporation.

Visit our website at www.skyhorsepublishing.com.

10 9 8 7 6 5 4 3 2 1

Library of Congress Cataloging-in-Publication Data is available on file.

Cover design by Sarah Pruski.

Print ISBN: 978-1-5107-1915-6
Ebook ISBN: 978-1-5107-1916-3

Printed in the United States of America.

For Sarah

CHAPTER ONE

From behind, the woman standing with a guy next to the Love's Truck Stop air pump looked like any other woman: long hair, too skinny, big purse, big sunglasses. But when the woman turned and smiled, Emily's chest tightened and her insides tingled in a forgotten but familiar way. Rumors of Jody's return had come as whispers around town, but until now Emily had lacked proof.

A warm breeze blew petroleum fumes and cigarette smoke into her face while she sought further confirmation of who she'd seen. Gas spilled onto her hand. Startled, she released the trigger on the pump and swiped her hand across her jeans. She sheltered her eyes from the sun to scan the parking lot. But the woman and the guy were gone.

Back on the highway, Emily tried to keep her mind as empty and barren as the farmland that rolled by. When that didn't work, she turned up the radio and hit scan, unable to settle on the station offerings from the nearest town—country or Christian or the same four pop songs on repeat interspersed with commercials for pawn shops and car lots. Midway through the miles she punched the radio off and tried to tell herself that her new fast food job and her time at home were temporary, though she'd been back a month already.

She hadn't meant to apply for the job. She'd talked to the woman at the temp agency like her mom had suggested. The woman had responded the way Emily had expected: sorry, but they didn't have anything for someone with her lack of professional experience. Best try fast food, the woman had said. The woman's coworker had lifted her eyes, and Emily had detected smugness in her smile. Angry and wallowing in self-pity, she had asked for and filled out a job application during her value meal lunch at a restaurant she'd spotted on the way home. She hadn't expected the manager to offer her a job—on the same day that she applied, after a rushed interview whose only purpose seemed to be to ensure she wasn't a criminal.

She had accepted. There was no choice.

Soon, though, she lied to the empty passenger seat, she'd get a call for a job she really wanted or some other professional job she didn't really care for, but at least it would be a real job, something that could make a dent in student loan and credit card accounts that sat on the brink of default and whose balances kept her up at night. That sounded good until the CDs and candle holders and assorted junk drawer contents in the last moving box she couldn't bring herself to remove from her car rattled in the back seat. If she took that last moving box inside her parents' house, she feared she'd never leave Drear's Bluff.

The dream of next week dissolved into the hot, stale air that surrounded her. She had sold her couch, her bed, her pots and pans. There was no need for those things now. Where she was headed, the cast iron skillet had been seasoned before she was born.

Her mom would cook the beans, potatoes, and cornbread the way her own mother had taught her. Dad would recite the Lord's

Prayer because it required no thought. And Emily would stare at her plate of food and let it go cold while pondering the headset and the cash register and the brown and blue uniform in her back seat, whose fibers still held its last tenant's stench of fryer grease and body odor—items for a life she had not expected to return to when she left for college, for a job that would not have been offered to her at all had she not removed the name of the state university from her resume—though two years hardly called for its inclusion.

Two years in, after failing to meet the grade requirements to keep her partial scholarship and other financial aid, she'd quit. Six months after quitting, she'd gotten a call from her mom asking why they had received a student loan bill in the mail when she wasn't supposed to graduate for at least two more years. Now, here she was. Back with debt for a degree she hadn't earned.

As the road came into sight—the one that led to her childhood home, and her parents, and their accompanying disappointment in her—she drove past it, beyond the mile markers, in a direction she had not driven in years, led on by a thought formed in the parking lot of the truck stop with no idea what she would find once she got there.

Drear's Bluff's main drag looked like every other small town. There were the necessities: a post office, a floral shop for homecomings and Valentine's Days and birthdays and graduations, and the feed store. Here, the men were men and women were women. Roles were handed out and passed down like the matriarchs' afghan quilts, biscuit recipes, and stories.

She slowed the car when she came to the Quik-a-Way gas station-slash-everything mart and roadside diner. Every Sunday for as long as the Quik-a-Way had been around, the old men sat at the counter, sipped their hot coffee, and waited for their wives to finish gossiping. They never tired of talk about the good old days, when the farms were theirs alone, no corporate middlemen to answer to, no undue rules and regulations. All the farmers, including Emily's dad, would pull on their green John Deere hats and disappear behind storms of dirt that trailed their tractors. They prided themselves on eating their Cream of Wheat and tightening their belts and working hard like everyone in Drear's Bluff had been taught. Folks liked to slap their knees and joke that there were only two classes of people in Drear's Bluff: poor and dirt-poor. The poor weren't really poor. They just liked to say they were. The dirt-poor were still dirt-poor but they liked to think they weren't. And most of the working fields, the ones that paid for supper, were good and gone.

Out of habit, she spied the parking lot for familiar vehicles. She didn't recognize any of them. These cars belonged to the current crop of seniors and juniors who were there to grab a burger or a Mountain Dew before they headed off to evening shifts at restaurants and stores in towns bigger than Drear's Bluff. They didn't know now, but in a year or two these kids might appreciate the simplicity and comfort of having somewhere to go every day that required no input, no guilt. You went to school. You ate lunch. You went home.

Once she left the highway and the outskirts of Drear's Bluff behind, the smooth asphalt shifted to a rumble. She cursed the potholes in the dirt road, unearthed by thunderstorms and hardened into craters that destroyed tires. The branches hung low and thick with dust kicked up from what little traffic barreled down the dead-end red clay road. The dust drifted into the car, coating the dashboard and causing her to sneeze. The soaring grain silos of Johnston's farm came into view. Along with their farm, they kept a stable of horses that they sometimes rode in the Old Fort Days Rodeo Parade. The horses dotted the horizon. As she'd done as a child, Emily adjusted her gaze so that the sky and grass looked connected by the barbed wire fence with a Frankenstein stitch, so that a horse looked like it'd been caught on the metal thorn. She navigated her car farther into the deep recesses of woods, past roads without markers and faded No Hunting signs riddled with buckshot, past the entrance to Lee Creek, where countless teenagers had indulged in their first drink, smoke, kiss, and heartbreak.

Two pale, skinny, and shirtless teenage boys walked along the side, near a dry ditch. One of the boys held a shotgun. The other, a red plastic gas can. Their ATV had probably run out of gas while they were out in the woods shooting songbirds for sport. Emily slowed the car when she passed them. She lifted an index finger off the steering wheel for a one-finger wave. Two sets of dead eyes stared back at her, like the boys had been beat on a few too many times. They returned the gesture and disappeared in the car's cloud of dust.

Her nerves pricked as she drew closer to that familiar plot of land. She came to the end of the road and paused at the faded black mailbox and the metal farm gate that stood wide open. Knots that had begun to cramp her gut told her to turn around, best to let some things lie, but a stronger current of curiosity and what ifs overtook her and she made the turn. Trees in desperate need of a trim scraped the sides of the car until she came to the clearing. Her heart drummed at the sight of the trees, the dirt drive that snaked up the hill, the chicken house, the uncut grass—all recognizable but unfamiliar.

She would have put the car in reverse and driven ten miles back to the highway, beyond the high school and the Quik-a-Way, back home, back from the past, shaking her head at the notions that had occupied her mind since she left the truck stop—but there was a witness. She leaned against the long metal panes of the chicken house and let a cigarette burn down in one hand while she gnawed on a fingernail of the other like it was sugar cane. Jody Monroe.

Adrenaline thrummed through Emily. She swallowed hard, tried to ease her mouth for speech. The rumors were true.

Jody stubbed the tip of her cigarette against the chicken house wall and flicked the butt to the ground. She unwound herself one appendage at a time, first dropping one arm, then the other, to drift over to where Emily had stopped the car. Any trace of Jody's mom in her looks had been masked by her unknown father's far more pervasive DNA, leaving Jody with an ever-present uncertainty of her origins and no way for her to answer that persistent question: "Where are you from?"

While her mom was straight out of a country boy's wet dream with her smooth, sandy blonde locks and plunging, sunbaked cleavage dressed to attract eyes like fruit flies to a rotting apple, Jody looked like she'd stepped out of a '90s photo shoot with ink-black, bed-head hair and heavy-lidded eyes. Tall for a girl. Skinny. Pure heroin chic.

Jody crouched down and propped her hands on the car's windowsill. Her worn black T-shirt swooped low. Her chest and cheeks had grown even sharper since high school, unlike Emily's, which were pasty except for the occasional sun splotch, with a strong affinity for shelving baby fat.

Thanks to the always-faulty A/C in her car, the rush of wind from the rolled-down windows had tornadoed Emily's hair. She smoothed it and pushed a strand of hair away from her face, conscious of the shirt and pants she'd worn for the failed temp agency interview, which did little to hide curves that would have been appreciated in a different era.

Jody's eyes didn't jump to the next distraction the way they had when she was younger. She surveyed Emily and said, "You smell like fries."

The semi-sweet, burnt-coffee smell of weed hung in the air, followed by the stench of ammonia and rotten eggs from the chicken house, delivered to their noses by an uptick in the wind.

Emily cleared her throat and positioned her shaking hands under her legs. "You smell like high school."

Jody's mouth broke into a smile. "What the hell are you doing back in Drear's Bluff?"

Emily had avoided church and inevitable versions of this question all month, even though she knew her mom told people that she was just taking a break for a semester. Emily hoped that they would forget the excuse when the semester ended and she was still there. She had left town a success—an acceptance to college!—and she had come back a failure. None of them wanted to broadcast that.

"I could ask the same of you," Emily said.

Jody swung her hand out. "Won the redneck lotto. Didn't you hear?"

She had not heard. In the years she'd been away, Emily had received unsolicited texts full of gossip from her mom along with questions about her grades and whether she'd gained any more weight, followed by complaints about how long it'd been since she'd come home. Her mom had sent one text about Jody. A rumor about her being pregnant. Emily remembered reading that text during the Principles of Biology class she was trying but failing to pass. She remembered how she had cried and the looks from the guy who sat on her right. She remembered her surprise at those tears and how she had blamed them on stress from homework and classes. She had asked for more information about the rumor. But that was all her mom had heard. Nothing more. Nothing to let her know if the rumor was fact. Nothing about where Jody lived now.

Emily had come here with Jody when they were younger but she couldn't remember it looking like this. Rust rained down the metal siding of the chicken house to the right. She could just see the roof of the mobile home that sat at the top of the hill. Gutted cars and discarded farm parts had been piled here and there. The property lacked a spread of trees to cover some of the depression. Other than one big maple in the front, there was nothing to recommend the place as fit for living. She did remember how Jody's grandma had watched Emily like she might try to steal one of her porcelain Precious Moments figurines or a chipped coffee cup from Dogpatch USA. Every other sentence from Jody's grandpa included the words "switch" and "kill."

Jody stood and stretched. "Grandpa got sick, and Mom sure as hell wasn't gonna come back to Drear's Bluff to take care of him. That left me. He passed about a year after Grandma."

"I'm sorry."

"Thanks. He was old, though. And ornery." She planted her hands on her hips and raised her eyebrows. "So college, huh? I heard you went." She whistled and grinned. "I knew you'd make something of yourself. You join one of them sororities?"

Emily wondered who had shared that bit of information. But word got around town whether you liked it or not. "What do you think?"

"Nah. I guess it ain't your style. Though I bet you would get on just fine with them girls. I hear they like to experiment," she said and winked.

Emily used to warm at such veiled references. At the rumors that flew around school about her and Jody just because they lived together for a handful of months when Jody's mom wasn't up to the challenge of mothering. Nothing had ever happened. Nothing but a close encounter in the woods across the creek. Her first kiss. Jody high on pot and the idea of leaving Drear's Bluff, which she did a month later. The moment shocking, quick, unforgettable, but not destined to happen again. They'd gone home and never spoken of it, though the moment reverberated within Emily still.

That was the worst of it, to be accused but denied the pleasure of what everyone thought.

"Well, I hear you don't even need to be in a sorority to experiment," Emily said. "Sometimes, all it takes is a little pot."

"That's fair." Jody laughed, but Emily doubted she got the reference. "You get lost on your way home? What are you doing all the way out here?"

Jody lived in the last house on a dead end in the woods. If you ended up in Jody's drive, you meant to be there. No lie would suffice. "I thought I saw you today, out at the Love's on I-40. I had time to kill." She checked her watch like it was no special thing to drive so far out of her way to see if an old friend happened to have returned.

Jody scratched her nose and kicked the dirt. "Must've been someone else. I been here all day." Something at the top of the hill distracted Jody. "I'd invite you up," she said, followed by a long pause. "Not really your crowd, though. I know how much you hate parties."

"I used to. People change."

"That's what they say. I have my doubts." Jody tilted her head. "You didn't really say why you're here."

Emily had toyed with various lies the whole ride over. "I don't want to go home," Emily said.

Jody chewed on a nail again, looking every bit like she was going to serve up some excuse and send Emily on her way. "Well, you've come to the right place, then." Jody pulled the handle on her door and opened it.

Emily stepped out. Before she knew what was happening, Jody wrapped her in a full embrace. Emily stiffened out of habit in Jody's presence, arms at her side. The scent of honeysuckle in Jody's hair sent her back to a time when Jody had teased the nectar out on its string and held it up for Emily to taste. She turned her head and let her nose graze the space behind Jody's ear. An ache bloomed in Emily from distant to present and settled in a spot below her stomach, casting nets to every nerve. She breathed in and held on until Jody made the first move toward release. Then, she let go as if ready as well.

Jody started up the hill and shouted out behind her. "Don't say I didn't warn you."

Underneath those words, Jody warned of something else. If Emily let her mind wander, she would remember. Instead, she locked her car and ran to catch up.

Behind the trailer, flames gathered in a funnel and spit sparks into the air while a handful of people stood around, their faces darkened by the shade of trees in the dying daylight. Emily half dreaded and half hoped that these shadows belonged to old high school classmates. Dread at the prospect that her life had taken a detour but ended up right back where she started, where they were. As for hope, she could continue the lie that she was in Drear's Bluff temporarily, boost her self-esteem by comparing her life to theirs, which she imagined included single-wide trailers, jobs at chicken plants in Fort Smith, babies with saggy britches and diaper rash.

They didn't disappoint. Most of the partygoers were already drunk or stoned. They looked like the type of kids who hung out in the dugouts before school, smoking and drinking whiskey out of Mountain Dew bottles. People who looked twenty years older than they were, the breakouts on their faces the primary marker of their youth. People who'd never set foot outside state lines.

She only recognized one of them.

Troy Barnett stood with a trio of girls who couldn't get enough of whatever lies he was telling them.

When Jody came to live with Emily and her parents, Emily had split her babysitting duties with her. Their only charge had been Troy, though he'd hardly needed a babysitter at his age. But Marjorie didn't like leaving him home alone while she worked at the Quik-a-Way. He'd scream if Emily tried to get him to behave, but he did whatever Jody asked.

Emily had last seen him when she'd come home for her mom's birthday the previous October. Somehow Marjorie had convinced him to come along as well. She and Emily's mom had gossiped about people the same way they had since grade school. Meanwhile, Emily had slumped on the couch, glazing over at the local news on the muted TV as Troy had gone on and on to Emily's dad—who humored him—about how many touchdowns he'd made, how many scouts were interested in him, and how many girls he'd banged. Her dad had unmuted the TV after that last bit of info.

By the end of that same month, Emily's mom had texted her with news about Troy's knee injury. By December, his subsequent addiction to pain pills. And by February, his withdrawal from high school a few months shy of graduation. One minute, Troy was the most valued football player in school. The next, a washed-up dropout. Football injuries and unplanned pregnancies had killed the dreams of Drear's Bluff's youth for years.

"What's he doing here?" Emily asked.

"Who?" Jody looked in the direction of Emily's stare. "Oh. He comes around." Jody knocked the metal leg of a guy's chair with her foot. "Move over."

The guy playfully smacked Jody on the leg before moving over to make room. Jody dropped a lawn chair to the ground and motioned Emily toward it.

"Jody and I let him hang around when his mom's on a tear," the guy offered.

Jody and I. Like surrogate parents. Jody cut her eyes at the guy but declined to elaborate. Emily drew her gaze from his face to his feet. He was the sort of man who would appeal to someone like Jody, what with his manly build, tan skin, and dust-covered jeans—like he'd been out herding cattle or fighting in the dirt outside a bar. He wore an irritating almost-beard that showed a lack of commitment. One side of his mouth had a lump from where he sucked on a wad of chew. Jody was just like her mom. They had a history of wanting the wrongest man they could find.

The guy tugged the bill down on his sun-faded baseball cap and glanced at Emily. The eyes and mouth and nose fit the features of a brown-haired 2A football star who'd been a few grades ahead of her in high school. A name came to her: August Ward. He'd been a hometown hero back in the day, on account of a touchdown that almost got them to state. Almost. Troy had been last year's version of him, and this year there would be another version of Troy.

August reached around to the cooler behind him and held out a can of Milwaukee's Best. Cold water dripped onto her pants and created a dark spot. She reached for the beer, and he pulled it away, holding it close to his chest, lips screwed up into a grin. "You're legal, right?"

She yanked the can out of his hand and glanced at Troy. "Like that matters." The fizz tickled her hand when she popped the tab and half-drained it while it was still ice cold and she could stand the taste.

Jody wandered over to a makeshift table fashioned out of two sawhorses and a plank of plywood and covered with empty bottles and balled-up napkins. She increased the volume on an old gray boom box, and thrash metal drowned out the buzzing of bugs in the thicket nearby. Jody swayed her hips and head like she had when they'd stayed up late and danced in their PJs before Jody left town. Pop moves set to metal. August drank in the sight of Jody and all the curves of her body like she was a cold beer, a look Emily thought must have easily landed him the hearts of women like Jody.

The beer hit her bloodstream, removing the already tenuous filter she had on her tongue. "Are you and Jody dating?"

He pursed his lips to keep from smiling and refused to answer. He leaned forward, elbows on knees.

She sucked down her beer quicker than she knew she ought to, urged on by the need to know who these people were to Jody and by how little she knew about Jody's life now. "She lived with us for a while."

"I know," he said. "After her mom had her accident."

Emily had thought she and her parents were the only ones who knew how Jody had found Connie on the floor, vomit in her hair and on her face. How she'd called Sheriff Jenkins, thinking her mom had died and not knowing who else to call or what to do. How Emily had felt when Connie had brought Jody to the house, how Jody walked right past her and quietly shut the door to her new room as Connie cried and thanked Emily's mom before taking off for parts unknown. Her heart broke a little knowing that Jody had seen that. Emily couldn't imagine being in a similar situation with her mom, who would never puke. It was unladylike.

All that shared history and knowledge—and she knew nothing of this man who sat next to her.

"Funny," she said. "I never heard her mention you."

"Is that any way to treat a guy who lets you drink his beer?"

She returned his smile out of spite and gulped down the last of the can, though her stomach had begun to complain about the volume of liquid and the speed with which it had been consumed. Her body grew warm, her nose numb.

"I'm not her boyfriend. Not anymore." He lifted his can and took a drink. "So have at it."

"Like she's yours to offer?" She couldn't help but laugh. "Thanks for your permission. But it's not necessary."

He leaned in close, so close she could smell hints of cedar and citrus in his cologne. His breath heated her face. She edged away from him, worried that she'd been too bold.

"All I'm saying is, do what you want. I don't give a shit what you do or who you do it with," he said. He leaned back, yanked another beer from the cooler and handed it to her. "Bottoms up."

She tapped her can against his and tried to ease the grip of tension in her shoulders.

The sun had disappeared below the trees, and dusk deepened the shadows and the chill. Troy wandered to their side of the fire and stabbed it with a long metal rod. Ashes spit into the air in complaint. He wiped his nose. Finally, her face seemed to register in the loose threads of his memory.

"I heard you was back," he said.

"I heard you dropped out." The same could be said of her. A part of Emily wished that her mom had told everyone the truth—not that she was on a break, but that she had quit—so the whole business would be over and she wouldn't have to keep lying. But her mom must've decided that was too sore a subject for public commentary.

"Missed too many classes. Would've had to retook my whole senior year. Fuck that."

"Definitely." She saluted him with her beer. "Fuck that."

Troy's smile faded. He struggled for words, like he had to formulate his answer without cheating off someone else. "Jody was always cooler than you." He threw a log on the fire and let it spray sparks as he wandered off to the woods.

Troy had always made sure that Emily knew it. Even with her pride at its lowest, the comment stung.

August's eyes stayed on Troy, as if waiting for him to do something stupid.

Jody slipped beside August and sat down. Her smile pitched to the side, like it was too much effort to lift more than one half of her face. She circled the top of the beer can with her finger. Without looking up, she wiped the water onto August's jeans, tilted the can, and held the beer in her mouth before letting it glide down her throat. Then, she leaned back in her chair, looking pleased at the gathering of people.

Troy came back with an armload of brush, bypassing the stack of logs for twigs and leaves. He dumped the lot of it onto the fire. The whole of his shirt was covered in some element of the earth. Dirt, dead or dying bugs, the broken needles of pines.

Jody bolted upright and waved the smoke away. "Goddammit, Troy! I'm gonna find a switch and beat your ass if you don't quit that." She picked up her chair and moved to a spot across the way. Some guy had arrived without Emily noticing. The guy brought out a joint and took a hit. When he passed it to August, he worked his tongue around the wad of chew inside his cheek and spit the lump on the ground. August inhaled, blew smoke out of the side of his mouth, and held the joint out to Emily.

Jody stared at her, expectant.

In junior high, police officers had come to school for the D.A.R.E. program. Emily remembered peering into a Plexiglas-covered suitcase and seeing all the drugs neatly organized, glued in place with labels describing what they were: heroin, cocaine, LSD, opiates, marijuana. For something so dangerous, the display made the drugs seem silly, not cool at all.

Emily had always declined when Jody offered her weed; Jody had always rolled her eyes. Finally, in college, after all that time saying no and craving that same stream of laughter that promised a release from her anxieties over classes and money, Emily tried it. The experiment had not lifted her mood, only heightened the memories of the smell that had permeated her clothes after time spent with Jody.

"No, thanks," she said. "Irritates my throat."

Lit by an idea, Troy ran outside the circle of partygoers and came back into the firelight within a minute. With an unsettling grin, he held a rusted cake pan out to Emily. Clumps of picked-at brownies littered the pan, a vessel of germs from greasy fingers and unwashed hair.

"You don't have to smoke it." Troy's eyes were glazed and piercing at the same time. "Go on," he said, and shoved the pan at her.

August glanced at Emily but looked away. He took another hit of the joint and passed it to the guy on the other side of her. "You don't have to do that."

"I don't need your input on the matter." Emily didn't bother looking away from him or lowering her voice. But she caught Jody staring at her.

Jody cracked a smile and said, "Always the good girl."

An old aggravation surfaced, the one she felt every time she was left watching Jody walk away with someone else. They'd peel out of parking lots, headed to mythical teenage places that Emily could only dream about. The invitation had never been extended to her, but still Jody would find a way to make her feel small, unwilling, unexciting. Jody was wrong. And Emily had a mind to educate Jody on all she didn't know about her.

She tried not to think about whose fingers had touched the pan or where they'd been and scooped a large piece and shoved it into her mouth. A mixture of flour clumps, what tasted like dried twigs, and sugar crystals without a hint of sweetness coalesced. She might as well have reached down and shoveled a handful of dirt into her mouth.

One of the girls that Troy had been talking to yelled from across the fire. "I can't believe you ate them." The girl laughed and plopped into a broke-down lawn chair next to another girl, nearly toppling over in the process. "They're nasty as fuck." Her laughter hung in the air as the rest of the partygoers' words died down, leaving only the music from the boom box until the song ended.

Troy glared at the girl. Night bugs sang out in the pause and one last log cracked and split in half. The girl looked around in confusion, her buzz killed by the sudden quiet of those around her. August drew his cap down.

Jody looked at Emily and smiled. A wild chill spread through her core.

Troy flung the pan at the girl who had laughed at him and those close to her scrambled out of the way. The metal corner hit the girl square in the eye, and August jumped out of his seat. She squawked and clutched her face. Troy was on her in two steps. He'd nearly run through the fire, like he hadn't seen the flames. The sharp clang of metal clattered in the air when his shoe made contact with the pan. He drew his arm back and made a fist. The girl lobbed her small hands toward his face. Limbs and hair and voices seemed to converge all at once as others in the group tried unsuccessfully to separate the two of them. The girls shrieked, some guys laughed. August finally got a handle on Troy's raised fist and dragged him away from the girl.

In the half light of the moon and the flames from the fire, the scene played out like some menacing shadow puppet show.

Emily spun her head to locate Jody and gripped the armrests when the motion made her woozy. She dropped her head between her knees. *Breathe*, she told herself, *breathe*. The sounds of metal and fists connecting with skin and the crackling of the fire mixed with voices and words that she had trouble catching. She lifted her head back up and begged the contents of her stomach to stay down. She ran her hands along her temples and down her jaw to drown all the yelling, screaming, grunting. Those noises were replaced with the scraping sound of her hands on her face, like old sandpaper on smooth wood. Up and down, up and down. Her bones, skin, and nerves seemed to crackle under her palms. Around her, people's mouths moved but she couldn't hear their words. Reverberations lit her toes and moved up her legs to her torso and then back down to her core, which felt like it had exploded into a ball of warmth and tingling, like the center of her body held and spun every inkling of desire she'd ever pushed down into its safe place, every undercurrent of every crush, every twinge in her stomach, every throb between her legs. She gaped at her stomach, expecting it to light up like a sleepy time Glo Worm doll. Instead of illumination, the core of her body pushed her, pushed her up, pushed her out of the chair. *Move*, her body said. *Move*. She let her hands fall from her face and gripped the armrests of her chair. Everything in her sparked.

"This is what they do. This. This." With a will of its own, her mouth moved and released bits of air when she held the *s* at the end of the word she repeated. She clamped her mouth shut. *I have to get out of here*, she thought. *I have to go away. I have to leave.*

"I have to pee," she told no one but the air. They wouldn't question that. That made sense. And no one would follow her. No one would want to follow her. Would they? Something was wrong with her. Words slammed against the inside of her head, fighting to get out. She had to get out. Go home. Home-home, her parents' house.

The canvas of stars above her spun. Or she made her own stars and they spun, she wasn't sure. She made her way to the trailer, glancing behind her to see if anyone followed. The moon came and went behind passing clouds. Voices behind her screeched into the air. She launched into a full run. Trees rushed by, the wind pushed at her face as her speed increased. Her body, Olympian, wild, triumphant in her escape.

But the tread on her shoes couldn't withstand a quick run through grass, and her feet slipped underneath her. She tried to break the fall with her arms but slammed into the ground near the back steps. The wind was knocked out of her, every bump on her spine was ablaze with shooting pain. Her wrist bones throbbed from hitting the ground. She had to get inside.

The stairs appeared to be close together and then far apart. Funhouse stairs. She waited for the bottom step to come closer and then crawled up. Only, she missed the second step and scraped her chin. She finally managed to scramble up the steps on her knees, pull the knob, and crawl into the kitchen.

From where she knelt on the floor, the kitchen cabinets looked enormous. The chairs, for giants. Baby bottles loomed to the ceiling. The rumor was true. She began to cry. *Stop, don't cry.* She tried to sit up but collapsed onto the floor to catch her breath. Fresh pain formed along her tailbone. Now would be the time for the ruby slippers, the clicking of heels, and the waking up, the night nothing but a dream. She placed her head on the cool floor and waited for the nausea to pass.

When she opened her eyes some time later, everything had shifted back to normal size. Jody and August stood above her, arguing.

"You told me we didn't have anything to worry about," August said.

"We don't."

"Then what the hell was that shit he pulled?"

Emily eased herself up on her elbows and sore wrists. They noticed her then and stopped talking. August took hold of one arm and helped her to stand. Every bone complained in response. She brushed the dirt and grime from her hands. Jody took her by the jaw and moved her head from side to side. Emily's chin stung from Jody's grip.

"She can't drive like this," August said. "Owen's been all over the highway. I'll take her home."

"No," Jody said. "She'll stay here tonight."

No. Not like this. She'd sleep at home. In her own bed. At her parents' house. "I have to go," she said. "Supper." She put one foot in front of the other, timid as the first step on a frozen pond, and walked through the dark living room to the front door. "I'm going now."

"You're not going anywhere." Jody yanked her arm and spun her. Emily nearly fell to her knees, sending fresh shots of anger from her joints. Jody had no right to see her like this. She shouldn't see her like this. Emily had to get to her car. She tried to free her arm, but Jody's grip held her tight and burned her skin like she was being wrung to dry.

"I'm fine." *I'm not myself,* she thought. *I don't know what I might say.* She twisted the front of Jody's shirt and sucked in air. "I have to go home. Mom's expecting me for supper."

"It's way past suppertime," Jody said and removed Emily's hands from her shirt. "And you aren't fit to drive."

August opened and then promptly shut his mouth, but his eyes tagged Jody's. They seemed to transmit secret meanings.

"You have something to say?" Jody asked.

August cast his eyes to the linoleum like he had everything to say but no authority to say it. He readjusted his cap and walked out the door.

Jody returned her focus to Emily. "Come on."

She led her through the kitchen. Emily slipped and struggled to lean on Jody. She couldn't control whether her mouth was open or shut and choked on her own saliva. Between coughing and bending over, a stuffed feeling charged up her throat. She thrust her hands out to catch her fall and landed on her knees. A burger, fries, beer, and the brownie came up and out onto the kitchen floor along with great gasps of air. She gagged and heaved until the final bitter strings of spit signaled the end. Cold blasts stung Emily's neck as Jody ran an ice cube along her skin and pushed errant hairs out of her face. When she was able, Emily opened her eyes and retched again at the sight of her own mess on the floor in front of her.

Embarrassed, she pushed Jody away and tried to regain some semblance of dignity and balance. Those efforts failed.

Jody wrapped her ice-cold fingers under Emily's arms and helped her to stand. Her hands moved to Emily's face and cooled her cheeks. "Let's get you cleaned up," she said.

The bedroom was dark, the curtains drawn. When Jody flicked on the overhead light, Emily groaned. She shut her eyes and waited for the piercing light behind her eyelids to recede before opening them again.

The bed took up the majority of the room. The bathroom door had been removed, leaving the toilet in clear view of the bed. If ever there was a room for romance, this was not it. Emily skirted the edges of the wall to get to where Jody yanked shirts and shorts from a dresser, tossing each one behind her on the bed.

"One of these ought to fit you," Jody said.

Emily held up a pair of men's gym shorts. "Who do these belong to?"

"Does it matter?" Jody yanked the shorts out of Emily's hands and tossed them onto the bed before stepping into the bathroom. Water rushed through a faucet, paused, and then sprayed little bullets onto the shower curtain.

Emily stared at the pile of clothing. It did matter.

Jody poked her head out from behind the bathroom doorframe. "Come on," she said and led her into the bathroom. She took the ends of Emily's T-shirt into her hands. Her fingertips grazed the skin at the top of Emily's jeans. Emily had no control over the goose bumps that spread across her skin or the shaking of her legs.

Jody must have noticed. Her hands slipped away, and she withdrew into the bedroom. "There's a spare toothbrush in the cabinet," she said. "I have to go clean up your mess."

Another drunk. Another mess for Jody to manage. Like Jody's mom. Emily's spirit crumpled like a helium-filled balloon whose contents had been sucked out and used for jest—emptied, wrinkled, and left on the floor. She hadn't felt so unbalanced, physically and emotionally, in years. Not since last she'd seen Jody. She didn't drink often, but when she did she could handle it. Pot's effects—and aftermath—had been elusive to her. Until now. She gripped the sink for balance. Steam had overtaken the room. She stripped off her soiled clothes and stepped into the shower. She let the hottest water she could bear run over her head in streams to drown out the embarrassment until the water ran cold.

In the bedroom, Jody lay lumped under the covers, and Emily wondered how long she'd stood under the water while time passed unnoticed. Her heart struggled to find its rhythm against the slow intake of Jody's breath. The harder she tried to breathe normally, the louder her breath seemed. The bedside clock blinked out the time as another minute ticked well past midnight. Her mom would be waiting, angry about the curfew she kept insisting on and Emily kept resisting. Had she been able to foresee the long strings of texts and late-night interrogations about her whereabouts that awaited her at home, Emily might have worked harder in school. The debate raged inside her: go home or get in bed.

She eased herself down under the covers and stretched out on her sore back. She moved the blanket up to her neck and waited for the A/C to kick on. When the whoosh of air filled the room, she eased the air out of her lungs. Exhaustion gripped her, but her mind raced. Off and on, the A/C went; in and out, she tried to breathe normally instead of in jagged gasps brought on by the embarrassment and confusion from the images and words that jammed her mind. Everything that had happened earlier with August and Troy and the fire. Her mind shifted back to the first sight of Jody by the chicken house and the last time she'd seen Jody before that, the night the bed shook with Jody's sobs. She'd made noises behind her clenched teeth, like an animal biting down and tearing at its victim's flesh. Emily had waited for her to speak, worried and eager for some insight into her rage.

After crying some more and huffing some more, Jody's breathing had quieted into the cadence of sleep. She no longer clenched her jaw. Her face relaxed. Whatever troubled her, Emily would have to wait until the morning.

Emily had torn her gaze away from Jody to stare at the stars on her bedroom ceiling. And then she had prayed: *God, make this terrible feeling go away.* Every time Jody slipped into Emily's bed instead of her own, she prayed. She couldn't describe the sensation as anything other than a new kind of pain, deep and pulsing. The hammering between her legs increased the longer she lay there. Ten minutes. Twenty. She squeezed her legs to try and shut down the feeling.

But her hands were beyond her control. They worked their way down her stomach and lifted the elastic on her pajamas. Slowly, she slid her fingers around and around. The pressure that had gripped her changed into the opposite of pain, bursting and spreading, thick and slow from the center of her body.

She lay there under the faded glow-in-the-dark stars, her body quiet. She eased onto her side toward the wall, away from Jody. The images and the worry and the words were gone. Sleep began to overtake her.

Then, Jody had sniffled. Clear as if she'd been awake the whole time.

The morning after, Emily had woken up alone. She'd eased open the door to Jody's room only to find the bed undisturbed and the closet full of empty wire hangers. The only items that remained were lined up on the dresser: Christmas gifts of perfume, an empty heart-shaped picture frame that had held a photo of Jody's latest boyfriend, dried flowers from when Jody had won the Miss Drear's Bluff pageant, gum wrappers. Downstairs, Emily's mom sat at the kitchen table, a coffee cup at her lips, her body stiff. Connie, she told Emily, had picked Jody up at the house early that morning. Jody would finish her senior year in another town.

"That's all I know," her mom had said and sipped her coffee while staring out the window.

Troy's voice rose above the memory, past the bedroom door, and into the dark room. A cabinet slammed, followed by a peal of laughter from multiple voices Emily couldn't place. She sat up in the bed and tried to orient herself in the unfamiliar room with its unfamiliar shadows and angles. Moonlight filtered in from the window in the doorless bathroom. Jody lay beside her, undisturbed. More laughter, heavy footfalls, and the slam of the back door followed. Finally, silence. Emily eased her head onto the pillow, drew the covers over herself, and looked at the long black strands of Jody's hair.

Jody had gone that night and not returned to Drear's Bluff until some time in the past year.

Here Emily was again, back in Drear's Bluff, barely a nickel to her name and Jody Monroe on her mind and beside her. They were not so much older than they had been, yet the years seemed a cave from which she had to claw her way out. Always worried about that night, not wanting to remember the details about why Jody had left.

Now those feelings, the remembrances, were there—under her skin and on her tongue.

She willed Jody to turn over.

Turn over, and I'll tell you everything.

CHAPTER TWO

A SQUEAL STARTLED EMILY AWAKE. Jody rustled beside her and pulled the pillow over her head.

Jody hadn't turned over, and Emily had slept fitfully, fighting heartburn and a headache. She sat up and tried to remind herself where she was. Were it not for the continued throb of her bones and skin scrapes, Emily would have believed that the previous night's events had been a drug-induced dream instead of her own stupidity. Giggles and gurgles came from Jody's side of the bed. The illuminated bars of a baby monitor rose from green to red as the baby raised and lowered its voice. When they were in school, Jody had sworn she'd rather die than end up like other girls who didn't have the good sense to use a condom.

The rumored baby. Was it a he or a she? Did it favor Jody or its mysterious father? She hated the thought of Jody sleeping with a man. She hated the undercurrent of possessiveness that plagued her when she saw Jody again. The way it kept pulling at her, begging to know more about what she had missed while they had been separated. Curiosity nudged her out of bed.

Emily searched the floor for her clothing but found nothing. She grabbed the baby monitor and slipped out of the room. Outside the bedroom door, Emily's clean clothes sat stacked on top of the dryer. Her car keys were on top, as well as her phone. She forced herself to check for the inevitable texts from her mom. There were none that she could see—her phone had one bar of service. She shrugged off the clothes Jody had lent her and replaced them with her own. They smelled like bacon and fabric softener, a comforting combination, though she couldn't remember anyone cooking bacon the night before. Less comforting was her missing underwear. She checked the pockets and inside the dryer and washer. At a loss, she pulled her pants on anyway, tucked the monitor into her back pocket, and made her way through the living room.

She'd been too drunk and stoned and sick the previous night to pay much attention to how Jody had made her grandparents' house her home. Judging from the outside, she hadn't expected much on the inside.

Most of the house was within view of the front door. A waist-high bar with two stools pushed up against it separated the living room from the kitchen. The fake marble linoleum that she'd puked on slightly assisted in lifting the conjoined rooms out of the gloom that the wood-paneled walls and brown carpet cast, even with the curtains held back to let the sun stream in. All the furniture appeared new if not fashionable.

Troy lay sprawled on the couch, bare-chested with his mouth wide open, fumigating the room. She grumbled as she passed him, cursing him for the pot brownies and making himself at home on Jody's couch, like he was a mainstay. Someone who stayed over all the time, the cushions not just accustomed to but welcoming his form.

A noise down the hallway distracted her from the tirade in her mind, and she made her way to a small bedroom. There he was. Rumor in the flesh. A jabbering, baby-boy replica of Jody smiled up at her from the crib he held onto for balance. That pull came at her again. Something about seeing him and knowing he belonged to Jody made her feel all twisty inside, in a way she didn't understand. She knew she should leave, put the baby monitor back in Jody's room, head home, prepare for another round with her mom over not coming home at a decent hour, not calling, not caring. Rinse and repeat. Same as the day before.

"Hey there." She gave the baby time to consider her while she considered his room, which had been painted a light shade of green. Brown baby furniture complemented the brown stuffed bear in the crib with a blue bow tie. The dresser appeared to have been built from some ancient wood that God had meant to endure long after the four horsemen made their ride. On top, a silver frame held a photo of him as a newborn balled up in a sleeping position on silky black fabric. The word that came to mind was not one she would have ever expected to use when referring to something of Jody's: expensive.

When she was sure he wouldn't scream, Emily hoisted the baby out of the crib and onto her hip. A rotten stench drifted to her nose. "Jesus. You smell." She looked around and found the changing table and draped him on it. "Let's get this filthy thing off you."

While she nearly gagged at the sight and smell, he chewed on a rattle and let her clean him. Once more, she considered her earlier plan of leaving him be, heading out of his room and heading home. But all that awaited her was an angry parent and anxieties about her new fast food job that would do nothing for her bank account, let alone her pride. The caretaking and the baby's chatter soothed her nerves. If she took care of the baby, maybe Jody wouldn't mind so much that she had had to take care of Emily the night before.

She didn't want to leave the house yet, not with that last picture of herself in Jody's mind: drunk and puking on the floor. She was more than that. More than another version of Jody's mom.

She lifted him onto her hip and headed out of his bedroom. Walking along the hallway, she patted his freshly diapered butt, enjoying something small in her hands and a purpose to the day.

She had little experience with what should come next, other than a vague notion that it should involve food. She eased the refrigerator and cabinets open as quietly as she could—not for the sake of Troy's slumber. She didn't want to wake Jody.

She followed the directions on a can of formula she found in the cabinet, and had the boy fed and next to her on the floor slobbering on a multicolored plastic chew ring by the time Jody emerged from the bedroom.

After Emily said good morning, Jody tapped the counter with her fingernails and glanced at the baby's breakfast dishes drying on a dishtowel.

"Everything all right?" Emily asked.

"Yeah. Just forgot for a moment that you were here."

The comment irritated Emily, but she tried to ignore it. "Thought maybe I'd help out this morning," Emily said. "You seemed tired."

Jody tugged on the refrigerator door and brought out a jug of orange juice. "Thanks," she said and drank from the bottle, something Emily would have expected from Troy. Emily hated to think that his lips had touched the same object. After she capped the juice, Jody asked, "How are you feeling?"

"Better. Just a little dehydrated." Emily turned away and hoped her shattered pride didn't show on her face. "Thanks for taking care of me. And for washing my clothes."

"Don't worry about it."

"I'm not worried. I'm sorry."

"No need to apologize." Jody scratched at her nose. "It's not like I haven't cleaned up after a drunk before." Additional apologies hung on Emily's tongue but she swallowed them, aware that they would only remind Jody of her mother even more.

She nudged her head toward the couch. "Is he always around?"

Jody focused her attention on a scratch on the surface of the bar. "Here and there. He babysits for me in a pinch."

Troy. The kid who tried to punch a woman in the face the previous night. "You're kidding."

Jody dropped her hands to her sides. "It's not like I have a lot of options."

"Um, there's my mom. Marjorie. Heather." She counted on her fingers and tried to think of any number of other options. "Sally. Misty—"

"I did ask them."

"Which one?"

"Your mom. When I was a little bit late or asked her to watch him at the last minute, she'd throw on the guilt trip. And she was weird."

"What? How?" Her mom had neglected to mention this detail. Her mom was controlling. Old fashioned. Eye-rolly. But weird? No. No one in Drear's Bluff was anything but boring and normal. Weird was the worst thing you could be. Weird was code for all the things they didn't say out loud about someone.

"I don't know. Weird." Jody discarded Emily's question with a wave of the hand. Clearly Jody wasn't in the mood for discussing it in more detail, or admitting how *weird* it was to choose Troy.

Silence filled the air where all her words wanted to be, asking for the scraps of their fractured friendship to be renewed. She fished around in her pockets for her keys and nodded toward the little boy. "He's real cute."

Jody smiled, likely because she was thankful that Emily had dropped the previous subject. "Thanks."

"Your mom seen him?"

She looked like she'd bit into something sour. "Are you kidding me? She didn't even show up for Grandpa's funeral. Her first and only grandchild is hardly reason to return to town. I'd rather Ricky not have anything to do with her anyway. She never did much for me."

Ricky. The faces of men around town popped into her head. None of them fit who Emily thought Jody would end up with. Emily tried to keep the question from coming, but she itched to know. She tried to ask it as innocently as possible. "Does he see his dad much?"

Jody looked at the wall for a while before speaking. "I'd rather not talk about him."

There seemed to be a lot that Emily didn't know and Jody didn't want to talk about. The flush of contentedness Emily had felt earlier slipped away, replaced by a chill.

"If you need it, I can help out with the babysitting," Emily said, offering one last option like a salesman who knows he's already lost the customer but somehow digs into a reservoir of hope that he can clinch a deal. "I'm around."

Jody laughed. "Didn't you drop Lucy's kid on its head? Not to mention letting Troy crash his bike into that barbed wire fence." Jody had ended up in the wire instead after yanking him off the bike. She'd gashed up the inside of her thigh so bad she had to get twelve stitches. Emily wondered what that scar looked like now.

She tried to hide her disappointment and disbelief at who Jody considered worthy of babysitting. The surrogate mom who'd taken Jody in when her own mom ran off? *Too weird.* Emily? *Fuck no. Red flag.* Painkiller-addicted high school dropout? *Absolutely.* "Who the hell doesn't know how to ride a bike at that age anyway?"

Jody leaned on the counter and nodded toward Troy, who slept on, oblivious to their noise and reminiscence. "He's a good kid. Mostly."

Again, Emily flashed to the rage he'd displayed around the fire—at a comment about his baking. "Sure, if your definition of good is no good."

A wave of laughter overtook Jody. "God, I've missed you." Jody wore a dreamy half smile.

The ball of tension that had built within Emily dissolved with Jody's words, those words she'd longed for, any words to let her know that they were okay again. Jody was like a book of stories she'd forgotten until she'd happened upon her the previous day. In that book of stories, Jody was in every one. Sometimes in the foreground, sometimes in the background. But always, always on Emily's stage.

Emily's head throbbed at her hangover and her shifting emotional state, one minute calm, one minute agitated. "I've missed you, too."

"Look. I appreciate the offer, but don't you have school?"

The question triggered her anxiety and sent it into overdrive. She considered possible answers and chose the one that required the least explanation and inconsistency: her mom's. "I'm taking a break for the semester."

"Break or not, you didn't go to college so you could become a babysitter," Jody said. "You need to find a real job and get the hell out of this town, just like we always said."

Jody's prized babysitter let out a half snore, half burp, behind Emily.

A real job? Oh, how she had tried. Instead, she had a brown-and-blue uniform in the backseat of her car. A handshake at the end of the interview. She'd walked out the back door of her new work-place and into the sunshine the day before smelling of the grill and fryer oil, holding a signed copy of her application for employment with a start date at the top scribbled in blue ink. In the ten seconds it had taken her to reach her car, the phrase *How do I get out of this?* had already begun to drum inside her skull.

"I'm not asking for a job," she said. "I was just offering to help out. Anyway, I should get going."

Jody breathed in deeply and then let the air sift out the same way, maddeningly slow. "Like I said, I appreciate it. But I'm good."

Rejection swelled at Jody's casual dismissal of an opportunity to renew their friendship. After all that time away, somehow in Drear's Bluff and in the presence of Jody she had shrunk inside, back into that small girl she felt like she'd been up until high school gradua-tion, as if all the time away had been nothing, with no learning or growing to show for it.

She wanted to ask, "What comes next?" A phone call, drinks, something? Anything? All she could think to say was good-bye.

Outside, the air held all the water it refused to share with the ground. It pressed against her skin, slowing her steps down the hill and toward her car. Fall had officially come that week, but the heat and humidity made it hard to breathe. She swung at the bugs that flew around her head. Daydreams that Emily had indulged of what her and Jody's lives would be like after high school didn't fit the images that surrounded her: the chicken house, the trailer, the abandoned car parts piled in a heap—the last remnants of Jody's grandparents' lives. Those daydreams had consisted of living in a city somewhere, anywhere, so long as they were too far to visit Drear's Bluff more than once a year. Eating dinner every night at restaurants with hip names. Only, she didn't know if that's what Jody had wanted. She didn't know how they would have made any of that happen or if Jody even remembered their shared dreams. She should have thought about that. An unsettling feeling washed over her—those dreams of her youth had a shelf life, and the expiration date had passed.

EMILY WALKED UP THE PATHWAY of cement circles that led from the drive to the kitchen door. Four circles still held a handprint and a name, one for each family member that had helped build the path on that long-ago day. She read the upside-down names as she crossed over each one: *Mom, Dad,* her own name. And at the end, *Jody.* Unlike the others, Jody had added a tagline: *Miss Drear's Bluff.* They'd laughed about it at the time. The silly pageant that Emily's mom had pushed Jody to enter. Not Emily, Jody. Six months Jody had lived with them off and on, and her name was hardened in the family history.

The whole drive home, Emily had tried to avoid thinking about what had happened at Jody's. Now, flashes of the previous night raised themselves like the dead to clatter and clang against the walls of her mind.

Once inside the house, she managed to sneak upstairs unnoticed. Out of habit, she headed toward her childhood bedroom. Surprise greeted her every time she did. Gone was her bed, the girl group posters on the wall, the wreck of lotions and hair ties and wadded paper along the dresser that her mom had always threatened to throw out if she didn't clean it off. Instead, she found a sewing machine, containers of brightly colored fabric and thread, and a glider chair for Emily's mom to sit in and rock without troubling herself to nudge the floor with her toes. Worst of all, the posters had been replaced by a menagerie of cross-stitched quotes, framed and forcing the viewer toward cheerfulness with words like *positive*, *happy*, *smile*, and *pray*.

Jesus, Emily thought, and headed to the spare bedroom where she slept now, Jody's old room.

After tossing on the daybed's hard mattress for a month, Emily understood why Jody was always sneaking into her room at night. The carpet offered more spring in its fibers.

After showering and covering the scrape on her chin from the slip she'd taken on Jody's back stairs, Emily gathered her wet hair into a ponytail and headed downstairs. The heavy scent of rose potpourri penetrated her nose once she hit the bottom step. In the living room, white cotton curtains fluttered with the breeze from the open window. White, the one color to interrupt an overwhelming palette of brown: the carpet, the wooden cross and the wall it hung on, the coffee table where her mom conducted her Friday night prayer circles.

In the hallway, recent family photos had been placed near the kitchen, while the dead hung near the entrance to the living room. There, faded photographs of Dust Bowl ancestors who had lived without the convenience of running water, refrigeration, and easy-to-clean tile waited for her. The prairie wind had both collapsed and preserved their faces. A permanent shadow covered their skin. They whispered to her: *You* don't have to sweep the dust off the floor every hour. *You* don't have to eat canned tumbleweed for supper. *You* dare complain?

Someone crinkled paper in the kitchen. Randy Travis crooned "Are We in Trouble Now?" softly on the radio in the living room. And she heard her mom's voice on the phone somewhere in the house. Words traveled to her: *Emily. Wish. Worried.*

Emily stopped at the last word. There'd been enough silence between the two of them in the past couple of weeks to invoke such a word. She could get back in her car and head . . . where? Those Dust Bowl faces waited. When she was a child, she'd imagined them judging her for crouching on the carpet to watch TV past her bed-time. For listening in on adult conversations she didn't understand. How long before they judged her for leaving Little Rock? For coming home. For quitting.

"Emily?" her dad called out. "Is that you?"

That brief dream of leaving dissipated. She nudged one of the frames off-center and headed into the kitchen.

Her dad sat in the sunlight at the small kitchen table near the window reading his *Handyman* magazine. Age spots had begun to crop up along the receded part of his hairline from too many days on the tractor without a hat. Steam from his coffee twirled up into the air but missed fogging up his glasses.

Emily dropped onto the calico cushion that covered a wooden chair and sat cross-legged. She tore off a piece of the warm monkey bread and shoved the sticky glob of prepackaged biscuits, sugar, cinnamon, pecan, and butter into her mouth to sop up her sour stomach.

"What time'd you get home?"

Emily focused on tearing off another piece of monkey bread and avoided his eyes. "Late."

Her dad held his mug in the air as if to think before he sipped. "You should've called. Your mom gets worried thinking about you out on the roads at night."

"She's something, but she ain't worried." They never talked in that house, not about real things. Not about things like worry. Worry was for people who didn't work hard enough or have faith—in the Lord, in the land, in all the hard-working kin who came before them and paved the road for their current comforts. This was something else. "I don't know why she insists on a curfew." Emily got up from the table and poured herself some coffee. Between that and the monkey bread, she hoped to combat the headache that drilled at her skull. "I'm not a child." Emily sucked sugar-goo off each fingertip and relished the ability that food had to anesthetize her from anything south of fine. "You pissed, too?"

Her dad shook his head and glanced back at his magazine. "I don't want to get into this again. You know the rules."

"What? I'm just talking."

"Maybe you ought to start listening instead."

"I am listening. And what I hear is Mom complaining about every little thing I do. She treats me like a kid." She tried to enjoy the taste of her breakfast but found it hard. "You told me that I could stay here as long as I needed, but she's making me feel a little unwelcome, to be honest."

He smacked her on the arm with the magazine. "You focus on finding a job, and I'll take care of the other stuff."

She couldn't bring herself to tell him that she'd accepted a part-time job as a fast food cashier. She might as well have been unemployed. The shame was the same—at least for her, and, she suspected, her mom. It was bad enough that everyone knew Emily was back in town and not at college, where she was supposed to be. But a fast food job on top of that? Shudder. Emily held onto the hope that a call about a better job would come soon and she wouldn't need to fess up. "Could you share that information with Mom? I think she might have other ideas."

Her dad returned his focus to the magazine.

Sometimes, she longed for his life. The results of his work in the fields were visible. He didn't have to answer questions about what next, or why haven't you done this or that. He'd taken her out on his tractor when she was younger and let her sit in his lap. Row after row, they plowed the field over the roar of the engine. Grass flew up and tickled her nose, unleashing a fit of sneezing that lasted a few days and earned him a good deal of heartburn courtesy of her mom's complaints. He'd never taken her out again. If she'd been a boy, he probably would have ignored her mom.

She picked at the sticky residue on her fingers. "I could take over the farm," she said, half joking, half hoping that he would consider it.

He laughed without looking up from his magazine. "You don't know the first thing about farming."

"I could learn."

"I thought you wanted to be a teacher."

She'd never been able to answer questions about what she wanted to be when she grew up. "I don't recall ever saying that."

"What are your friends from school doing?"

She knew he meant well, but the question made her feel like he thought she was incompetent and incapable of figuring things out for herself. She thought that about herself, but didn't want anyone else to. "Last I heard, they were in the same position."

The few friends she'd had in high school had faded into Drear's Bluff or the surrounding area as young wives and mothers or were currently in the process of ignoring her. Most from college had moved on without her after a few failed attempts at common ground, but none could understand why she had decided to quit halfway through.

He peered at her above the rims of his glasses. "What's this about?"

She slumped in her seat. "I have no idea what I'm supposed to do with my life."

"I don't think anybody does until they're doing it. You just have to keep looking and trying different things. Some people never figure it out."

"Thanks for the reassurance," she said, which made him smile. "I guess you got lucky."

"Farming?" He scoffed and squinted at something he saw out the window. "You know better than to romanticize that."

"Who's gonna take over for you when you retire? Are you gonna keep working until you die?"

His eyes narrowed. "You think I'm that old?"

"No, I'm just thinking about the future."

He patted her on the arm. "You're gonna figure it out. Give it time." The scruff of his beard grew darker at the dimples when he smiled. Something in how his eyes crinkled at the edges reassured her in ways that little else could, not the Bible or the pastor or anyone else. Usually. Today, not so much.

"You ought to get a move on." He said the words before Emily heard her mom coming, like he'd sensed her arrival, the same way he had sensed Emily's desire to bolt out the door. She shoved a final piece of monkey bread in her mouth and hustled up the stairs to her bedroom.

She kicked a box of clothing out of the way and crouched on the floor of the spare bedroom with the knee-high green bottle that she and her dad had found at a flea market in Fort Smith when she was a kid. She was surprised it hadn't been exiled to the barn with most of the belongings she hadn't taken with her when she moved out. Over the years, her dad had dropped his spare change into its mouth, and Emily would extract the coins for slushies at the Quik-a-Way, armband day at the state fair, and other such trivial events that had come her teenage way.

She and Jody had used them for penny poker years ago. Dad had taught them different hands while Mom was at the store or visiting friends. Now, Emily considered heading to Oklahoma, maybe try her luck at the Cherokee Casino.

She flipped the bottle upside down and watched the mostly copper-colored coins twirl down the spiral neck and drop one-by-one onto the carpet among the change and wrinkled, half-damp dollar bills she had pulled from the pockets of all her jeans, shorts, and jackets. She counted out the change until needles shot through the soles of her feet. Forty-four dollars and six cents. All she owned, there on the floor.

"Goddammit," she said.

Emily startled at the presence of her mom standing in the doorway with a laundry basket. She was already decked out in a full face of makeup and a dress that barely cupped the awful inheritance that Emily had received in adolescence, those breasts that caught every crumb and stare.

"You always were a jumpy child."

"You were always sneaking up on me." Emily rubbed her toes to bring blood back to them. "How long have you been there?"

"Long enough." Her mom dropped the basket on the daybed. She walked over to where Emily sat on the floor and brushed Emily's still-damp ponytail with her fingers, pulling at the tangles. Emily could feel her follicles strain to stay attached. "Did you color your hair?"

"No." She pushed her mom's hands away. "It's just wet."

"It's nice," she said. "I noticed you didn't come home last night."

She'd likely been up all night. But Emily was an adult. She should be able to come and go. "I ran into Jody while I was out. We went back to her house."

Emily heard a sharp intake of air and its forced exhalation, a noise Emily had grown to equate over the years with displeasure.

"I didn't know you two had stayed in touch," her mom said.

Emily swiped at the thin layer of sweat across her brow. Her mom always switched the A/C off at the end of August to save money, despite the persistence of heat. "We didn't. But I heard you did." Emily didn't look at her mom but could feel her silence like a water-soaked wool blanket thrown on top of her. "She said you baby-sat Ricky. Why didn't you tell me you'd seen her?"

Her mom walked over to the bed and began the customary bed check—tucking each corner so tightly that Emily had to kick herself free in the middle of the night. The clothes that Emily had dropped on the floor after her shower became her mom's next focus. She shook them out and inspected them like they might hold some clue to Emily's behavior. "I wish you had called."

She hadn't expected her mom to answer the question. Avoidance was easier. She focused her attention back on the floor. "It was late. I didn't want to wake you." The coins on the carpet glinted up at her.

"Were you drinking?"

Emily shuffled the coins. Somewhere in the pile, there was an Indian head penny. Her dad had always remarked on the luck of finding one before dropping it in with the common coins. She'd never known the pennies to work any charms but she sought them out just the same. The search gave her something to do with her hands, which had begun to shake with a simmering anger when she thought about why her mom had withheld such information.

"I'm really not comfortable with you drinking while you're living here."

She doubted that the drinking was what her mom was uncomfortable with. All the words her mom didn't say shifted the air in the room the way she could sense a thunderstorm coming by the intensity of her headache. "Would you rather I drive home after drinking?"

"I'd rather you not drink at all."

"There's a lot of things I'd rather."

Her mom cleared her throat and waited a while to speak. "We said you can stay here as long as necessary until you find a job and can get a place of your own, but I'd prefer you not crawl in at all hours from who knows where. It worries—"

"I just told you I was at Jody's. And no, you didn't tell me I could stay here as long as I needed to. You told me just yesterday I need to get a move on and find a job and get out as soon as possible."

"I worry," her mom continued, "because I don't want something bad to happen to you. Just the other day, this girl was out jogging and was yanked off the road by this guy and . . ." She lifted a hand to her chest.

The only people Emily had ever seen run or jog outside instead of on a treadmill were athletes on the track at school. They lived in a land without sidewalks. There's no way the story was local. "Um. I don't jog. Did you see that on Facebook?"

Her mom pursed her lips.

"I don't understand what the big deal is. And I don't understand why you would lie about not seeing Jody."

"The big deal is that this isn't a motel. And I didn't lie."

"Oh," Emily said. "Interesting."

Her mom looked toward the ceiling. Moral support from God, Emily supposed. "I don't understand why you're so mad at me. I'm not the one who decided to drop out of school. If you hadn't, maybe you wouldn't be living here today. And I would be real careful accusing someone else of lying."

Emily deflated at the reminder and the conversation she imagined between her parents after her mom had hung up the phone and learned that Emily had not only lost her scholarship but had lied about it for six months, all the while responding to her mom's inquiries about how her classes were going with a simple reply, "Good." Here she was, about to lie to them again, this time about a job she couldn't bring herself to tell them she'd taken. The depth of their disappointment was too deep for her to dredge.

She fought to hold back her tears. "I'm sorry," she said. Her mom didn't reply. The only sound that followed was the click of the door as it shut.

Sorry. The worst word in the English language, right after *college*. Dropping it around these parts was a sure-fire guarantee for absolving sin. But her sin felt fresh and raw every day she stayed in that house.

CHAPTER THREE

ON THE FIRST DAY OF her new job, Emily walked outside the house and shielded her eyes. The sun was an offense, as was the sound of her dad on his Bush Hog out farming land that could have been hers to handle instead of a cash register. Her longing for it had grown since she'd talked about it with her dad. A job that had been passed down through generations, one without an employment application or timesheet, one that didn't require a degree—one that would have gone to a brother if she'd had one. She burned at the thought—though she knew the farm would grow fallow under her bored and inexperienced hand. She couldn't see her dad, but she heard him behind the house cutting zigzags across the expanse of fields. The cat lazed in a slash of sun on the wooden boards of the porch. The kitchen window slid open and her mom yelled out her name.

When Emily turned around, all she could see of her mom was the white of her forearm. She waved money as if she were at a drive-through window. Emily hated the reminder of what awaited her at her new job. She and her mother had made tentative peace over breakfast by acknowledging each other with "Good morning." That's all either would offer in the way of an apology. Emily walked over and looked up.

"Where are you off to?"

"The library," Emily lied. "Job searching. I'll be gone all day."

Her mom nodded. "Could you drop by the store on your way home? We need toilet paper and eggs now that you're home." Her mom had spent the better part of Emily's teenage years complaining about the expense of toilet paper and the speed with which it "disappeared," as if Emily were hoarding it or doing terrible things with it under the cover of night.

Emily considered how long it would take to "drop by" the store when she already had to drive forty minutes to work and back. A flicker of guilt crossed her mind, but she pushed it away. "Can I keep the change? For gas?"

Her mom sighed and slid the screen closed. She returned and slid it open again. Another bill, twenty dollars this time, appeared between her fingers. "Go on and fill your tank. You can pay me back when you find a job."

Emily hesitated. Taking that money felt like betraying herself. But she took the bills and shoved them in the pocket of her pants. "Thanks."

A wave of hot drive-through-leftover air hit her in the face when she opened her car door. She cranked open every window. She popped the trunk and sifted through shoes, CDs, and random trash that littered the space. She found an old sweatshirt and placed it on the vinyl front seat to keep from burning her legs. Once situated, she put the car in reverse and headed toward her new job.

For three weeks, she set her alarm clock, slogged to work for her shift, and yanked the pants of the too-small uniform up her thighs in the handicapped stall at work. She read through the new employee handbook. She dropped coins out the drive-through window when trying to hand change over to a customer, cursing under her breath that they hadn't used a debit or credit card. She scrubbed the men's urinals and the women's trash bins. Once, her drawer had come up short, and she'd had to recount it three times. Each count produced different results, with the ultimate result being that she owed the drawer eleven dollars out of her own pocket because she couldn't figure out where the money had gone.

All that, she could handle. All that, she could leave behind each work day when her shift ended and she made her way back home, back to her bed for a late afternoon nap that left her wondering what hour, what day it was when she woke up. The thing that pricked her, though, the thing that broke through the calm was the warning she'd gotten from her teenaged supervisor after a woman had complained about her language. Language that Emily had used off the clock while on her break, hovering over a plastic tray that held a paper-wrapped cheeseburger and fries, checking her email on her phone, and receiving yet another rejection for an office job she didn't want but longed for if only to escape the confines of that shitty little fast food joint. Emily couldn't even recall saying "Fuck you" to her phone, but apparently she had. It was her word against a customer's, and the customer was always right. Her acne-pocked supervisor had sat her down and told her that she needed to watch her language. This might be a national chain, he said, but it was a family business. And the family had a strict policy against the types of expletive-laced insults that Emily silently hurled at the boy's face while he admonished her.

She took Sunday shifts, which no one else wanted because the church crowds were almost worse than post–football game crowds. It gave her something to do other than consider her life. After the rush, the dining room looked like a tornado had ripped through. The bathrooms were in the same condition, only at times there was actual shit on the floor.

But after the sit-down with her manager and the paltry net pay on her first check flaring her temper, she said to hell with it and called in sick the next Sunday.

She'd planned on sleeping in, lying about having a stomachache, but her dad had asked her to attend church, for once. Like the old days, he'd said: it would be good to see her sitting there beside him.

She said okay. He'd asked nicely.

"Wear something nice," her mom had added.

Hanger after hanger, Emily riffled through the musty dresses she hadn't taken to college in a vain search for something that could accommodate the freshman fifteen she'd put—and kept—on. Not one of Emily's moving boxes contained a dress. She'd flung those into the giant green Dumpsters behind the dorm the first day she'd arrived.

At the back of the closet hung a dark blue, high-collared dress with a droopy white bow ill-designed for flair or fashion. The fabric was thick and structured at the shoulders, like something a soap opera actress from the eighties would wear, but shorter. She suspected her mom had bought the dress years ago, worn it out, and shoved it in the closet when she grew tired of it.

The dress was tight, but it fit better than anything else she could find. The mirror reflected an image of her mother as she might have appeared before she'd gotten pregnant with Emily, her only child by her only boyfriend who had become her only husband.

The way her mom told the story, she'd been a Southern belle. As if there had been any in Drear's Bluff. Maybe they could be found in the old money families in the antebellum homes they featured on those TV shows her mom liked. In Drear's Bluff, girls were more likely to wear something with their asses hanging out and on display. Girls washed their dirty panties in the sink, got saved on Sunday, and prayed to God that their periods would come next month. That was the tradition they could hang their hats on.

She surveyed herself one more time in the full-length mirror on the back of the closet door. Normally, she didn't care what she looked like, but the out-of-fashion dress highlighted all manner of imperfections that she'd tried to ignore over the past few years as her pants had become tighter and tighter. But she wasn't going on a date. She was going to church.

BY THE TIME THEY REACHED the church's gravel parking lot, most of the spaces were filled and the sun had climbed past the steeple to wash the building and lawn in harsh daylight. The steeple perched on top like the last piece on a mad stack of playing cards. The shutters near the sounding bell hung haphazardly. Like the houses the church abutted, white paint chipped along the wooden clapboards, revealing the gray, faded wood beneath. None of the churchgoers milling about seemed to notice. But then, they hadn't left town. Their perspective didn't require adjustment.

Inside, clusters of bedazzled women, ironed old men, and wrinkled children moved in a procession down the stained red aisle runner to their seats. Her dad slipped off to talk with a group of middle-aged men who, unlike their ironed elders, all looked like they shopped at the same store: dark jeans that they had convinced their wives passed for pants, dusty cowboy boots, button-down shirts in need of starch, and big brass belt buckles.

Emily followed her mom as they snaked down a row and waited while other families did the same. The crowd had thinned out over the years, but the diehards creaked into the pews as always. Some of Emily's classmates were there, now with children of their own. People extended pleasantries to Emily's mom over the heads of their neighbors. In turn, the neighbors shifted in their seats to see who their neighbors were talking to. When they noticed Emily, they waved and shouted out, "Welcome home," like word had gone around town that she meant to stay. People she never imagined she'd see again would become a part of her daily life once more. There would be children's names to remember. Ailments to check up on: *Oh, and how is your rheumatoid? Your daughter's asthma? So-and-so's broken wrist?* They would all want to know what was going on with her after the service when everyone clustered outside the church for small talk. Anonymity, lost.

But she knew people's attention spans for life outside town were limited. When she had come back for holidays, they'd asked polite questions about her studies, church, and boys. But they didn't have much to say on any of those subjects and quickly moved on to the latest town gossip. Now that she was back, there was nothing more to talk about. Two years and six months away, and she was once again surrounded by strangers, though she knew everyone by name.

Marjorie Barnett, Troy's mom, heaved herself and a giant quilt purse down the pew and sat in front of them. Emily never did understand how her mom and Marjorie had stayed friends all those years, what with Mom steadily shifting her preferences to designer jeans from Dillard's and Marjorie continuing her proud display of screen-printed American flag T-shirts from Walmart. Nor did she understand why Jody and Troy seemed to be friends now. Nothing made sense.

"If I didn't know better, I'd think you were avoiding me," Marjorie said to Emily.

Emily had been avoiding her, but only because she didn't want to be offered a waitress job at the Quik-a-Way—again. The only thing worse than serving strangers was serving former classmates and current students.

"So," Marjorie said. "Got any updates on your love life?"

Marjorie and the other women who surrounded Emily's mom had always asked her a litany of questions: was she dating anyone, had she thought about coloring her hair, maybe wearing something with a little more color? A skirt instead of slacks? That's all Emily needed, they'd offer with a wink. They had to know the full details of every person they'd ever met: where they grew up, if they were married or why not, if they had kids or why they didn't want them, who their pastor was at their previous church, and what opinion they held on the subject of welfare and the sorry state of our government.

But the love life question, of all questions, had made Emily pause, reaching for the correct response when she was younger. She'd wanted the right words to fall out of her mouth, words that would make the questioner stop asking. Back then, all she could ever muster was a "No, ma'am" or a "Yes, ma'am," and slither away to her seat and burn with self-defeat.

That was then.

"I went on a date recently," Emily lied to Marjorie.

Her mom looked like she was bracing for impact. Marjorie leaned over and smacked Emily's arm. "You go, girl!"

Emily rubbed the sting and swore she'd never use that phrase again now that it'd come out of Marjorie's mouth. Emily was surprised that her mom hadn't shared her assumptions about Emily's sexuality with Marjorie.

Emily hadn't gone on any dates. In Little Rock, she had looked at online dating sites, but there was always a reason not to engage. Though she was sure these women were lovely and had great personalities, she couldn't imagine taking off her clothes or getting excited when they took off theirs. The ones who did look good to her were always in some far-flung part of the state, like El Dorado or West Memphis. The bios of the remainder made her question whether they were men posing as lesbians for unseemly motives. Though she didn't put much weight into her mom's nightly-news and Facebook-fueled terrors, Emily didn't want to take a chance at ending up with her head in a box.

"It was just a date. I didn't cure cancer."

"Does this fellow have a name?" Mom asked, with emphasis on the word *fellow*.

Emily hoped her mom could see the hate in her eyes. "Sam," she said.

"Sam what?"

There was no need for her mom to insist on such minor details as a last name for a first date. She and Emily's dad had been together since they were fourteen, married since they were eighteen. Hell, they were named Best Couple in their yearbook all throughout high school. It's like they were ordained for each other from birth. Her mom didn't know anything about what it was to date, let alone when you went against the grain.

"Collins," Emily said. "Sam Collins." She pursed her lips in anger.

Her mom narrowed her eyes. Some other question worked its way up but she didn't have a chance to voice it.

Marjorie gasped like Emily imagined she did while reading her Harlequins during a long and unexciting shift at the Quik-a-Way. "Well, what'd y'all do? Where'd you go?"

"We went to Fontainebleau," she said. "This new French place in Fort Smith. Very expensive." The name didn't register for Marjorie. It shouldn't have, given that the restaurant didn't exist.

In reality, she hadn't gone anywhere, with anyone. Nowhere but online. These alleged experimental and wild lesbians that populated college campuses were no more than a myth to her. She figured that must've been something that happened in cities. But then Sam had arrived. For months, they sat next to each other in class without talking. Then Emily saw Sam holding hands with another woman out at the strip mall. Emily did a double take and followed them for a while to be sure that what she was seeing was real. She couldn't believe it when it was. Not only that it was someone she knew, but that they'd held hands in public. Jealousy, something she hadn't expected, washed over her. She had rushed to her car.

Her mom made a show of checking her watch and craning her neck to look for any sign of the pastor.

"And?" Marjorie asked. "What else? What's he look like?"

He. Emily squirreled around in her mom's open purse and found a piece of gum, a distraction while she cooked up a lie to mess with them for not wanting more for her than a man. "Tall, dark hair. Handsome, obviously." The way they liked their heroes.

Sam was not unattractive. But neither did she look like the far-flung online lesbians Emily daydreamed about in moments of boredom or at night, under her covers. But in Sam's presence, after she'd seen her at the strip mall, Emily got nervous. She'd catch herself wondering what it'd be like to kiss her. The wonder grew each day and then they'd ended up at a house party held by a fellow classmate.

Almost everyone at the party was male. Some guys had dreadlocks. Some guys had liquor. Some guys had weed. Some guys kissed in a corner. Emily watched, dumbly, until Sam walked over to her with a bottle of rum. Through the course of the night, the liquor eased their tongues. The temperature in the living room rose as more and more people crammed in. The music vibrated up through her feet and throbbed in her ears. To hear each other, they had to stand close. Sam's breath had tickled her neck. There was nowhere for their bodies to go but toward one another or out of the crowd. Sam had grabbed her hand. Emily had followed.

"How'd you leave things at the end of the night?" Marjorie leaned in with her chin on her fist, deeply invested in the outcome.

She glanced at her mom, whose face had fallen into such a state that it almost broke Emily's heart.

In a stranger's bedroom in that strange house, Sam had slammed Emily's body into the closet so hard that the sliding door had come off its track. And Emily had liked it. Sam slid the jeans down Emily's hips and kissed the space between her legs. Emily's fingers tangled in Sam's hair and she stood on her tiptoes and arched closer until her body hummed and surged, and finally, stilled.

"A kiss on the cheek. Then, we said goodnight."

Emily never returned to class after that. Six months later, Emily's limited savings had reached its end and her mom had called after receiving Emily's first student loan bill at the house.

"That's it?" Marjorie huffed. "I was hoping for something a little more exciting than that. I depend on you girls to keep me entertained."

"Sorry to disappoint," Emily said, and scratched at an itch that seemed to come from deep within her.

"When will you see him again?" her mom asked.

Where there had once been confusion and discomfort on her mom's face, now there was something else.

A woman without a man? There was something worse.

"My friends—" She paused to consider that there were no friends. Not Sam. Not Jody. No one. "They say to give it a few days for the phone to ring." She placed her hands on the tops of her thighs and wiped away the creases the way her mom had always done to signal that the conversation was over.

Marjorie patted Emily's arm. "Don't you fret. He'll call."

"Oh, gosh," Emily said in the flattest monotone she could muster. "I certainly hope so."

When it was over, Emily had searched the floor for her clothing and her keys, rushed through the loud and packed living room and out the door. Emily missed one text and then three more until finally Sam left a voicemail, which Emily ignored for two days. She deleted the message after Sam called her a coward and before Sam could finish asking what happened and why wouldn't she just talk to her?

Sam was nice. Sam was good, actually great. But when Emily thought about occupying a space next to her during the day, at a movie, in a restaurant, sitting on the couch wading through a slew of TV shows, walking hand in hand at a strip mall for everyone to see? Discomfort lined the edges of those images. When she thought on it too long, her guts constricted in an impossible-to-ignore way.

Emily wanted those things. But she didn't want them with Sam.

While Emily rubbed the spot on her arm to erase Marjorie's intentions for her, Emily's mom and Marjorie indulged in a barely whispered round of gossip centered on how the high school counselor got caught cheating on her husband with a student in the soda-soaked earth beneath the football bleachers. Emily focused on the Sunday service program. Same sermon, different day—except for the part where Jody arrived at the end of the pew with Ricky on her hip. Emily choked on her spit and coughed so much that one of the old ladies in the pew behind her reached over to pound her on the back. Jody made her way down to the empty spot next to Emily.

"What are you doing here?" Emily asked, her voice cracking.

"Nice to see you, too. You left these." Jody twirled Emily's missing underwear on her index finger. Emily tried to snatch them from her, but Jody held onto them and prepared to launch them like a football that would fly across the congregation and land on the pastor's microphone.

But she didn't. Jody held them out to her and laughed. "No hard feelings, yeah?"

Emily balled them up in her fist. "What's wrong with you?" she said under her breath. She tried not to focus on whether there'd been any unpleasantness lurking in the crotch before they'd been washed.

Her mom's eyes shifted between them and then at the underwear. She considered Jody before placing her arms around her for a quick pat and release. "Nice to see you here." She then pushed past Emily to scoop little Ricky out of Jody's arms.

"Seriously?" Emily said as she was shoved aside. Though irritation lingered at her mom's comment, she derived a bit of satisfaction that her mom got so wound up about the perceived evidence of her and Jody carrying on, in church of all places, the last place that Emily—and, she suspected, anyone—expected Jody to turn up on a Sunday.

"About time you brought this little man to church," Marjorie said, and squeezed Ricky's cheek. "I hardly believed he existed since we ain't seen you anywhere. But Troy talks about him all the time." She cut her eyes at Jody. "Y'all seem to be getting on well these days. Shame you been hiding out from the rest of us."

"I'm not hiding. I'm busy," Jody said.

Busy drinking, smoking, hanging out with teenage boys like Troy.

Mom continued to plant lipstick kisses all over Ricky's face and the white collar of his shirt. Jody reached over to wipe the spot with a tissue but Mom swung him away. "Oh, you'll have to get used to it, Jody." She dipped Ricky and then hoisted him in the air, which unleashed a string of baby laughter from him. "All the ladies love little Ricky." As if to help make her point, the old ladies sitting behind them proceeded to coo and purr at the little boy, who took delight in their attention.

Jody surrendered any complaints she might have about the stain on Ricky's collar. Instead, she returned her attention to Emily. "Nice dress."

"Nice hair," Emily shot back. The words made no sense, but she wanted the attention off her. Being back in Drear's Bluff had thrown her off balance. She had always abided by the polite-church-people dress code from her youth and hadn't thought to break the habit. Had she known Jody would be there, she would've worn dark jeans like her dad.

Jody frowned in response but her hands worked their way up to her thick black mane that fell in pretty swoops. She sat quietly next to Emily while they waited for everyone around them to settle into their seats, almost the same as when they were teenagers. Emily's legs stuck to the lacquered wood and sweat pooled at the base of her bra. One bead escaped and drifted down her stomach to wet the front of her dress. The close collar threatened to suffocate her, and the tight-fitting fabric had traveled from her knees to the middle of her thighs. She yanked the sides down as best she could while sitting. Jody's fingers brushed Emily's knee when she tried to help her pull the hem down. A shot of electricity socked Emily in the gut. Her cheeks warmed and she was certain all eyes were on her and Jody. Flushed, she located her program and waited for her heart to beat the embarrassment and growing irritation out of her.

"Oh, bless his heart," Emily's mom said beside her. Emily followed the direction of her mom's gaze. Mr. Johnston walked down the aisle, his wife at his side. Mr. Johnston's arm stuck out of a sling, in a great bulb of white bandage. Dark red and orange burns marked parts of his face. Everyone looked. Some stood and clapped as he passed. Someone yelled out from behind Emily, and the Johnstons looked in their direction. Mr. Johnston's eye, the one that wasn't bandaged, looked shot full of dye, the pupil swimming in a sea of red.

Marjorie shifted in her seat to talk to Emily and Jody. "He ought to let one of them boys take over before he gets himself killed."

"What happened?" Jody asked. A catch in her voice caused Emily to look over at her.

"You haven't heard?" Marjorie asked, incredulous.

"I haven't been able to get out much these days." Jody kept her eyes trained on Mr. Johnston.

Emily ran through the town connections in her head, trying to figure out why Jody would care. The Johnstons—including their three sons, all handsome and muscled from years of helping out on the farm—lived on the same road as Jody, leading Emily to wonder whether one of them had found his way out to Jody's house one night.

Marjorie rattled off the less important details, like what she'd been doing the day of Mr. Johnston's accident, who had called whom, bits and pieces of information offered by customers who came into the Quik-a-Way for gas or a burger. Then she finally answered Jody's question: "His nurse tank ruptured. Blew ammonia right in his face." She nudged her head toward him. "Could've killed him right then and there. Real dangerous stuff. Makes you wonder about them using it to grow our food. Really does make you wonder."

Jody's face stayed blank and indecipherable as Marjorie fished for an ally in her complaint.

Emily's mom kept a hand to her chest.

Emily's body vibrated with discomfort at the auditory torment of Marjorie's voice, the mental torment of waiting for the clock to inch forward, and the physical torment of Jody's warm thigh against hers.

Jody fidgeted in the pew, her eyes on the stained carpet as if the answer to a puzzle were contained within its fibers.

"I think the pastor is waiting for everyone to be quiet," Emily said, but Marjorie went on like she hadn't heard. Emily imagined the pastor holding his wrinkled ear against the little door beside the pulpit, listening for the right time to make his entrance but holding back because it sounded like people still stirred in the pews, when it was really just the sound of one person giving her opinion on a subject that didn't concern her.

"Shame," Marjorie said. "Those old men are starting to lose their sight and minds. And before you know it, they'll end up killing themselves or someone else." She tapped the pew in front of Mom to ensure she was listening. "You tell Emily about Mr. Prescott driving his car into the cheerleaders outside the high school during one of their car washes?" She chuckled. "I shouldn't laugh, but my word, they're out there practicing flips and whatnot in dripping-wet bikinis with their butts hanging out. I can't believe the principal lets them wear that. Mr. Prescott dang near killed every last one of them. Put a few in the hospital."

Emily's mom opened her mouth in an apparent objection, but Marjorie brushed the air with her hand and redirected her attention to Emily and Jody. "Really, just gave them a fright, is all. But it could've been worse. If that sheriff of ours had any sense, he'd have taken Mr. Prescott's license. He sure doesn't have any problem taking other people's licenses away. I asked him about it when he come into the store. I asked him, I said, 'Owen, are you gonna let that old man run down every single person in town?' He got real mad 'cause I didn't call him Sheriff, and he stormed out like a teenager. He likes to tell it different, but he didn't earn that job." The puff of air she exhaled brushed Emily's arm, and Emily scratched at the spot. "His daddy would rise from the dead and die again if he knew how that son of his has tarnished his good name."

Emily squeezed her eyes shut and mumbled, "Stop talking, stop talking, stop talking."

"What's wrong with you?"

Emily opened her eyes to Marjorie's lip and eyebrow curled in confusion. Rather than answer, Emily rubbed her eyes with the palms of her hands until she heard the creak of the pew as Marjorie turned back toward the front. She felt Jody stiffen next to her.

The clock read a quarter past and everyone had begun to fan themselves with their programs by the time the pastor strode to the pulpit. Her dad sat next to her mom and read the program like it was the morning paper after a double take at Ricky, a glance at Emily and Jody, and a quick lift of his eyebrows to her mom. Her mom still held onto Ricky and bounced him on her legs to lull him into a state of quiet.

A hush came over the crowd as the pastor opened his Bible and coughed into a white handkerchief before launching into the week's sermon on a Spirit-filled marriage. The pastor stayed rooted to his spot, the microphone too far from his mouth to amplify whatever words of wisdom he might have. The pastor cleared his throat and the speakers screeched in response.

Emily swiped a hand across her forehead to catch the sweat before it dripped into her eyes. She discarded her wilted program in the hymnal tray and tugged at the hem of her dress again, causing her mom to shift next to her and glare.

Hot, Emily mouthed.

Her mom leaned down, nearly squashing Ricky in the process, and retrieved a giant travel mug from beneath the pew. The Quik-a-Way logo on the front had long since faded. Emily took the mug, expecting water, but gagged at the saccharine aftertaste of diet cola. Her mom took the mug back and shushed her.

The longer Emily sat there and the more monotonous the pastor became, the less she could focus on anything but how Jody had rejected her offer to babysit and why she had decided to show up to church out of the blue. And Troy. Always she circled back to Troy sleeping on Jody's couch and Jody thinking nothing of it, like he didn't just crash there, but lived there.

She turned to Jody, the way she'd done all those years ago when something big inside her had to be shared before it ate her up, even though most of the time it was nothing more than the girlish frights of other, more popular girls and the menacing glances of boys. Jody shifted her eyes around the room and scratched her neck.

Emily grabbed the wilted program she'd discarded and the little pencil from the holder and began to circle different letters to send a secret message as they'd done when they were teenagers. She passed it to Jody, who waved it away, but Emily poked the corner of the program into her arm. Jody took it and fanned herself. Emily nudged her again, pointed at the program and mouthed the words, *Open it.*

A baby's wail punctuated the end of the pastor's line about something great the Lord had said. Assorted ladies testified with their hands in the air as their husbands shook their heads and spit chew into plastic cups. Jody used the commotion to decode the message: *Go outside.* She grumbled but then nodded.

Emily rose from the pew and felt a tug at her hem.

"Where are you going?" her mom asked.

"I need some air," she said. "Too hot."

"Now?" her mom whispered.

"Yes, now." She grabbed the wadded-up underwear by her side and thrust it at her mom. "Here. Hold my panties."

"Oh my g—" She quickly grabbed them from Emily and shoved them into her purse. "I can't believe you sometimes."

Emily ignored her and made her way past Jody's knees and the knees of all the other people seated in the row and hurried toward the church doors.

When she stepped outside she drank in the fresh air, thankful for relief from the hot room and the distance between her and everyone else. She sat down on the church steps and waited.

A prayer for rain seemed more fitting than the usual fare, an afternoon thunderstorm to wash away the dust from the cars and the coat of frustration that had layered itself onto her since she had moved back home. She closed her eyes and let the blinding sunlight beat down on her face.

Before long the doors opened, and Jody sat down next to her.

A faint memory came back to Emily, one where she and Jody had sat on those same steps and peered down the road waiting for Connie to come cruising into the church parking lot in her white Chevrolet—though she rarely did.

Next door to the church a subwoofer thumped, and gravel crunched under the tires of a car pulling out of the driveway. She had watched Jody disappear into similar cars—usually with some boy that Jody had taken a liking to, or one of the girls from school with their dark makeup and shredded jeans. Any manner of illegal substance was liable to be stuffed in between or under the seats. Emily was left waiting at the curb of the school parking lot, lined up for the bus with all the other losers without a car, wondering what charms those kids held that she didn't. Not much had changed, from what Emily could tell.

She nudged her head toward the car. "You know him?"

"Why would you think that?" Jody placed her head on her knees and hugged her legs tighter, looking all of sixteen in her sundress with her painted toes sticking out the bottom of her skirt. A breeze picked up. Jody removed the windblown hair from her lipstick and pressed her lips together to smooth out any patches.

Emily looked away from the spaghetti strap that trickled down Jody's shoulder. "Looks like someone you'd know," she said.

"What'd you want?" Jody asked.

Everything. She wanted to inhabit the same space as her without that clawing need to know that they were okay and she wasn't the only one stuck in the pattern of remembering their shared past. "Nothing. We used to do this all the time. Skip sermons and talk. Remember?"

Jody didn't say anything. Instead, she picked at the paint on the stairs.

"You could've called," Emily said. "I would've come to get my underwear."

Jody hugged her knees and bent over them to laugh. "Where's the fun in that?"

Emily had often been the unwitting object of Jody's fun.

Jody leaned over to bump Emily with her shoulder. "Oh come on. You know I'm just playing. Like you said, we used to do this all the time." She leaned back and sunned her face, eyes closed. "I'm glad for the break. I forgot how much I hate church. It's so fucking boring."

"You never could stay awake during service."

"Not with those Boone's Farm hangovers," she said. "I bet Marjorie keeps it behind the counter so the kids can't steal it. Thank God for fake IDs and Fort Smith liquor stores."

While Jody reminisced, Emily hung on to the way that Jody had dismissed her three weeks before, with not even a simple, "Hey, let's hang out some time." She didn't know how to ask for what she wanted from Jody; she never had. "You're lucky you never got arrested," Emily said.

"Sheriff Jenkins—the old one—knew we were just kids fooling around. He didn't go around bugging people like Owen does. Unlike his dad, Owen's just playing cops and robbers."

"Well, it is Owen we're talking about," Emily said. "Didn't he put Johnny Day into the hospital after hitting him too hard during practice? Over a girl, I think."

"That must've been before I moved to Drear's Bluff. But sounds about right."

"His dad got him off."

"Well, shit. That's not saying much. I could talk my way out of anything with Sheriff Jenkins." A range of emotions crossed Jody's face. She looked off into the distance. "Sometimes, I wonder if maybe he ought to have put me in jail."

Emily's insides itched with questions. "You're wrong about the Boone's Farm. The county's still dry." She glanced at Jody. "And that wasn't all that gave you a hangover."

Jody shoved a flop of hair back behind her ear. "That was a long time ago." Not so long considering what Jody's friends had passed around the fire the night that Emily had gotten sick.

Emily breathed in, gathering the will to broach the subject at the top of her mind. "Besides personalized underwear delivery, what are you doing here?"

"At church?" Jody huffed. "Everybody's always telling me I need religion. But when I show up, everyone's got something to say about it. Nothing nice."

"You just said you hate church."

"So do you. But here you are." Jody chewed her bottom lip like she was trying to keep a lid on something. She glanced at Emily but went back to picking at the paint. "That's awful about Mr. Johnston. And unusual for something like that to happen, yeah?"

A fly buzzed around their heads, and Emily swatted it away. She sat back, disappointed that Jody had gone off on another topic without answering her question. "Not really. Accidents happen all the time on farms. A tractor overturned on Mr. Garrett and crushed his chest. And one of the Harris boys lost his arm when he got caught in the hay baler. That's just this year." She knew plenty about farming. Her dad just didn't give her a chance to show it.

"How do you know about all that?"

"Mom texted me every time something happened, big or small. Didn't matter." Like Jody getting pregnant. Except the part where Jody had returned and she'd babysat for her. She'd left out those details.

"Thought you didn't like gossip."

"I don't. She started texting after I stopped answering her calls."

Jody scratched at her legs. "I had no idea about Mr. Johnston or anyone else."

"You should get out more," Emily said. "Where've you been all these years anyway? You didn't say." Sometimes, she thought of Jody as a missing kid. Gone in the dead of night with no word, no forwarding address, no phone number. Nothing.

"Everywhere. Mom was living in Spiro near this gypsy camp when she came to get me. She was hot on one of them, but kept saying his mom put a hex on her." She rolled her eyes. "Since then, I've lived in Hackett, Pocola, Roland. The finest towns that Arklahoma has to offer. I been to 'em all."

"You didn't answer my question."

"What question?"

"What you're really doing here at church."

"Jesus H. Christ. I'm used to getting the third degree from Marjorie and your mom, but you? Are you mad at me or something? Is this about your offer to babysit?" she asked. "You don't have to be embarrassed, if that's what you're getting at."

"Why would I be embarrassed? I was just offering to help. That's what friends do. But like you said, you have a babysitter. Troy."

"Oh," Jody said and drew out the vowel so long it felt like a weapon. "I see."

"What?"

"You know what."

After all this time away, Jody could still find her weakness, like a cadaver dog sniffing out the body. Emily choked back her pride and a surprising appearance of tears that had pooled in her eyes. Over babysitting. How far she had fallen.

Behind the church doors, the piano swelled, and the choir launched into the first verse of the invitational.

"We should get inside before service ends," Emily said.

They stood and brushed the backs of their dresses, releasing the dirt and paint chips to the ground. With the sun at Jody's back, the outline of her body shone through the dress. The swell of her calf, the knob of her knee, the lines of her inner thighs as they rose and came together. The only thing separating her skin from the world, the thin fabric.

When Emily pulled the heavy church doors open, the third refrain met their ears. The pastor spotted Emily and Jody as they headed down the aisle. He opened his arms to welcome them toward the pulpit. Emily shook her head and slipped into the pew to stand alongside her parents. Ricky dozed in her mom's arms. Her mom's forehead wrinkled into a frown when Emily came up beside her. Instead of asking if she was feeling okay, she leaned over and sniffed to see if Emily smelled of cigarettes. Emily mock-coughed in her face a couple of times until her mom went back to singing and slowly rocking.

After four hypnotic chants of the chorus, "I come, I come," Emily wished the sinners would make up their minds about coming sooner. Every time she shifted, she accidentally knocked into Jody. If she placed her hand on the seat back in front of her to steady herself, somehow Jody's hand would end up there as well, convincing Emily that Jody's sole purpose that morning had been to taunt her.

The choir used to get through the invitational with one run through the song. Sometimes, the sinner who went up to the pulpit wanted to get saved. Back when Emily was a teenager, they had peer-pressured each other to get saved so they could end service, but a scan of the crowd revealed hardly any teenagers there.

She crossed her arms tight against her body, stood knees apart, and suffered the sweat that dampened her bra and soaked the back of her underwear. She tilted her head up to find a pocket of air and looked at the water-stained ceiling. The brown, rackety ceiling fan distributed dust from its blades. All those years of contributions, and Emily couldn't say that the money had gone to any use. She imagined the vapors of women's perfume and the body odor of men drifting up to the ceiling while they suffered below in the stuffy room. She shut her eyes and considered getting saved to distract herself from the dread rising up her throat about the next day and all the days after that, when she would wake up in her childhood home—not a dorm, not an apartment—and get dressed for minimum wage work and come back at the end of the day to have supper with her mom and dad.

Finally, a guy Emily didn't recognize stepped out into the aisle and walked toward the front. The pastor placed an arm around him. They both kneeled so the guy could admit he was a sinner. Emily didn't care as long as he hurried up. The church had become small and hot and too much. Once the pastor stood, the choir and organ wound down and the pastor let everyone know that the guy had confessed and asked Jesus for forgiveness. Then, he handed the guy off to the deacon, who held him by the shoulder. After the usual spiel about God's grace and the Holy Spirit, the pastor released everyone with a reminder about Wednesday night service. The deacon guided the guy through a door past the choir so he could give him a talking-to and the little yellow book about how great it was to give your life to Jesus. Emily could have saved him the trouble and given him one of the books she'd collected over the years.

She needed out. Out of the pew, out of the church.

Outside, everyone gathered for small talk. Emily's mom still held Ricky as if he was her own. Emily's dad held Emily around the shoulders the same way the deacon did to the guy, as if both of them were prone to escape. When she turned to locate the person her mom was waving over, she realized that her dad's grip was less about her and more about his physical reaction to seeing Marjorie.

Her dad released her and tapped Emily's mom on the shoulder. "Dot, take your time. I'm gonna head over to the feed store with some of the guys. I'll catch you two at home." He kissed her mom on the head before ambling over to the blue jean brigade of men who seemed in similar need of escape from wives who couldn't be dragged away from conversations.

Marjorie registered his departure with the slip of a smile.

Once, when they were younger, Jody had told Emily she'd heard that Marjorie had taken a shine to Emily's dad way back in high school, before he and Emily's mom started dating. Emily had no idea if the rumor was true. It was impossible to know the truth about anyone in this town, but she didn't have to strain to imagine how suffocating the unwanted romantic attention of someone like Marjorie could be. From what Emily could surmise, if Marjorie couldn't have Emily's dad, then she would do what she could to be a constant source of consternation to him.

"Why don't we head on over to the Quik-a-Way for lunch? Marjorie's got a high chair just fit for this little man," her mom said to Jody. Marjorie grumbled under her breath.

Jody reached over and took Ricky from Emily's mom, who frowned. "I need to get Ricky home for his lunch and nap."

Go, Emily thought. *Take your spaghetti straps and your painted toes and go, like you always do.* But she didn't want her to go. Not yet. Not without knowing if she'd go another three weeks without seeing her.

"Don't be silly." Emily's mom reached over to stroke Ricky's arm and wormed her fingers around the soft flesh for a better grip. "He can eat at the Quik-a-Way." She reached out with her other hand and tried to pull him toward her.

"He'll eat at home." Jody swung the hip that held Ricky away from Emily's mom and released him from her grip.

"We can still go to the Quik-a-Way," Marjorie said.

"We always go to lunch after church." Emily's mom crossed her arms, staring first at Emily and then Jody. "It would be nice if you would join us. It'd give us a chance to catch up." She faked those words so hard that anyone who didn't know her might believe she actually wanted to reconnect with Jody instead of judge her as she'd done mornings before and would do mornings again if Jody made church a habit. Though Emily found that possibility hard to believe.

"Another time," Jody said, and made Ricky wave bye-bye to everyone. Marjorie smiled and dragged Emily's mom away, her displeasure trailing behind as high notes at the ends of her sentences. Jody grabbed the diaper bag from where it sat on the ground. She dug inside for her cigarettes and a lighter, inhaled until the flame caught. With Ricky on her hip and the bag slung over her shoulder, she made to leave without a final word or a simple good-bye.

"You could come around sometime," Emily said. "We don't have to be strangers."

Jody narrowed her eyes and flashed something else that Emily couldn't translate. "I promised Ricky we'd watch Elmo and read some books."

He was just a baby. It wasn't like Jody would leave him alone. They'd both be there.

"And I've got shit to do tomorrow." The cigarette bobbed up and down when Jody spoke.

Nobody said today or tomorrow. "I said sometime."

"Sometime," Jody said. "Yeah. Sure."

They'd been best friends. Now Jody treated her like someone she'd run into at the grocery store and didn't have advance notice to avoid by ducking down an aisle. "I guess I'll see you in a couple of years, then," she said.

Jody looked startled that such words could come from Emily. She squinted in the sun. "What's that supposed to mean?"

"Forget it," Emily said. The words scorched her mouth like a shot of hot sauce.

"Things aren't like they were in high school. I can't drop everything and be your only friend. I have a kid. And responsibilities."

Anger came back to Emily, hard and hurtful. All those times she'd wanted something she didn't even understand. How Jody had made her want it. This time, her high school self rattled through the haze of memory and shook the older version. Jody was nice when she wanted something. She was sweet when she was low. *Remember*, the voice said, *how she leaves as soon as she's done with you? Remember how Jody up and left, back to Connie, to finish high school in another town? Remember that? Now look at you. Not jumping, but asking Jody how high. How high, how long will you wait?* She couldn't help but wonder why she'd found those yesterdays with Jody so magical.

She forced herself to stare at the cracked slab of sidewalk instead of at Jody. When she finally looked up, Jody's face was expressionless.

A thin trail of smoke snaked off the tip of Jody's cigarette and formed a sort of halo around Ricky, who rubbed at his big baby eyes. Jody tilted her head and exhaled as gracefully as a silver screen siren.

"We'll hang out soon, okay?" She nudged Emily on the arm. "I promise."

Emily tried to remember why she had decided to show up at Jody's door, expecting what exactly? What she hadn't considered was how she might feel when she saw Jody again. For some reason, she thought she'd moved past all that. Yet she had not stopped twisting around thoughts of Jody since the truck stop. Seeing Jody today, in that dress, knowing that Troy was probably waiting for her at the house, and Emily being left out of her world once again, was too much. An ache had lodged itself inside Emily's core and it showed no signs of easing.

CHAPTER FOUR

EMILY WISHED THAT SHE HAD driven her own car to church that morning instead of getting a ride with her parents. She wished that she had gone to the feed store with her dad instead of agreeing to go to lunch at the Quik-a-Way with her mom and Marjorie. She wished that she had said what she'd wanted to say to Jody. Such wishes were worthless.

The bell above the door marked their entrance. One half of the store held aisles full of standard gas station fare like chips and soda and oddly paired household items: the tampons next to the bleach. On the other side was the diner.

The previous owner, Mr. Woodrow, was one of those old men who liked to append the phrase, "from my cold, dead hands," to any conversation that veered dangerously close to the topic of change or selling his store, especially to a woman. But when he couldn't pay his bills and the bank took over, Marjorie had bought the business thanks to a small business loan, making her the first official female business owner in Drear's Bluff and the whispered reason why Mr. Woodrow had had a stroke.

Marjorie had redone the interior with orange booths and old-school black-and-white tile. Harsh overhead fluorescent lights unified the two areas of the building and ensured no one looked their best or occupied the booths too long.

The store was warmer inside than out, a biosphere of grease, humidity, bleach, and tinny country music coming from ceiling speakers that hadn't been replaced since the eighties. Much like Emily's mom, Marjorie boasted a strict policy of not turning on the A/C in September, defiant to Mother Nature and anyone who dared to complain. Drear's Bluff had no other option for food, snacks, and minor necessities. Most people didn't complain. At least not to her face.

On the diner side, a blonde waitress in a tight and short skirt bent over to pick up napkins that a table full of teenage boys had dropped onto the floor. When she stood, Emily recognized her. Heather. She looked ten years older than she ought. She wore their senior T-shirt with Sharpied autographs from their fifty classmates. Emily couldn't believe she still owned the shirt, let alone wore it. Emily had thrown hers out the day they gave it to her in a fit of mild teenage rebellion.

She and Emily had gone to school together since kindergarten but they'd never been what Emily would call friends. Heather had been the poor kid, the dirty kid, the one who didn't fit. The one that women like Emily's mom tried to help but the kids tried to avoid. The kind of kid Emily had been, too.

For years, Emily had sat with girls like Heather at lunch or when required. She'd watched other girls in school—the cheerleaders, the smart ones, the hoods, all of them—drift down the hallways in their groups. They whispered and giggled and told each other secrets that Emily longed to share. If her mom hadn't taken Jody in, she would never have talked to a girl like Emily. But Mom had. And Jody did.

Heather shot over to them and hugged Emily, which she awkwardly received. "Hey, girl." Heather had adopted that grating upspeak that spread among girls like a virus. "I heard you were back." Emily had heard via text that Heather had cheated on her now-estranged husband with Owen. "Haven't seen you around. We ought to get together soon."

"Sure," Emily said with no intention of following through.

Heather's smile held an air of hope, one that twinged a bit of guilt in Emily, who had only been nice to Heather when no one else was around.

"Heather, these tables are a mess," Marjorie said. "Deep clean, my foot. This is nothing short of an embarrassment." She swung a hand to the empty booths. "Dot, go on and sit up at the bar."

Heather began to complain, but wandered off to find a cleaning rag instead. Emily didn't know how anyone could stand working for Marjorie, whose eyes found errors where others found none.

Emily slid onto the stool next to her mom and placed her head on the counter.

"That's the first time I've seen Jody since her grandpa's funeral," her mom said.

Again, Emily wondered about her mom's continued failure to disclose that she had babysat Ricky, long after the funeral.

Marjorie placed a large glass of Dr Pepper in front of Emily.

"Mothers these days," Marjorie said. "Talking about sleep schedules and feeding schedules. I tell you what, you feed the kids when they're hungry, and you put them to bed when they're tired. And you spank their little butts when they misbehave." She propped a hand on her hip and nodded toward Emily. "You so tired you can't even hold yourself up?"

The heat of the day and the residue of her interaction with Jody had sapped her of energy. Emily propped her head up enough to slump over the drink. She drew the soda through the straw and let the syrup and carbonation sting the back of her throat.

"I heard Troy on the phone with Jody the other day," Marjorie said. "I'd sure like to know what's going on with those two. Ever since he quit school, he's been up her butt. Ain't been to church in I don't know how long. Sleeps all day, comes home late. Tells me he's cleaning the grill until four in the morning, like I'm some fool who doesn't know the Sonic closes at midnight and doesn't have the sense to call and see if he still works there. Then, he went and lost his license, so I don't know how he's getting to wherever he's going. And now, he's stopped coming home altogether some nights." Marjorie wiped the spot where Emily's glass had begun to sweat and pool on the counter. "Lord help me if those two are carrying on. I don't think my nerves could take it."

"That's ridiculous," Emily said, but the insinuation further lit the ill temper she'd acquired since Jody had shown up at the end of the pew. She gnawed on her straw until the edges were mangled with bite marks. "If you're so concerned, why don't you ask him what he's doing and where he's been instead of making assumptions?"

Her mom widened her eyes. "Emily," she whispered.

Marjorie stopped wiping the counter to gape at Emily. "You can't ask a teenager why they do what they do." Marjorie went back to wiping the same spot she'd wiped down five times. "They'll just lie."

"They're friends," Emily said. "Nothing more." But doubt antagonized her, too.

Mom yanked the menu out of its slot to peruse the options even though she knew them by heart. "Jody's older than him. And a mother." As if those details resolved the matter. She dropped the menu back in its slot next to the napkin dispenser.

"A single mother," Marjorie said. "Probably looking to find that kid of hers a new daddy. I'll be darned if I'll let that happen."

"With his grill money?" Emily asked. "I highly doubt that."

Marjorie took the menu that Emily's mom had handled and gave it a good once-over with her rag. The little bell above the door dinged and a party of five walked in.

"Where did Heather get off to?" Marjorie grumbled, and shoved the menu back in its spot. "I swear that girl is bound and determined to test me." She let the people stand there and wonder if they should seat themselves or wait. "Watch my register," she said.

Emily made swirls on the counter with the water that dripped from her glass while her mom looked out the front window. Soon, she poked Emily on the arm and nudged her head toward the door.

A sheriff's car had pulled up to the gas pump. Connie emerged from the passenger side and leaned against the door in a yellow spaghetti-strap dress spattered with embroidered white daisies that looked to have been purchased from the juniors section of Kmart. While the gas pumped, Owen pressed up against her, and they proceeded to morph into all hands and heads and hips bobbing.

"I didn't know she'd come back," her mom said. A gallon of Roundup couldn't kill the weed-like hold that Drear's Bluff had on people like Connie. Even when she did manage to leave, she turned up again eventually. Emily brushed away the thought that the same could be said of her.

Marjorie glanced out the window and then ripped the lunch party's order off her pad and shoved the paper across the metal pane to the cook. "Oh for crying out loud. Like I don't have enough to deal with today."

"I'm sure she won't stick around long. She never does," Emily's mom said with a mixture of disappointment and judgment.

"Good. It'll save you the trouble of getting her saved again. Poor Deacon Jones can't handle seeing her dunked and come up in that wet cotton dress again. And without a bra? At church? My God." Marjorie could barely get the words out amid her laughter. "He nearly croaked right there on the altar."

Emily's mom looked away. "That's an exaggeration."

Emily knew her mom was more than a little embarrassed that everyone knew she was the one who had convinced Connie to get saved. "The Great Connie Crusade," Emily had heard Marjorie whisper to some of the other prayer circle ladies afterward. At the time Emily had barely known Jody, only that she was the new girl in school. She didn't recall Jody being at church that day and wondered how she'd managed to miss that particular comedy. And she wondered what happened for her mom to have stopped trying. When did she realize that Connie would never change?

She tried to imagine what life must have been like for Connie growing up in Drear's Bluff. Too much church shoved down her throat? Too many people caring about her sins instead of themselves? Maybe that's why she'd gone and done the opposite. Emily pressed into her chair's hard frame and considered all the speculation that would occur once word got out that she was broke and working at a fast food joint in Fort Smith. Not to mention those other unsavory details.

"Don't go getting mad." Marjorie grabbed her soda and downed it. "Lord knows you tried. Like taking in Jody when Connie couldn't be bothered." She wiped the wet off her mouth. "Some folks aren't fit for saving."

"You act like I singled her out," Mom said. "I was just being nice."

"Sure you were," Marjorie said. Before Mom had a chance for a rebuttal, Marjorie left to check on the other customers.

Outside, Connie picked at what Emily guessed was a loose button on Owen's shirt, collateral damage from when Connie had no doubt tried to yank the shirt off him earlier that day.

Emily's mom surveyed the diner to see who might be within earshot. "I don't approve of Heather cheating, but I'd hate for her to see them two together. She thought for sure she and Owen had something."

"Whatever she thought they had, Connie's got it now," Emily said, though Owen's particular *whatever* wasn't much, if anyone asked her.

"Y'all need something?" Heather came up behind them.

Mom tapped Emily's leg with her foot. "Could you be a love and see if Marjorie's got any fresh iced tea in the back?" Her nose crinkled. "She knows I don't like the kind from the machine."

Heather tilted her head, somehow missing the display outside the store the same way she missed current fashion trends. "Sure," she said. "You want more soda while I'm at it?"

"No, thanks." Emily propped her chin in her hand and played with her discarded straw wrapper.

When Heather left, Emily and her mom returned their attention to Owen and Connie. They were practically dry-humping right there in the broad daylight. Connie reached down between his legs and grinned up at him like she'd just found twenty bucks in her pocket on laundry day.

After filling the tank, Owen walked inside the store while Connie stayed outside to reapply her lipstick in the side mirror.

"Good afternoon, Owen." Mom threw on her most dazzling smile, the one she saved for those she planned to talk about later. "How are you doing today?"

Owen pulled his wallet from his back pocket and propped himself against the counter. "Mrs. Skinner. Good to see you." Either Emily's face didn't register with him or he didn't care because he didn't say hello.

"You remember Emily," her mom said. "My daughter."

Owen rotated toward her and considered her like he would a weed in the garden, something to be yanked. "I might've heard your name a time or two." He used that particular Southern lilt that blurred the line between a compliment and a curse.

Mom gauged the location of Marjorie and Heather. "Is that Connie I see out there by your car? I wasn't aware she was back in town. You all out for a picnic?"

"Just a little ride, is all."

Marjorie took her time meeting Owen at the register. Owen grabbed a pack of gum off the shelf and slid it toward Marjorie to ring up. She grabbed his card and swiped the machine so slowly that it beeped in error. She nodded toward Connie sitting in his patrol car. "Nice to know where all my taxes go. Hauling out the trash."

Emily's mom stiffened. Emily knew Marjorie's confrontational style had always made her uncomfortable. But Marjorie said what Emily wished she had the courage to say every time Connie showed up out of the blue like nothing had ever happened. Like Jody hadn't sat there all those times waiting by the phone for a call from her mom to say where she was, what she was doing, if she missed her at all.

Marjorie never let things go unsaid. She pressed and pressed until she got or said what she wanted. Her mom's style, a style Emily realized with some annoyance that she had adopted, didn't get her anywhere but wondering.

Owen ignored Marjorie's comment. "Taking a break from catching criminals. Speaking of, where's that son of yours? I ain't seen hide nor hair of him since his DUI."

Emily's nerves pricked at the mention of Troy. He was probably in Jody's house that very minute, doing things that Emily didn't want to think about but still pictured.

"Under the influence of a prescription that he needed for pain," Marjorie said. "It's not like he was out there on the roads like some hooligan on alcohol or drugs."

"Mmm-hmm," Owen said.

"What's he supposed to do? Suffer? Not go to work?" Marjorie swiped the card once more, pounded the keys of the register, and shoved the receipt into Owen's hand. "And you took his license away, so it's not like he can be out on the roads. So I don't know why you're expecting to see—"

Owen laughed as he walked toward the door. "You all have a nice day." He waved behind him and the little bell dinged as he exited.

"I rue the day his daddy passed and—" Marjorie stopped herself and breathed a heavy sigh. "I'm not going to let him ruin my day."

After the lunch order came for the party of five, the diner fell into quiet—or as quiet as Emily imagined it could be with her mom and Marjorie's never-ending chatter. The minutes, and her thoughts, ticked by with a thud: Troy hanging around Jody's house, how Jody would allow him to come over to her house but not Emily, why Jody would invite her up to the party but then dismiss her.

A desire to say all those things set fire to every part of her, so much that she couldn't sit still as she waited for her mom to pore over the menu again only to pick the garden salad.

"How long are you gonna be here?" Emily asked.

"Why?"

"Because I wanna borrow the car for an errand if you're planning on staying a while."

Her mom studied her nails. "Well, I don't know. I can't predict. Where is it you're wanting to go?"

Marjorie cleared her throat. "Oh, Dot. Give the girl your keys. It ain't gonna hurt you to sit back and relax a while. Lord knows we got plenty to catch up on and it's so hard to get you alone." For years, Marjorie had made similar references to the presence of Emily's dad or other friendships Mom had tried to cultivate.

Mom considered and finally dug through her purse and handed over the keys, but not without giving Emily a strict timeline: one hour, tops. Emily mouthed *thank you* to Marjorie, even though she pitied the woman for holding on too hard—something Emily knew plenty about—but there she went, down that same road herself.

But this time, she wouldn't stay silent. She wouldn't let Jody slip away so easily. She longed for those old days, those old feelings, way back before everything changed. Or at least understand why that might not be possible.

On her way out the door, Heather stopped her. "You're leaving?"

"Yeah. I need to head to Jody's for a little bit."

A frown formed on her face. "I knew you and Jody'd be at it as soon as you got back." Then, she narrowed her eyes. "You think people don't talk about you anymore, but they do."

Shock hit her system, and anger pushed at Emily for all the things that these women said about her and wanted from her. But what did they give her in return? What did they want other than the girl she had been? Quiet. Unseen. Unheard.

"Let them talk," she said.

CHAPTER FIVE

As EMILY NEARED JODY'S DRIVE and the metal gate, her gut said: *Go home.* All the lines she rehearsed along the way came out the same, like a desperate, childish plea: *Why can't we be friends again?* But she'd driven all that way. Though she didn't know how to say it, she wouldn't go home until she did.

After she passed through the gate and beyond the line of trees, a chicken ran across her path and she slammed on the brake to avoid hitting it. The door to the chicken house was cracked open. A handful of other chickens pushed through the opening to wander out as well. She cut the engine and peered around the property. No one appeared to be around, but a truck sat in front of the chicken house. No sound filled the air but the low clucks of the chickens. She considered heading up to the house but noticed in the rearview mirror that one of the chickens had escaped through the open metal gate and into the road. She hopped out of her car and managed to grab it before it had a chance to run away. She tucked the chicken under her arm and pulled the gate closed. She tried to corral the other chicken house escapees with her feet, but only managed to get one to cooperate.

When she pulled the chicken house door open wider to step inside, the odor hit her nose—that strong, ammonia-ridden, god-awful smell. But inside the building, there was a heavy overlay of something metallic, chemical. She placed the chicken on the ground, yanked the neckline of her dress over her nose and stepped inside. The windows had been covered with newspaper, lending a sepia tint to the space, which was practically empty except for a couple dozen uncaged chickens. All looked healthy and happy, only halfway interested in her intrusion. There were no cages, manure pits, feeding belts. The chicken she'd captured ran for the door again. Emily caught it before it had a chance to escape and shut the door behind her.

"Jody?" No answer. "Hello?" A thin line of light came from the bottom of the egg room door near the end of the building, along with the sounds of someone moving around or talking.

She had no phone number for Jody. No email. She didn't want to wait another three weeks for a chance meeting. She wasn't sure her nerve would last that long.

After running her hands along the wall and finding no switch, she made her way across the dimly lit building. It was slightly longer than the trailer and far larger than necessary. One of the chickens squawked and scattered when she walked by. Soon, her shoes were covered in chicken shit and straw. The noise grew louder as she neared the egg room.

She heard a buzzing noise. Music. Pounding, like someone was banging their fist on a table. Something felt off, enough to keep her from knocking. Instead she placed her ear against the door to better listen, but heard nothing more than those same noises amplified. Images of Jody and Troy came at her, mixing with Marjorie's words. She wanted to walk away, but she couldn't. Her body shook with nervousness at what she might find. If what Marjorie had implied was true.

She eased her hand on the doorknob and rested it there before slowly testing to see if it was locked. The knob twisted easily and a rush of cold air hit her face when the door cracked open. Fluorescent tubes flickered on the ceiling. Plastic containers of different sizes and corroded propane tanks had been piled into a corner with bicycle tubes, garden hoses, and duct tape scattered amongst them. August and Troy stood with their backs to her against a bare wall with no window, in front of glass jars, cans of starter fluid, and a pile of batteries. Winding plastic tubes ran from a propane tank to a glass container full of what looked like a white paste. Other identical containers were lined up along the base of the opposite wall.

An assortment of coffee filters held what looked like rock candy. Beside those were bulk packages of cold medicine, and beside those was Troy, bringing a large metal flashlight down onto a wooden table over and over. Little bits of pill dust fogged the air.

"What are you doing in here?"

Emily startled at August's voice and knocked over a jar on a shelf next to her.

"Fuck," August said.

Troy turned, eyes blazing and red-rimmed, his brow leaking with sweat. Before she knew what was happening, he bounced and headed toward her. Emily bolted out the door, slamming it behind her to stop his progress. She raced across the length of the building, toward the door, losing a shoe in the process. She stepped on something—a chicken maybe—and almost lost her balance, but she ran and ran, past the door and toward her car, before Troy slammed into her and she hit the ground. She gasped and tried to gather air back into her lungs, but his arms were around her, squeezing her so tight she thought one of her ribs might crack.

"Get off me!" she screamed, but he kept squeezing. She squeaked out another plea, begging him to stop before she passed out.

He did, but only because August was yelling and pulling him off her, the same way he'd pulled Troy off that girl.

Emily lay there on the ground, letting her body settle after the assault. When her ears stopped ringing, she eased onto her back. She watched as stars spiked her vision. Questions rang out like alarms in her head.

Emily tried to sit up, but her whole body ached. Troy stood legs wide above her, his face contorted by anger.

"*You fucking idiot,*" she screamed. "Are you trying to kill me?"

Troy came at her again. She tucked herself into a ball but August held him away. Troy hurled obscenities at her until he finally calmed down and didn't need to be restrained. He stood behind August, his face easing off the rage that had occupied it moments earlier.

August held his hand out to her and she knocked it away.

Troy leaned around August. "I can see your panties," he said with a hateful grin and spit at the ground.

"Fuck you." The dress she'd tried to keep down all morning had edged up around her waist.

"Goddammit, Troy," August said and shoved him. "Shut up."

"You shut up!" Troy looked like he would launch at him now.

She heard the pounding of shoes on the ground. Jody came running down the hill. Her breathing was ragged when she got closer, and she looked at all of them. "What the hell is going on down here?"

"What's going on? *What's going on?*" Emily pointed toward the chicken house. "You fucking tell me because what I just saw in there ain't fucking chicken farming."

Jody stared at her. Then at August and Troy.

"Did you know about this?" Emily's throat ached from screaming all her sentences and trying to regain her breath after having it knocked out of her. "Do you know what they're doing?"

"How did she get in there?" Jody asked.

August raised his head and huffed toward the sky. Then, he looked at Jody with another one of those looks whose meaning only they knew. Only this time, Emily could decode it. Someone had screwed up. That someone was Troy.

Jody's hands curled into fists. She ran up to Troy and launched them at his face. "What the fucking fuck, Troy? Huh?" He crouched over and guarded his face. "You stupid little shit."

Emily watched as Jody whaled on him with her fists. Unlike with Emily, Troy took it. He didn't bother to fight back but ducked and tried to protect his head. August kept yelling at Jody to stop and tried to pull her off him. He did, but not without Jody landing one last blow to Troy's head. Troy yelled out at last.

"Jesus, Jody," Troy said. He wiped his mouth to check for blood. "You didn't—"

"Don't speak," she said, finger in his face. He opened his mouth in complaint. "Don't say a fucking word, Troy. Not one goddamn word." They glared at each other for an uncomfortable amount of time.

August braced, as if ready to intercept incoming blows from both of them. Emily sat on the ground, numbly trying to make sense of what had happened, what might happen next.

"Get out of my fucking face," Jody finally said to Troy. "Right the fuck now."

Troy stood his ground, fists clenching and unclenching. Finally, he muttered under his breath and disappeared back into the chicken house. August stopped next to Emily to say something he couldn't seem to release from his mouth. He abandoned the thought, followed Troy, and shut the door behind him. A moment later, Troy stepped out the door again and lobbed something in the air toward Emily. She ducked and heard a thud coincide with a new tirade from Jody directed at Troy. The shoe Emily had lost during her run out of the building landed beside her hand. She heard a click from inside the chicken house as the lock slid shut.

She looked up at Jody, who raised her hand when Emily began to speak.

"Wait until we're in the house," Jody said. "I have to get back to Ricky."

Emily stared at the building, slack-jawed. That was it? They would go back to what they were doing? Jody would go back to the house?

"Come on," Jody said, and motioned for her to get up.

A muscle in Emily's back strained when she eased herself off the ground and onto her feet.

With each step they took up the hill, Emily's brain churned with what she'd seen and how Troy had tackled her, and her confusion at Jody's reaction shifted to understanding. Jody knew what they were doing. Now Emily knew.

Inside the trailer, Ricky lazily chewed on a plastic ring inside his playpen. Jody headed to the bar and stared at her phone for far too long.

Emily tried to keep her voice calm. The pressure in her head increased from clenching her jaw. "What the fuck, Jody?" she asked. "What the fuck is going on?"

Jody dragged her purse across the bar and scrambled around in it until she found a pack of cigarettes.

"Are you gonna answer—"

"Troy gives me a cut of what he makes. That's all I know. I don't know anything about how it works. I've never even been in there."

Jody had spent so much time looking at her phone that Emily thought for sure she'd have at least come up with a decent lie. Something to explain why she let a teenage dropout and an ex-boyfriend cook meth in her chicken house. But there it was, the bald-faced truth. Emily could hardly believe what she'd seen, what she'd heard, how calm Jody was now, almost as if Emily hadn't been tackled, August hadn't had to referee again, Troy hadn't been beaten by Jody's fists, and they were discussing the fine print of a new phone plan.

"If you're not involved, then why were you down there that day I came out here?"

"I was checking the lock." She looked up at Emily, almost accusatorily. "I guess I should've checked today, too."

She rubbed her eyes and tried to find the words. "This is like the worst stereotype of the South come to life. All you need is a Confederate flag over the fucking door. And you're just . . . You agreed to this? Are you crazy?"

"Fuck you." Jody crumpled the empty cigarette pack and threw it at Emily, where it pinged off her chest and landed on the floor.

"Jesus," Emily said. "If you were so hard up for money, you could have asked my parents. They would have helped you."

"Your mom's charity ended when she kicked me out."

"What are you talking about?"

"She found a bag of pot. Why do you think I had to leave? She didn't even give me a chance to explain before she called Mom and told her to come get me."

All those wasted moments of guilt and shame and feeling downright wrong about what she'd done in the bed the night Jody left. If only she had known. If only her mom had told her the truth that next morning when Emily had asked where Jody had gone.

"You're just like your mom," Jody said. "You've always thought of me as some redneck with a sad, stupid life. You've never even tried to understand me."

"No I'm not." Emily struggled to regain the thread of their conversation after what Jody had revealed. "I never thought—"

"You did. And you still do."

Emily drew her hands into a position of prayer by the sheer force of her need to plea. "I never, ever thought that. But this is crazy. This isn't you."

"It is now." Jody paced the room and then slid down the wall into a crouched position, head against the wall. Her fingers wiggled like she craved a cigarette.

Emily shook her head, not believing the turn the day, her life, had taken. "How did this happen?"

"Debt. Bad luck. Motherfucking life." Jody held her fist to her mouth and didn't speak for a while.

"What about all this?" She waved her hand around the room. "Didn't your grandpa leave you everything?"

"He left me a trailer and some land."

"Isn't it paid off?"

"Wow. You've never lived on your own, have you?" Jody rolled her head toward Emily, an eyebrow up. "Yeah, the land and trailer are paid off, but there's property taxes, a car payment and car insurance, a telephone bill, food, toilet paper, tampons, diapers, doctor's visits . . ." She ticked the items off on her fingers. "Electricity, water, what else?" She looked around the room and then flicked a finger in the air. "Oh, and let's not forget a credit card bill I won't be able to pay off thanks to a deadbeat boyfriend who disappeared along with everything in my bank account and who doesn't pay child support *and* who I don't want to talk about right now in case you were going to fucking ask me again."

Jody banged her head against the wall a few times.

"Try finding a job when you're unwed and pregnant. I even put on one of Grandma's rings, like I was married. Not even the temp jobs would hire me, not with a fucking kid on the way." Jody glared at Ricky, happily playing on the floor, like he was something to hate. "'Come back later,' they said. But you know good and well they threw my application in the trash as soon as I walked out the door.

"I had to get on WIC." She shoved the heels of her hands into her eyes and exhaled bitterness and exhaustion. "That was just about my breaking point. You should've seen it when I pulled out my vouchers. Whether it was the checker or the assholes behind me in line with their noses all up in the air, staring at me and Ricky like we were nothing but losers. They judged everything coming down that conveyor belt. I couldn't buy a goddamn candy bar without everyone looking at me like I was trash."

"I know, but—"

"That's the thing. You don't know. You don't know a thing about it. My credit card? Maxed out. I'm not out buying bling or some shit. I used it to keep the lights on. To have heat. To buy Ricky a coat. I'm not doing this because I want to. I'm doing this because I have to. You have parents who can help you. I don't. I'm all on my own. I've got no one."

Jody chewed a nail so aggressively that a trace of blood appeared on her bottom lip while Emily tried to find the words to express her worry and confusion, finally settling on, "This doesn't sit right with me."

"It didn't sit right with me either. But it's what I've got to do. And it's just until I can get back on my feet and save up a little. It's not like I'm making a career out of it. And it's good money. *Really* good money. Look." She held out her hands, stating her case. "Nobody's getting hurt. It isn't like there are drug lords or motorcycle gangs or guys with guns and all that bullshit they show on TV. Just a bunch of teenagers and lowlifes itching to get high, is all. They're gonna get it somewhere."

Now it was Emily's turn to chew on her nails. She bit one down to the nub. "Are you dealing?"

"What?" Jody jerked her head to face Emily. "Of course not." She scrunched her face and turned away in disgust. "Oh my God. Why would you even think that?"

"Because I just found a meth lab on your property." Jody's reaction cut at Emily, like she ought to be ashamed for asking. "I saw you in high school."

Jody would stand close to someone and lower her voice. Hand something mysterious to a classmate or some random stranger those times Jody let her go cruising with her on Grand Avenue in Fort Smith. Emily had never said anything. She'd checked over her shoulder to see if anyone else had seen them and had felt relieved when they hadn't.

"I was buying it, dumbass. Not dealing it," she said. "And just because I smoke a little weed now and then doesn't mean I'm doing meth. I told you, I let Troy do his thing and he pays me. It's down the hill. I barely even notice when they're here. I just happened to be taking out the trash when I heard you all screaming at each other."

"What if someone else finds out? What if it wasn't me who came over today?"

She pushed her hair out of her flushed face. "Nobody's come around. Not all the way out here." She glanced at Emily. "Least not till today. Somehow you keep showing up."

"Sorry to inconvenience you."

"I don't mean it like that." Jody propped her head back against the wall.

"It's not my fault that this happened. Any one of those people at the party could've wandered in."

"No. Not when the door's locked, which it's supposed to be. Which it was not today, thanks to Troy." She eased off the wall and sat cross-legged. "Those people didn't just wander out here. They're friends."

Unlike me, Emily bristled.

"You've lived in town too long. It's like you've forgotten what it's like to live in the woods. The nearest neighbor is at least half a mile. Nobody gives a shit what you do as long as you don't go bothering them. And nobody goes wandering onto someone's property unannounced unless they want to get shot."

She leaned back on the wall. "All I ever wanted was to be on my own. Be an adult. If I could do it all over again, I sure as hell wouldn't do it the same. But I'm not stupid. And I hate you thinking that I am."

Her stare drew Emily like a magnet. She wore those sorry eyes. The ones that normalized the situation. The ones that said, *Yeah, I'm a jerk. But I'm your jerk.*

Emily sat down next to her. This time, the sitting didn't take so much effort thanks to a rip along the seam of her dress from when Troy had tackled her, but her back flamed in spots. "I don't think you're stupid."

Her current complaints about living at home felt small in comparison. "You're not alone. I don't want you thinking that because it's not true." Emily drew her eyes toward the floor. "I know things haven't been great between us, but I'm still your friend. I still care about what happens to you. And Ricky."

Ricky chewed his toy and watched them from the playpen, like he knew they were dealing with something big and that he was a part of it.

"When you showed up that day, I was glad. I feel like it's been forever since I've had a friend, a good friend, you know?" Jody paused. "I wanted to call you. But I was scared about you finding out. You always seem to know when I'm hiding something."

"It's not like I'd tell anyone."

"I didn't know that. We hadn't seen each other in so long," Jody said. "I understand if you want to go back home and never come back. Just please keep this quiet. If anyone finds out . . ." She shook her head at the unspoken thought. "I could lose Ricky, everything." She pointed at Emily. "And I know what you're about to say. It's too risky. But I'm telling you, I don't have a choice right now. I wish there was some way I could make you believe me."

Emily didn't know how she was supposed to know about this and pretend she didn't. This was not how their lives were supposed to play out. One night when she was supposed to be studying for a history exam, Emily had been glued to the computer looking at all those before and after pictures of people who'd used meth: faces busted out with scabs and their eyeballs floating in their sockets.

Around Fort Smith, raids and explosions weren't exactly nightly news, but they were there. All around the country, all around the state. In Fort Smith. Here. In Drear's Bluff. At Jody's.

Emily's mind raced back to those crystals in the meth lab that had looked like rock candy. The night she'd eaten the brownie, she'd crunched down on something hard but breakable, like rock salt but bitter. She recalled those guys from around the fire, the way their teeth and skin seemed to have aged them by ten years at least. In a year or two, Troy might look like them. His waxen hair and charm had already left him. But Jody's skin held none of those abscesses, nor did August's.

"This is so fucked up," Emily said.

A flicker of recognition, something, flashed across Jody's face. But then it was gone. They sat for a while in silence. Ricky chattered to himself in baby talk, and Emily considered what disasters might await him in life with what was going on down the hill. But then, what disasters awaited without the basic necessities that money could provide?

Emily checked the time on her phone. An hour had already passed. No screaming texts from her mom. But then, she had no service. "I should go."

"Your dress is wrecked. You want some clean clothes?"

The last time she'd borrowed clothes, she'd ended up having her underwear thrown at her in church. Hard to believe that'd been earlier today. "No. I'm fine."

They made their way outside. Emily led and Jody trailed behind, quiet.

In the car, Emily slipped the key in the ignition, not finding the words to grasp all the complications that now weighed on her mind.

"Hold on a sec," Jody said. Loose strands of hair drifted across her face. "What'd you come over here for anyway?"

Those reasons seemed small now. "I felt bad about how we left things at church."

Emily waited as Jody seemed to search for words. "You came all this way for that?"

"I would've called, but I didn't have your number."

Jody scratched her head and looked like she was being forced into contrition. "Goddammit. You know I'm no good at this." She paused. "I'm not good at much," she said. "I'm sorry. About everything. You've always been good to me. I haven't deserved it."

So many times, Jody had said that Emily was the only one who knew her, who'd seen her cry. Euphoric recall would unleash its magic and make Emily forgetful of how hard and dismissive Jody could be.

"You're just saying that 'cause you're nervous I'm gonna tell on you," Emily said.

"So what if I am?" She laughed but then grew serious. "Sometimes, I wish I could go back to what it was like before I fucked up and got saddled with a goddamn kid. Cut me some slack, all right? I miss you."

The small gift of affection did little to comfort Emily. But like butter set out on the table too long, Emily softened despite her intentions otherwise.

Jody slapped the hood of the car and then walked back to the house.

With all those long-buried feelings dredged for release, Emily eased the car into reverse and headed back toward the Quik-a-Way.

CHAPTER SIX

SUN GLIMMERED OFF THE WAVES that trickled in from the sloped and ever-widening gap of creek bed to where Emily and Jody lay in the sun. They had found a patch of dirt amid the stones and dropped the blanket on top. Though November was around the corner, an Indian Summer loomed high and bright. The trees still held their autumn leaves. A breeze rustled through the limbs and snatched one weak leaf from its bough. The leaf floated down and rested in the pack and play, where Ricky lay asleep in the shade of the tree. The gray boom box filtered pop music through its black mesh circles.

A few days after Emily had left Jody's house, a call came from an unfamiliar number. It didn't take but a second to determine it was from Jody, who after a quick and awkward chat to catch up, asked, "You wanna head to the creek? Might be our last chance till next year."

Emily said yes and hung up the phone, knowing full well why Jody had called, despite Emily's reassurances that she wouldn't tell anyone what she knew. In the days since she drove out of Jody's driveway, she wrestled with *What now?* With both knowing and pretending not to know.

Heather had let it slip—willingly, no doubt—to Emily's mom that Emily had gone to Jody's while she and Marjorie ate lunch after church. Her mom had approached the news the same way she did most topics that made her uncomfortable: "Oh."

To ease her anxiety, Emily ticked off a mental list of things to be worried about and why she shouldn't worry:

Worry: the safety of Jody and Ricky.
Don't worry: the trailer is at the top of the hill, far from the chicken house.

Worry: someone might find out. People talk.
Don't worry: Jody lives too far away from anyone else for them to notice. It's in a chicken house. No one, as Jody said, would wander into a chicken house. No one but me.

Worry: what if Troy leaves the door unlocked again?
Don't worry: he won't make that mistake again.

The thought that slid in between all those worries was the thing that Jody had said, the thing that kept Emily awake at bedtime and drifted back to her at work when the rush of customers had subsided: Jody had said that she missed her.

Though she fought tumbling down into any feeling other than friendship for Jody again, her body tugged at her with flashes of their conversations and these new flashes of Jody's skin.

Jody slathered sunblock on her arms and legs and stomach. Little beads of sweat that refused to mix with the white lotion popped up along her skin. She handed the bottle to Emily and proceeded to lie down on her stomach.

"Get my back, will ya?"

Jody reached around and pulled the string of her bikini top, leaving the whole of her back open to Emily's hand, the stretch of skin like water after a drought. Emily drew her eyes along the ridges, down and around the backside until they rested at the crook below Jody's swim bottoms. The fabric rode up on one side and revealed the places where the sun had deepened the hue of her skin despite the claims on the back of the sunblock bottle. Emily drew the bottle above the sweep of Jody's lower back and squeezed. Liquid dripped and pooled in the two dents above her tailbone like oil in a frying pan. Dipping her fingers into the liquid was no less likely to singe and scar.

Jody cocked her head, expectant, her eyes hidden behind her mirrored sunglasses, hiding the X-ray eyes that appeared to know what Emily was thinking and feeling even though she aimed to keep all thoughts stored so deep they couldn't be read.

Emily placed the bottle on the blanket. "There you go," she said and pretended not to understand the full meaning of the request. But another part of her, not so deep, fantasized that the request wasn't so much about arm reach as Jody wanting Emily's hand on her back.

The liquid squirted through Jody's fingers as she twisted her hand around to her back. Her elbow jutted in the air as she tried to reach. In doing so, she lifted herself up. "Get the top at least so I don't burn."

Emily tried not to stare at the curve of Jody's breast and its cradle within the cloth triangle of black bikini top. Unlike Jody's sunglasses, Emily's were tinted and revealed every glance and aside.

"Fine," she said and placed her hand at the lowest curve of Jody's back and swooped the excess sunblock up along the bumps of her spine, across the shoulder blades, and down again. One hand could administer the whole business, so slight was Jody in the shoulders. Skin draped delicate as a silk shift on a storefront mannequin. No freckles, no moles.

Jody placed her head down on the blanket and smiled with what Emily interpreted as victory.

"I hope you burn," Emily said.

Jody laughed. "You're the one who needs a tan. You're white as Marjorie."

The last time Emily had seen her was at the Quik-a-Way, along with Owen and Connie. "Has she ever come around looking for Troy?"

"She doesn't even know where I live."

"Everybody knows where everybody lives."

Jody didn't speak for a good while. "Why're you talking to me about Marjorie? You're ruining my day."

"You're the one who brought her up, asshole," Emily said. "That reminds me, I saw your mom at the Quick-a-Way."

Jody stayed quiet a little too long. "You sure it was her?"

"Positive." She recalled the unfortunate image of Connie's hands down Owen's pants at the gas pumps. "From what I can tell, she's dating Owen."

"Dating?" Jody rolled onto her back and laughed. "Mom doesn't date. She fucks a guy and takes whatever he'll give her. Though I can't imagine what Owen could possibly offer her besides bad sex in the back of a patrol car."

Emily wondered if Jody knew from experience.

"When was this?"

Emily had to think. "Last Sunday, after church." The same day that she'd found the lab. A day that felt ages ago and unreal.

"Why didn't you tell me before now?"

"Because I had just stumbled upon a meth lab. I was a little pre-occupied."

Jody's mouth twisted on a thought. "You talk to her?"

"No," Emily said. "She stayed outside. Owen was giving Marjorie a hard time about Troy." Emily rubbed her hands to try to remove the sticky aftermath of sunscreen. "You don't think he'll head out to your house, do you?"

"No. He has no reason to. He caught Troy speeding one night and Troy just happened to have taken too many pain pills. That's all there is to it." Jody flipped back to her stomach. "Owen doesn't have it out for Troy. That's just Marjorie being Marjorie. And Owen can't just go wandering around my property, so there's no reason to be paranoid. Troy's been doing his thing for months now. I don't know how many ways I can tell you everything is fine before you'll believe me."

Emily grumbled and headed toward the water, muttering to Jody that she had to rinse the sunblock off her hands. The water was what she needed, ice cold and baptismal. She waded in and walked away from the edge, away from Jody and the agonizing lure of curves and requests to touch them and demands for information while Jody hid illegal activities. She walked to where the water lapped at her shoulders. The scooped neckline of her bra showed through the battered white T-shirt she wore. Prevention against the sun, she'd told Jody, and pulled the fabric down to cover herself. Silty mud stirred up around her toes. Ahead, on the other side of the creek, stood a line of tall trees along a crest, where years ago, she and Jody had climbed out of the water and kissed in the woods.

Earlier that day, they'd put their swimsuits on under their clothing and headed to the creek on an old ATV Jody's grandpa had bought and fixed.

They'd raced up and down the dirt road. Emily had to grip tight around Jody's waist lest she fall off when Jody tugged the wheel to make a hard turn. Emily had wondered if Jody weren't trying to toss her off for sport. When the exhaust pipe scorched their legs and sweat dripped down their backs, Jody navigated toward the creek. The roar of the engine died down in their ears while they splashed around in the water. Jody was skinny as always, but with enough curves attached to her frame to attract the eyes of boys and men alike.

Jody had torn through the water and up the slope. By the time Emily took hold of the tree roots and scrambled her way to the top, Jody had already stopped in the middle of a thicket and sat down. She unrolled a Ziploc sandwich bag she'd tucked into her swimsuit top, reached inside, and pulled out a lighter and a joint. She inhaled long and deep.

A thick curtain of evergreens with points driving high into the sky blocked out the sun. The ground was slippery from the previous night's dew. No gnats bugged or mosquitoes bit them. There were no birds or squirrels. Something felt out of order, like life had been sucked out. Emily had raked her hands along her arms and fought a swarm of goose bumps.

Jody lay down on the forest floor with her hands clasped across her chest. Aside from the joint sticking straight out of her mouth, she looked like a corpse.

Emily spun her head in the direction of some distant tree branch that had cracked and then back to Jody. "What are you doing?"

"Smoking," Jody mumbled.

"We should get back."

Jody sat up and crossed her legs. "Why? It's not like anyone would miss us or wants us around. At least not me." She'd jabbed a stick into the ground repeatedly to make a hole. The last bit of the joint flamed to an end. She released the smoke slowly before shoving the remains into the hole and covering it with dirt. Another jab at the ground and she was done. She stood and wiped the forest debris off her swimsuit. "I'm out of this fucking town anyway."

"What are you talking about?"

"I'm talking about getting out of here. Running away. Haven't you been listening?" Jody had threatened to run away about once a week since she'd moved in, complaining about Emily's mom and her rules, her own mom and how she ran off on her, and school. Emily had heard her. She just hadn't believed her. This time, something in Jody's tone told her she should. "You're barely sixteen. Where are you gonna go?"

"Anywhere. I can get a job now." Jody lodged her hands at her sides. "I'm leaving and never looking back."

Emily wanted to say, *What about us? What about me?* "When?" she asked.

"Soon. And don't come looking for me."

"Oh, I won't," Emily said. How could Jody leave her alone in Drear's Bluff? What was she supposed to do? Go back to hanging out with Heather?

Jody placed a hand on Emily's shoulder and let out a sad little sound when she looked at Emily. "I don't mean that," Jody said, "about not coming to look for me. I'd tell you where I went. You're the only one I'd tell." Jody dropped her arms but held Emily's stare. "We'll always be friends. Like the song says"—Jody laughed and opened her hands, palms up as if to receive the baby Jesus—"friends are friends forever."

Emily hated that song. Every other line evoked the Almighty Lord. The girls in choir practically circle-jerked to the song's false promise that friendships could never be severed. Emily knew better.

Jody was proving that. Emily shifted on her heel and started walking the way she had come.

"Don't be mad at me." Jody ran to catch up with her. When she did, she stopped in front of her, slung her arms around Emily's neck, and pulled her so close their noses almost touched. "We'll still be friends." She held her like that, uncomfortably close, until Jody leaned in and pressed her lips against Emily's.

Emily jerked away from her. "What are you doing?" And then, "Oh my god. You are so high."

"Maybe I am." Jody laughed and kissed her again, working her tongue into Emily's mouth out of what felt like spite. And what worked its way through Emily was not annoyance or disgust but a deep, unnameable something that Emily's own tongue sought more of until Jody pulled away in surprise.

Jody's eyes were glassy. Her smile lopsided. "Now you're high, too," she said and walked back toward the creek ahead of Emily.

Not long after, Jody left just like she'd promised, only not how she'd planned, and with them never speaking again about what had happened.

Now Emily rubbed the silty mud into each palm. When she drew her hands out, she could still see and smell the sunblock. She walked back through the water and up the bank to where Jody propped herself on her elbows and watched. At least that's what Emily assumed, not knowing where her eyes landed behind her sunglasses. She felt silly in her T-shirt and bra, the jean shorts made even longer by the water that wept down her legs, a swimsuit for country trash. She wrapped her towel around her before she sat.

Jody turned on her side, all legs and torso. Tendrils of black hair floated down to join the curve of her breast, accentuated by the way she lounged on her towel.

"I been thinking . . ." Jody said.

Emily kept her eyes on the creek. The wind hit the water on her skin. She drew the towel tighter around her body.

"You could stay with me. Help out with Ricky."

Emily glanced at her and then turned back to the creek water, wondering if Jody was toying with her again. "What are you talking about?"

"I was thinking you could babysit while I look for jobs and try to get out of this hole I'm in. And get away from this mess with Troy."

The look on Jody's face said this time she was serious. Emily had known there was more to this invitation than getting together as friends. Emily wanted to say no, if only to show Jody that she wouldn't come running every time she called. But more than the desire to prove her wrong, there was the desire to be near her—even if it meant babysitting. But ignoring what was going on in the chicken house? She wasn't sure she could do that.

"I told you I'm not going to tell anyone about what's going on," Emily said. "You don't have to keep me close. I'm not a risk to you."

"You think I'm some kind of asshole?" Jody asked. "That's not why I'm offering. If it makes you feel better, I'll let you clean the house and get groceries."

"Like a nanny?"

"Sure, I'll give you a job title if you want."

"I already have a job."

"Since when? Why didn't you say something?"

"Because I'm a cashier. It's embarrassing. And as much as I hate it, I doubt that babysitting's gonna pay as much as I'm getting now, which is not much, by the way." It was hardly enough to cover the gas to and from work. At the rate she was going, she'd be thirty-five before she could move out of her parents' house. And she'd still have that student loan to pay.

"I bet it's more than what you can pull in working forty hours a week."

She found that hard to believe. Besides, they barely let her work twenty.

"How long is Troy gonna be around?" she asked, trying to sound like she was changing the subject while also negotiating the fantasy of quitting her job and living with Jody.

Jody scratched her arm. "I told you. It's only for a little while."

"How long?"

A ripple broke along the water. The dark, triangular head of a cottonmouth skimmed its head along the surface. Emily dashed her feet onto the blanket.

Calm as could be, Jody found and flung a rock at the snake, which disappeared back underwater.

How long had that snake been there in the water while she'd waded, thinking about the past?

"He's only there a few more months. Maybe less. I just need to find something steady that pays well so I can make it on my own." Jody tilted her head. "Besides, we always wanted to be roommates. Remember?"

The wind picked up and goose bumps ran along Emily's arm. Perhaps she hadn't been the only one to remember those dreams, or the day in the woods. "I remember."

BY THE TIME EMILY RETURNED home from the creek, the sun had already set. She turned off the engine and propped her head against the headrest. All the windows in the house were dark except those in the living room. The TV created sporadic shifts of light behind the thin curtains.

She had gotten up early that morning and would need to get up early again the next. She was tired and wanted to wash the creek water off her. She missed being able to come home and not speak to anyone. Her roommates had either not been home or not been talkative.

Outside the car, a brisk wind promised a late evening thunderstorm to cool the air. All the creatures seemed to have taken to hiding in anticipation, leaving a hush. Many nights like this Emily had sat on the porch steps with her mom after doing the dishes. There'd been comfort in the habit. Now the air felt sticky and her pulse high. Things had been easier then, and Emily wasn't sure what had changed.

Once again, she walked over those cement circles with their names. At the sight of Jody's name, she returned to a series of what-ifs she'd entertained on the ride home. What if she said no? What if she said yes? Neither answer came without complications.

The rote actions of living in the same house most of her life led her to the door, into the house, and across from her mom in the kitchen, who asked her if she wanted supper.

"No, I already ate."

Her mom put away the leftovers and an empty plate she'd already taken out. "Where were you all day? The library must close at some point."

Emily rubbed her face. She considered lying again, but the sun and debating Jody's offer had depleted her. "At the creek with Jody."

"Oh," her mom said.

"I'm going upstairs."

Before she could get to the hallway, her mom called out behind her.

She longed for a shower. The daybed, even though it was hard and hurt her back. The door that could be shut but not locked. Headphones. Music. Quiet. "Yeah?"

"Any luck on the job search?"

Rejections or no word at all while she sat eating her comped meals and collecting the bare minimum wage that businesses were legally compelled to provide.

"Nothing yet." She turned to leave but knew she wouldn't get far.

"You spend a lot of time at the library on the computers. Maybe you'd have more luck with the papers."

"People don't do that anymore. It's all online."

"I don't understand how—"

A simmering irritation broke to boiling. "Of course you don't."

Every day since she'd been home, she'd had the same or a similar conversation with her mom. She'd tried everything and come up with nothing, nothing but her current job. Panic wore on her, panic at not having found a good job—a *real job* as everyone liked to say—at having to move back home, at credit card bills and student loan statements and résumés and cover letters and dead-end desk jobs that didn't seem worth having even if she could get them without a degree, though everyone fought for the opportunity to win them. That panic rested as a lump in her throat, a reminder of what a failure she'd been and continued to be. It was hard to focus with the daily pressure of her mom's expectations and requests for status updates. *Fuck it,* she thought. *Fuck it all.*

"I got a job. Okay?" She held her hands in front of her, as if offering a gift. "I get to press a button and say 'Welcome!' every time this annoying buzzer goes off. I get to fill cups with Coke. I get to give bags of burgers to people and pretend that I am so thankful for their order instead of hating every minute of my day."

She studied her mom's face. There it was. There was the crushed pride that Emily knew she'd see on her mom's face at the latest twist in Emily's downfall—and how it would affect her mom, who didn't have to work. Her mom's parents had taken care of her and then Emily's dad had—and still did. She didn't have to wonder how she'd afford a phone to get her a job that would one day allow her to maybe find an apartment so she wouldn't have to live at home. She didn't have to try and try and try, only to get a low-wage job with a bad outfit and worse tasks. But still, her mom worried that somehow this meant *she* was less-than, not just Emily.

"I didn't tell you because I knew exactly what you'd think," Emily continued. "But don't worry. It's way over in Fort Smith, near the Oklahoma border. So you don't have to be concerned about anyone seeing me and thinking you're a failure, too."

Her mom stepped back and raised a hand to her chest. "I never said—"

"You don't say a lot of things."

"What's that supposed to mean?" She wrung her hands as she seemed to work through some thought that she didn't share with Emily.

"Like how you didn't tell me that Jody was back in town or how you babysat Ricky. I know why. I know exactly why."

"I'm not . . ." Her mom cleared her throat and clapped her chest as if she'd swallowed wrong. She moved a hand to her mouth and held it there for what felt like an age. "You had a really hard time after Jody left," she said.

After weeks of Emily barely eating, barely speaking following Jody's departure, she'd gotten re-baptized at her mom's request. Emily shivered at the memory of the cold water dripping down her back.

With all those constrictions she felt and talk of sin, church might as well have been a finishing school for the burial of desires so river deep that no one could drag any sin out of her. After that, bags full of dresses and shoes appeared. Nudges were dispensed when a cute boy walked by. Every night, Emily would get on her knees and pray, thinking that maybe it would make a difference.

She'd left the house. The town. And slowly, she'd tried to unburden herself of the guilt she carried about why Jody had left. Then she'd gone and committed the one sin that her mom was most afraid of, only it wasn't with Jody. Emily had fought too hard already to feel normal in a place that couldn't accommodate any deviation. She wouldn't tamp down her feelings for Jody or anyone else anymore, and she wouldn't let her mom try to drown them this time. Pot was likely just a convenient excuse her mom had used to get Jody out of the house once it became clear how close they'd become.

Time hadn't erased her feelings. And prayer hadn't changed a thing.

"She was my best friend, and you promised Connie you'd take care of her," Emily said. "But you didn't. You kicked her out instead of helping her like a good Christian." Her mom looked like she'd been slapped. All that pent-up anger flooded Emily. "All because you can't stand to think that your daughter might be something that makes you sick."

Her mom's face reddened and her eyes widened. Emily willed her mom to say something, anything to refute her.

"You're such a fucking coward," Emily said, her voice breaking. "You can't admit why you really kicked Jody out. You can't even talk about me behind my back with Marjorie the way you do about everyone else. I don't even get that much from you."

"What's going on in here?" Her dad's voice startled her.

Her mom rarely lacked for words. If her mouth wasn't expressing her feelings, her body did it for her. The silence of both alarmed Emily.

"Dot?" her dad asked.

A deep, guttural noise came from her mom. She quickly shoved her hand over her mouth to cover any other noise that might escape. Tears streamed down her face. She rushed past Emily, failing to contain the wail that echoed through the hallway and followed her up the stairs.

Her dad raised his hand. It shook in the air until his fingers curled into a fist, his index finger slowly inching in her direction. "You've crossed a line this time."

"But she—"

"Enough! I don't want to hear it. I don't want to hear any of your excuses." She'd never seen him angry. He'd never yelled at her. Never raised a fist. "Your mother only wants the best for you. And you . . ." He began to choke up.

She opened her mouth to speak, to apologize. But her dad had already turned to leave.

"I can't even look at you right now," he said.

She watched as he retreated, pushing down the horror of what had just happened, of dropping the finely tuned filter, of saying things good people weren't supposed to say.

But I'm not a good person, she thought.

CHAPTER SEVEN

SHE BELONGED HERE.

That's what Emily told herself as she stood in front of Jody's door one week later. That's what she had to believe. She had no choice. She couldn't stay with her parents. Not after what she'd said. They wouldn't allow it.

Three days after their confrontation, three silent days of beating herself up and trying but failing to find the correct words to describe how sorry she was, her dad indicated that given everything that had happened, it might be best for her to leave. He also said he'd help her with a deposit on an apartment if necessary, but that hopefully she'd saved some from working the past month. He hadn't looked up from his *Handyman* at that last part.

An apology wouldn't have helped. Every interaction was tainted with the words that she'd said. There was no way to take them back.

And there was not enough money for a deposit, not with first and last month's rent. Not with the second month or the third or any of the months that followed. Not with the bills that already ate most of her paycheck. She scoured through the rentals in Fort Smith, closer to work and away from Drear's Bluff, looking for a roommate. The only options were located in the bad parts of town and the rent was still too high. There was no one she wanted to share a place with. No one but the one who had already offered a room and a job, someone who had seemed happy when Emily called and asked if the offer still stood, and whose door she stood in front of now.

Though she'd made her decision, a storm of doubts had gathered about moving in with Jody.

Emily had said yes and told herself that the chicken house was too far down the hill to hurt her if something bad happened. She had said yes and prepared herself to say that she didn't know anything if anyone came asking. She hadn't noticed anything off before she'd wandered into the chicken house. She told herself that no one else would either. The land and surroundings had appeared calm, quiet, uninhabited even. Every other piece of land on that dirt road—save Johnston's farm—looked the same: weathered and on the edge of foreclosure. Appearances suggested nothing more than the usual downturn in people's luck and bank accounts. Yes, she had said, with reassurances of the move's temporary nature, to get her out of the house. Long enough to find a real job. Long enough to save up for a deposit on an apartment. Just long enough.

In the back of her mind, she held on to Jody's assurance that the lab—and Troy—would be gone in a few months, maybe less. Once that happened, maybe Emily wouldn't have to leave either. She shoved all the worst-case scenarios to the back of her mind and tried to focus on those dreams they'd had instead, the ones that Jody remembered, too.

Even though the door she stood in front of was now technically her own, she knocked and waited for an answer. The doorknob jiggled in her hand and a thin line of the particleboard door that had not been stained appeared as a half moon at the top of the metal casing. She turned the knob to go inside, but not before pushing the casing back to cover the exposed piece.

When she yelled out hello, Jody popped her head up from behind the bar between the kitchen and the living room.

"You don't have to knock. Go on and get settled." Jody swiped the back of her hand across her forehead and nodded toward the hallway. "Ricky puked lunch all down himself, me, and the floor. I've got to clean him up and put him down for his nap."

Emily didn't have the energy to clean up baby puke. "You want some help?"

"Nah," Jody said. "Take today off. But tomorrow, he's all yours."

One thing Emily hadn't given up just yet: her job. Something within her said, *not yet*. If she wanted to stay with Jody, she'd have to babysit. Full time. There was no way to do both. So she made a plan: she'd call in sick for a few days, see how things went with babysitting before quitting.

Emily carried the few moving boxes she'd brought with her into the back room at the end of the trailer, past Ricky's room.

Emily and Jody had stayed in this room on a handful of visits to Jody's grandparents' house. Not much had changed since then. The room was small and spare with no bed and a stack of milk crates in place of shelves lined up against the wall. She'd used similar plastic cubes in her dorm room. She reminded herself that she was Jody's roommate now, not a guest. If she wanted a dresser and bed, she'd have to go out and buy them.

She shoved her boxes next to the windows that marked the front of the trailer. Another thing on her list of to-dos: buy curtains to cover the blinds. The room needed some color, something to help her forget her mom's affinity for all shades of brown.

The closet door rattled on its track and resisted when she slid it open to hang her collection of monochromatic T-shirts. On one of those previous visits, Jody had thieved some of her grandpa's beer from the fridge and they'd crashed into the closet door while dancing like fools, Jody's grandparents unaware as they slept at the opposite end of the trailer. Jody had insisted they couldn't hear the closet door falling or her and Emily giggling and shushing as they lay half on top of it and half on top of each other. With the slight buzz of beer and the danger of getting caught, Emily recalled wanting to stay in that moment. But Jody had rolled off her and placed the door back on its track, not so much correcting it but fixing it with a permanent screech and resistance whenever one tried to pull it open.

She shoved away the memory of that other closet door that had come off its track, not wanting to cloud her day further.

Much like the closet in the spare room she'd vacated, this closet retained a handful of items. Emily scraped the metal hangers full of old jackets along the wooden pole and out of the way. At the very back hung the red satin dress that Emily's mom had bought for Jody's pageant.

Jody rustled outside the bedroom after closing Ricky's door. Emily considered shoving the dress back but held it out into the light. She called out to Jody.

When Jody walked in, her eyes widened.

Emily laughed and moved the dress away from Jody's hands when she lunged for it. "You kept your pageant dress."

Jody's face flushed.

Emily laughed again and held the garment up to Jody's skin. "Your color almost matches."

"You're such an asshole." Jody yanked the dress away but laughed along with Emily. She held the dress out in front of her and plopped down onto the carpet. "Lord." Her fingers glided over the satin. "Who keeps a stupid dress?"

Emily followed suit and sat cross-legged next to her. "Mom still has dresses from when she was my age."

"That explains your church dress."

Emily cringed at the reminder. "Shut up and give it back." Jody did as requested. Emily unfurled the dress from its ball and held it out in front of them. "You kept it because it matters."

"No. I didn't know what to do with it." Jody folded her hands into her lap. "I should have burned it. That would have been a fitting end."

None of the popular girls had paid much attention to Jody. That changed when Emily's mom convinced Jody to enter the pageant. More than once afterward, Emily had heard girls whisper not so quietly about Jody's lack of name brand clothing and who she'd slept with this week, comments that would send Emily into a silent rage, especially when they began to include her in those rumors.

Instead of fighting back, Jody had meandered to the dugouts with the hoods, who smelled of cast-off cigarettes and didn't care that she'd worn a dress and stood on a stage to be judged.

The shimmery fabric slid through her fingers. Jody had looked beautiful that night. "Mom and Dad were so proud of you."

"Your dad always just seemed to tolerate me."

"That's not true. You were in and out a lot." Emily's dad had never taken to Jody but couldn't say no when her mom asked him to consider giving her a home. He'd always been polite. But Emily suspected he knew that someone would end up getting their feelings hurt. "You should have seen Mom when you walked out on that stage and they called your name. I guarantee it's one of the proudest moments of her life." Even though she meant what she said and there was no lie in the words, their truth cut.

"It wasn't much of a competition. Those other girls looked so stupid in their poufy dresses and hair. No one should wear that much makeup. It's like they went to the mall and got it done for free at Dillard's. And you're forgetting that they held the pageant in the cafeteria. Besides, it should've been you in that dress."

Emily spread the dress over her lap to hide her thighs. "It wouldn't fit on me."

"That's not what I meant," Jody said. "Your mom should have told you to enter, not me. You were prettier than all of them. You still are."

The words were nothing more than a consolation prize, something Jody had to say because she was feeling low about herself remembering the way things had changed after the pageant. "Mom knows I hate dresses."

Jody twisted her fingers and began to speak but stopped herself.

"What?" Emily asked.

"I'm sorry that I let your mom do that." Her eyes glossed over. "I shouldn't have."

"You don't have anything to be sorry about."

Jody sniffled and wiped her eyes along her forearm.

Emily continued, "I'm glad Mom cared about you the same way she cared about me. You deserved someone to fuss over your hair and makeup and tell you you're pretty."

Jody hunched over, arms around her legs. "Why do I always want to cry around you?" After a while, she lifted her head. Her face was red, but her eyes were dry. She pulled the dress off Emily's lap, leaving a cool, tingling sensation as the silky fabric left her skin. "Should we burn it?"

Emily rubbed at her legs. "Do you think you still fit in it?"

"I sure as hell don't want to find out. Not with all this baby weight."

The dress would have slipped off Jody's shoulders. Jody ran her fingers along the fabric, as if to lock the folds and stitches into her memory. Emily understood the desire.

"I can drop it off at the Goodwill the next time I go into town, if you want."

After another round of hesitation, Jody spoke, "I'll take care of it." She picked the satin hanger off the floor and placed the straps on the cushioned part. "Your mom wouldn't let you take the bed?"

Emily hadn't asked. She'd grabbed her things and left as soon as Jody had confirmed that her offer was real. "Nope."

"Figures." Jody held the hanger high in her hand and draped the bottom of the dress over an arm. "I'll find some blankets so you can make up a pallet for the night." She examined the dress for a while and then seemed to realize that Emily had been watching her.

"I won't tell," Emily said.

Jody smiled, held the dress against her, and danced down the hallway.

Watching her walk away, Emily felt as dirty as if she'd been watching porn. The craving came on like a fever, as if a coal had been stoked within and blurred the edges of reasonable thought. Rather than push it away, she sat on the floor and let the desire consume her.

A HANDFUL OF ASPIRIN HAD done nothing to dull the pain of having only thin blankets to cushion her back all night. The floor couldn't hold all the blame. The ever-present anxiety of her job and her student loan and credit card payments kept Emily awake. She hadn't talked to Jody about how much she'd get paid for babysitting, or if Jody instead intended to give Emily free rent. At the creek, Jody had said she could pay more than what Emily was making. Full-time pay.

But she had not thought through the details of her move more than that, only the pressing need to find a place to live after her dad asked her to leave. The same way she hadn't thought about how losing her scholarship would lead her back to Drear's Bluff.

And then there was the chicken house, and the dangers it held, looming at the end of the hill. A few more months. She just needed to wait a few more months before Troy and August and the lab were gone.

She stared at the water-stained ceiling of her new bedroom and wondered how long it'd take until her body and mind adjusted to the feel of this worn carpet on her bare feet, these walls that met her in the dark when she got up in the middle of the night to pee, a baby crying out for food or comfort or other anguish at ungodly hours. Emily had rolled out of the tangle of covers and off the floor when Ricky sounded the alarm at six a.m. She'd gotten up, fed him, and tried to stay awake while he did the things that babies do.

Eventually, Jody emerged from her room wearing a plain white T-shirt, too-big slacks, and the knockoff Doc Martens that Emily's mom had bought her years ago because her own shoes had been so worn. She flipped her phone between her index finger and thumb. "I have to take off here in about ten minutes."

Emily sat up from the couch where she'd been fighting off sleep. "Where are you off to?"

Jody grabbed a fistful of Cheerios out of the box. "An interview. They called this morning." She shoved the cereal in her mouth and crunched.

Not the outfit Emily would have chosen for an interview. "Don't they usually schedule those things instead of calling and asking you to show up on the same day?"

Jody shoved another round of cereal into her mouth. "I don't know," she grumbled and chewed. "They asked if I could come in today, and I said yes because you're here. It's factory work. I might be able to pick up these one- to two-week jobs that cover people's vacations and sick days. Maternity leave, too. That's a big one," she said. "They told me I might go perm eventually."

"What's the name of this place?"

Jody scratched at her head. "Just this temp agency."

"You don't know the name?"

"Why do you care?"

"I'm just asking a question. I've been looking for jobs for months and haven't found anything besides fast food, so I find it curious."

Jody closed the cereal box and followed it with a swig of milk. Then she wiped her mouth with the back of her hand. "If this is what it's gonna be like living with you, please shoot me now." Jody shifted to look at Emily. "If you have a problem babysitting today, you need to tell me now so I can call Troy."

"What's he gonna do, put the playpen in the chicken house with him? Lord knows he would."

Jody pointed at Emily. "Stop being an asshole and just promise me you'll take good care of my kid."

"Of course I will."

"If you're here and Troy's down there, I can be elsewhere."

The annoyance of Troy's presence and her babysitting duties had distracted her from the larger question that worked its way into her thoughts. "But if he's busy making you so much money, why do you need a job?"

"I told you already. If I want Troy out of here in a few months, I have to start looking for something permanent."

Emily threw the blanket off and stood up. Her head still roared and her eyes felt devoid of moisture. "All right, give me the rundown. Like how often to feed him and whatnot."

Jody looked at her watch and grimaced. "There's no time. Just try not to kill him."

She hurried around the room looking for her purse and keys. When she found them, she shoved lotion and assorted female necessities into it. The bag fell open enough that Emily could see the handle of a pistol.

The sight of it stunned her, though it shouldn't have, given what she'd seen thus far.

"Is that a gun?" she asked. There seemed to be some new revelation each minute that passed.

Jody followed the direction of Emily's eyes. She pulled the flap over. "It's no big deal. I'm a woman alone in the woods. I had this before all that."

Troy. August. Emily. They were all there. "You're not alone," Emily said and plopped back down on the sofa while Jody rounded up the rest of her things.

When Jody leaned over to give Ricky a kiss and a hug, her fresh shower scent permeated the air. Emily's body betrayed her and fluttered with the promise of a hug as well.

"Good luck with your interview," Emily said, emphasis on the last word as she took in Jody's appearance once more.

Instead of the nail that Jody favored and gnawed to jagged edges, she bit her bottom lip, smiled, and then shut the door.

RICKY HAD TAKEN TO STORY time like Jody had taken to the suggestion that she get saved at church. After his screams morphed into spasms, Emily admitted defeat. She placed Ricky in his playpen and let him get stoned on TV from the safety of his baby jail.

She hovered in front of the open refrigerator and foraged in both the refrigerator's freezer and the storage freezer on the back porch until her fingertips stung. Nothing magically delicious awaited her like at her parents' house. She could've gone for some of that leftover monkey bread or sausage gravy today. Instead, she found cans of golden hominy and black-eyed peas and a box of dried spaghetti—minus an accompanying jar of Ragu. She stood on her tiptoes and wiggled her fingers along the second shelf of the high cabinet. Her fingertips grazed the smooth triangle patterns of a glass jar and the ridges of metal on top. She reached farther into the cabinet to pull out an unsealed jar of Muscadine jelly that had probably been gathering dust since before Jody's grandma died. She shoved it to the far end of the cabinet.

She tried to occupy herself on her phone, but she barely got one bar of service in the house. She walked around the yard with her phone held high in the air. The service bars flickered at random times and disappeared with a shift in the wind. When she did get service, it sucked all her power.

Finally, out of options that didn't include daytime soaps or talk shows, she glanced at Jody's closed bedroom door. She couldn't help but wonder what else Jody might be hiding besides a meth lab, a gun, and the name of her baby's father. Hell, maybe she'd gone full redneck and Emily would find moonshine, a banjo, and a whole other family. After checking on Ricky in his playpen, she peeked out the front window to look for Jody's car and then opened the bedroom door.

The bed had been made, the carpet free of discarded clothing. She navigated the narrow passage along the bed toward the dresser and opened a drawer. The gym shorts Jody had given her to wear lay freshly laundered on top of a pair of sweatpants, a sweatshirt, and assorted T-shirts with assorted logos, none fit for anything more than chores or laying about the house. She lifted the clothes out of the drawer and held them to her nose. The faint scent of Downy fabric softener clung to them. Underneath the pile of T-shirts she found the scratched-up Snow White keychain that she had given Jody. Emily's dad had bought it for her on a trip to Disney World. Jody had found it in Emily's near-empty jewelry box and twirled it in her fingers. Emily didn't know why she liked it so much but had let her keep it.

That fever-like craving came over her, remembering and hoping for more small pieces of their life together to appear. Shame swelled. She had no right to Jody's private things, but like an addict in search of a bigger, better high than the appearance of a simple keychain, she opened five other drawers. Jeans, T-shirts, socks, thin blankets. One drawer held nothing but stacks of old bills and a sheet of uncut wallet-sized pictures of a newborn Ricky from the J. C. Penney portrait studio. She opened one of the small drawers at the top of the dresser. Instead of lacy panties and barely-there G-strings—the anticipation heated her skin and made her feel dirty, like when she'd found *Cosmo* magazines hidden under the Bible in her mom's bedside table, page corners turned down on articles that described things she didn't want to think about her mom doing to her dad—she discovered disappointing piles of neatly folded, solid-colored utility underwear Jody had probably bought three to a package and tossed absentmindedly into her cart at Walmart. Emily pushed the drawer shut without disturbing the contents and moved to the closet and the boxes on the top shelf. Through the bathroom cabinet. Under the bed. Behind a small box that sat on the floor. The same anticipation and letdown met her everywhere.

Not one drawer or box held evidence that Emily had ever been in Jody's life. No record existed of the time that Jody had spent living with Emily and her parents. No photographs of moments big and small, like the tenth-grade Halloween dance where they'd dressed like Madonna circa "Like a Virgin," or Christmas morning with their matching iPods, or that visit to the state fair where Emily and Jody had cheesed with cotton-candy mouths. No knotted friendship bracelets, matinee movie stubs, passed notes with acronyms—nothing to verify those claims of *forever forever forever*. Forever, blotted, except for that Snow White keychain.

All those other things resided in a shoebox at the bottom of Emily's closet.

Dejected and erased and feeling sideways about it, she opened the door to head back to the living room.

Troy stood propped against the wall just outside Jody's room, smiling so hard his lips looked like they'd bleed from the effort.

"Jesus!" Emily clutched a hand to her chest. She hadn't seen him since he tackled her. She tried to appear strong and unfazed, but she didn't like being alone with him in the house without Jody or August to intercept his fists should he decide to use them for the smallest slight.

He held a peanut butter and jelly sandwich in his hand and bit off a giant chunk. "Whatcha doing in there? Sniffing Jody's panties?"

"None of your damn business." She shut the door behind her and rushed past him. "Why are you here?"

Troy burped. The smell of peanut butter drifted to her nose. "Just picking up some things before I head back to work."

"What could you possibly need from the house for"—she gestured with air quotes—"'work?'"

"None of your damn business," he said in a high feminine voice—a poor imitation of how she spoke.

"Well get it and get out."

He held up his sandwich. "Already did." He shoved the rest in his mouth and scratched at his crotch. "Good luck babysitting," he said, mouth full. "I recall it ain't your strong suit. If it weren't for Jody, I might be scarred for life from that barbed wire fence. Or even dead if I'd have hit it right." He grabbed his throat with both hands and—she gathered—mimicked choking on the blood rushing out of his make-believe injury.

She rolled her eyes and headed for the couch.

He moved toward the front door and opened it before pointing at her. "Don't you hurt my little buddy, you hear? No more leaving him alone while you snoop. TV ain't a good replacement for real care and attention."

She wanted something to throw at Troy's head. "Oh, shut up."

He held his hands to his face and exhaled deep and long into an imaginary pair of panties. She turned away so she wouldn't have to see, but that did nothing to silence his stupid cackling before he closed the door and she was left in the quiet of the trailer.

In the living room, she stewed in her anger and concern that Troy would say something to Jody about her snooping. After lunch, Ricky finally dozed off and she laid him in his crib. She clicked off the TV, leaving the drone of the refrigerator to accompany her dishwashing. While sponging bits of smashed peas off a plate, she noticed August's truck down the hill. He wandered in and out of the chicken house carrying boxes to and from the back of the truck. She told herself not to look. If she didn't look and she didn't know, she wouldn't have to lie about more than what she already knew. She was a nanny now. Sort of.

Still glancing out the window, she sunk her hands into the sudsy dishwater to retrieve the next item and pricked her finger. She swished her hand around the sink to find the offender and retrieved a blunt steak knife. The soft skin of her index finger ached but the knife hadn't drawn blood.

After the dishes, she shoved the baby monitor in her back pocket, peeked her head into Ricky's room to check on him and headed outside with the trash.

Bits of charred paper floated in the air along the side of the house, where Emily stood watching the week's refuse burn and turn the sky above oily black.

"Hey," August said and made his way around the side of the trailer.

Hay's for horses. Her dad's corny joke. If only it could make her laugh now.

"Saw the smoke." A toothpick hung from the corner of his mouth. "Wanted to make sure everything's okay."

Like she couldn't be trusted with the simplest of tasks. "I know how to burn trash. We didn't get county trash pick-up till high school and—"

"Settle down, Scarlett. I'm just making sure you're not burning down the hill."

"If anyone's gonna burn shit down, it ain't gonna be me."

He looked off to the side as if he needed a clear space to generate his next sentence. "Jody told me you'd be moving in."

"You jealous?"

"Damn, girl. You got a real hair up your ass." He smiled; she grimaced. "I told you before, there's nothing going on between me and her. Not anymore."

Jody had said she kept a gun because she was a woman alone in the woods? Emily wished. Troy and August always seemed to be around.

"Is Ricky yours? Is that why you're still hanging around and making illegal substances with a teenager in Jody's chicken house even though y'all broke up?"

August shook his head. "You are something else." He smirked and readjusted his cap. "No, he ain't mine. I haven't been with Jody in a long time."

"How long did you date?" Her irritation heightened at the things he'd seen and shared with Jody.

When he spoke, his toothpick stuck to the dry skin of his bottom lip. "About six months."

Emily hadn't known Jody to stay with anyone longer than a week. "What happened? Why'd you break up?"

August considered her question a while before answering. "She fell in love with someone else."

"Who?"

He shook his head and threw his toothpick into the trash barrel. "Just some guy she met while I was in Alaska for work. I had the distinct pleasure of returning to our glorious state to find Jody with a baby, unwed, and living in a mobile home."

"That's a real sad story. You ought to write a book." She shifted to face him. "Are you still in love with her?"

"No. Are you?" He pointed behind her. "You might want to get that."

A large piece of diaper box had flown out of the barrel and was dive-bombing a patch of dry grass at the edge of the lot. She took off toward it.

"Fuck you," she yelled behind her.

"What's that? I can't hear you."

The blades of grass cut at her bare legs and itched. The box had kindled the patch of ground and roused up a good bit of brush that would need to be tamped down. "Goddammit," she muttered. All she was wearing were granny house shoes with thin plastic soles and a strap of fluff across the top. August came up behind her and stomped the ground with his work boots.

"My fucking hero."

He laughed and nearly lost his balance going after the remainder of the fire. Instinctively, she reached out to steady him.

He grabbed hold of her elbow. "Thanks for not throwing me in."

"I would've, but you're signing my paycheck this month." What an irritant that was.

When they were certain that danger had been averted, they headed back to the barrel and he shoved the remaining trash down with a metal rod.

She lifted a leg to scratch at her ankle where the late-season chiggers had gotten her. "How'd you get mixed up in all this anyway?"

"Same as you, I suppose."

She doubted their addictions were the same. "You got student loan debt, too?"

"Funny," he said. "No. I got an elderly dad with medical bills and a farm and house that's about to go underwater."

Stories like his were all too common. Farms in shambles. Acres of land wasted away until deer season and the pittance hunters paid to use it. Such talk didn't garner much time or attention at her mom's prayer circle though, close as it was to the pride they swallowed every time they passed another For Sale sign. Or yards and lives that rotted around them, an embarrassment they all pretended not to notice.

"I'm sorry to hear that."

"That makes two of us," he said. "Look. Anything I feel about you living here ain't got nothing to do with anything but me trying to keep shit real quiet and real safe. You being here is just one more thing to worry about."

"I'm not the one you should worry about."

"Believe me, I know exactly who I should worry about. What concerns me is someone getting caught up in something if they don't need to. There are other ways to make a living, you know?"

"This coming from someone who's making meth in his ex-girlfriend's chicken house."

He took his cap off and smacked her on the arm with it. Despite her desire not to, she laughed and swatted him back.

"All I'm saying is, maybe this ain't the best situation for a girl like you," he said. "Didn't you go off to college?"

College might as well have been a dirty word in Drear's Bluff. If you went, you were considered uppity, too good to hang with hard-working folk. And if you didn't have something to show for the effort, well then you must be stupid. Fuck it. Might as well admit it. She was stupid.

"I hated college. Everything about it. I lost my scholarship, so I quit." The fire weakened in the barrel. "I've been lying to everyone about going back. So you can stop thinking that I'm somehow not fit for this position because you're sorely mistaken." She'd thought it would be hard admitting it to someone besides her mom or dad. But it wasn't. As soon as the words left her tongue, she felt lighter for it. "Besides, they don't hand out jobs just because you once showed up to a bunch of classes. You actually have to find those on your own."

She watched him form a thought and then trap it before it could get to her. He wiped some mystery element off his hands that Emily couldn't see. "College or not, you're a smart kid. The more people who know, the more nervous I get. And that has nothing to do with you personally or anything else."

She didn't like this turn in conversation. He was supposed to ease her anxiety, not increase it. "According to Jody, there's nothing to worry about," she said. "Is that true?"

"True enough."

"Then why does Jody have a gun?"

August shrugged. "Shit, I'd be more shocked if she didn't have one. If that's what worries you, then you definitely need to head on home."

"I can't go home. They kicked me out. So you're stuck with me whether you like it or not. Three more months and then you won't have to worry anymore."

His brow creased. "What's in three months?"

"The lab. Jody said it'd be gone by then."

He spit chew onto the ground. Dust crowned the spot where it landed. "Right."

She hadn't expected the edge in his voice or the way his eyes caught hers and wouldn't let go, like he was holding her by the jaw. Those boyish good looks and Southern charm, gone.

"I best get back to Ricky," she said.

BY THE TIME JODY RETURNED, Emily's patience had been sucked out by Ricky's boundless energy and the chatter in her head about the reality of what was going on around her. Never before had she felt like such a foreigner in her own town, her own skin, her own life. For

hours, a list of pros and cons she should have thought about before
moving in with Jody picked at her insides.

Pro: Not living at home.

Con: Meth lab.

Pro: Jody.

*Con: Jody has a meth lab in her chicken house. Jody. Has. A. Meth.
Lab.*

But did she? Jody had said that it was Troy's, not hers. But the
lab was on her land.

No matter how much Emily wanted to pretend that she was just a
roommate and didn't have a stake in any of this, her mind wouldn't let
her off the hook. Regardless of who did—or knew—what, they were
all involved. That's all that Owen or any other person associated with
crime and punishment in a small Southern town would care about
when it came to people like her and Jody and Troy and August. The last
thoughts she had before Jody walked in screamed the loudest: *Don't quit
your job, apologize to Mom, move home.* Those options plunged her back
into the depressive state that had clutched her for months.

When Jody opened the door, Ricky scrambled off Emily, insert-
ing a foot in her rib while doing so, and crawled across the floor to be
swooped up into Jody's arms. His laughter filled the room when she
planted kisses on his face.

Emily hauled herself off the couch. "I guess this means you got
the job?" Though Jody had insisted that she had nothing to do with
the lab other than collecting a cut of the profits, Emily couldn't shake
the thought of Jody standing at the corner of playgrounds and truck
stops, opening her jacket to display rows of plastic baggies like they
showed in cheesy anti-drug ads, enticing people with a seductive
grin.

Jody didn't react to the sarcasm in Emily's voice. "Yeah." She propped Ricky on her hip. "It's odd hours, but they say it'll be steady as long as I'm willing to come in when they call." She ran her hands over Ricky's skin, as if searching for bumps. Satisfied, she looked up at Emily, still smiling. "That all right with you? You're not gonna run out on me now, are you?"

Emily closed her eyes and scratched at a spot behind her ear. There was no point in asking about the job again. Jody would just lie. "No. It's fine."

Jody placed Ricky on the floor and dug through her wallet. She brought out a one-hundred-dollar bill. "Let me pay you before I forget." The words came out carefree, as if dispensing hundred dollar bills was an everyday thing.

Was this for the day? The month? Time seemed to slow and wait for Emily. "That's a lot of money."

Jody lifted an eyebrow and held the bill out to Emily. "So?"

"You can pay me later, when you have something smaller." *And less meth-y*, she thought. "It's not like I really did anything."

"Ricky's alive, and for that I'm willing to pay whatever I need to. Troy gets to focus on other things that help us all out." She didn't specify what those other things were. She didn't need to. "You should take the money." The words came out smooth, uncomplicated.

There in Jody's hand was one-third of a loan payment, minus the interest she'd accrued in late payment fees. One day's work. More to come. More than anything she'd be able to make at the fast food joint or the Walmart or any other shitty little job that she could find in their shitty little town or their shitty little county in their shitty little state.

But there'd be no going back if she took it.

Pro: Making bank.

Emily took the bill and slipped it into her pocket.

As soon as the money was transferred from Jody's fingers to Emily's, Jody's face relaxed and her smile lifted. "Now that that's settled, help me bring in the groceries. I got us some steaks and corn. We can put those on the grill. Oh, and they had some good wine on sale."

"I thought you only drank beer."

"I drink wine." Jody headed toward the door. Before she exited, she leaned her body against the doorframe. "I thought we could celebrate my new job and you moving in. Wine's better for that than beer. Doesn't that sound nice?"

Once more, the words caught in Emily's throat, but not due to the pros and cons and the money that itched her skin through the layer of inner pocket fabric. She cleared her throat and nodded. "Yes. That sounds great."

CHAPTER EIGHT

For two weeks, Jody had placed money in Emily's hand at the end of each day. Remarkable, she had thought after the first week, the amount of money that could be made. Cash, she had discovered, held more sway than a paper check with her name laser printed on a line next to a box with a sad dollar amount. She had finally quit her job. She had finally paid a student loan bill. She had finally felt some relief after fretting over her bank account for months.

While Benjamin had graced those first bills, on subsequent transactions with Jody, she welcomed George, Abe, Ulysses, and Andrew. The stacks grew, and one day she took them all out of the shoebox she kept in her closet and held them in her hands: $1,400 and change. That long-ago day on the carpet in her childhood bedroom, holding forty-four dollars, now a speck of a memory, barely recognizable, barely worth a thought.

Much like the money, Jody's "factory shifts" magically materialized. After the second random factory shift, Emily almost confronted Jody about what she was really doing when she left the house, but something told her to keep her mouth shut. Though Jody had said that they'd all be guilty by association, a small part of her held on to the hope that she could deny knowledge of what was going on if the worst-case scenario came to pass. She was just a babysitter. She stayed in the house all day. She never went inside the chicken house. If anyone—like Owen—were to find the lab, her suspicions about Jody's real job wouldn't matter. Only what Jody had told her: that she was a factory worker. The less she knew, the better her chances of not going down with the rest of them.

Emily tried not to think about the money, and whatever else likely passed between Jody's hands and those of people Emily would never see or know. It was better that way, she told herself again and again, trying to trick herself into believing it was true.

As the weather grew colder and the leaves began to drift to the ground, Jody spent more time away from home, Troy spent more nights on the couch after spending all day in the chicken house with August, and the majority of her days were spent alone with Ricky. During those hours, she paced the house and peered out the windows. Owen's patrol car hadn't come up the drive, nor had any others. The local mailman in his little white Toyota didn't even drive out this far anymore. Jody had a P.O. box in town. And Emily's phone had gone silent since she moved in with Jody, and not due to the poor service. Her mom hadn't sent one text. Nor her dad. That unnerved her more than anything. She'd never had to guess at the status of her dad's affection for her and didn't like not knowing. With every tick of the clock, Emily felt more and more like one of those old ladies in the black-and-white films her dad liked to watch, a shut-in, locked away from the world.

One day when Jody didn't have "work," Emily finally made the trip into Fort Smith to return her work uniform after her supervisor threatened to "take action," whatever that meant. She used the threat as an excuse to get out of the house for a change. August had come up to the house that morning, a harried look on his face. He and Jody had gone outside to talk. When Jody returned, she was in a mood, and there was no point in Emily sitting around and waiting for it to pass.

She went to the movies. She ate buttered popcorn for lunch. She walked through Central Mall and tried on jeans and shirts and shoes and rings—real rings, not the kind she'd bought when she was younger, the kind that turned her skin green. The diamonds and sapphires and rubies sparkled under the perfectly placed store lights that set the mood for a big purchase. For the first time in her life, she could afford these rings—one of the smaller ones. She could buy one for herself. And for someone else.

"I'll think about it," she told the salesman when she handed over the last ring.

When she returned to the house, ringless but with the soft buzz of an imagined future that she'd indulged on the long ride home, August's truck was gone and daylight was drawing low. Jody was in the kitchen, staring into the refrigerator.

Jody lifted her head when Emily entered the house but didn't smile. The way her eyes shifted downward ever so subtly gave Emily a knot in her stomach, like she ought to be embarrassed or ashamed. "You forget to go shopping?" Jody asked.

"Shit. I'm sorry. I got caught up," she said, remembering the smoothness of the platinum rings against her fingertips and the glint of the jewels. "There should be enough to make a sandwich."

"I ate supper. I'm just bored." Jody pushed the fridge door closed and sighed. "But we do need more food."

Emily dropped her bag on the carpet and joined Jody at the kitchen table. "I feel like I go every other day. Food seems to disappear around here." She paused before adding, "Troy staying over again?"

With all the money he had to be making—an assumption she held based on how much she had saved—she also assumed that he could find a different place to live and someone to drag him back and forth until he got his license back, if ever. She hated not knowing if he'd be there when she returned from town or turned a corner.

"I don't know. I haven't seen him."

Unlike Emily, Troy had not received an invitation to move in. But he'd taken up residence on the couch with such frequency that there had been more days with him than without. His socks lay in wads around the living room floor. His shoes stunk. If he was in the house, Emily felt like he was always within earshot and she could get no time to herself. When he was not in the house, it was just a matter of time before he showed up again.

Worse, he'd become a fixture at the kitchen table at suppertime. He didn't wait until they all sat down before he dug into the Hamburger Helper, heaping spoonfuls onto his plate, leaving the bowls of salad and creamed corn untouched. Little bits of food hung from the bottom of his lip. He chugged an iceless glass of Dr Pepper and burped. The plate, when he finished, was near licked clean and left on the table for someone else to place in the dishwasher. The whole table moved when he pushed his chair out and headed to the bathroom Emily had to share with him. No matter how many times she scrubbed, she could smell his urine around the toilet, the walls, the floorboard.

Jody's indifference to his presence and their living situation bothered Emily so much that she had to clench her fists and count to ten. "What's up with August?" she asked after her anger had eased. "He seemed aggravated this morning. Everything okay?"

"Yeah," Jody said. "Nothing to worry about." She propped her chin on her hand. "He heard Marjorie talking at the Quik-a-Way about how your mom is worried about you being out here with me. Has she called or texted you?"

"No. Last I heard, she still hates me." Emily hadn't told Jody why, other than because she had quit school. There didn't seem to be a good reason to stir that pot. She slumped in her chair. Her mom had stopped talking to her, but not about her. Of course. "Maybe we should go to church on Sunday," she said. "Everyone'll be there. We can show them there's nothing going on and everything's fine. And I'm sure Mom's aching for another hit of Ricky." Maybe it'd soothe some of that hurt between them. Every day she didn't hear from her parents, the divide felt more staggering and difficult to navigate.

Jody sat back in her chair. "That's not what you'll be showing them."

Emily's face heated at the reminder of what people around town thought and said about her. For churchgoing people, they had filthier minds than anyone she'd met. "Are you worried about me being out here, with you?" The words flew out of Emily's mouth before she had time to censor herself. "You afraid of what people might think? Because I'm not. Not of that. But if you are, then say so."

And then what? Emily had nowhere to go, nowhere else she wanted to be. But sometimes the thoughts in her head made her want to run, anywhere, away from all that temptation and rage that ate at her insides.

Jody hung her head and twisted her fingers in her lap before she looked up. "I don't give a rat's ass what people think. I just . . . You get so mad if anyone implies anything."

"Can you blame me?" Nothing could undo everyone's memories of who she had been in junior high and high school, how she'd acted and responded, her former self unbreakable and forever binding. "It bugs the shit out of me, yeah. 'Cause I'm sick of hearing it. But I don't care what they think about me anymore. I only care if it means someone might start coming around, sticking their nose where it shouldn't be." Thinking they'll find something dirty, but finding something worse.

Jody twisted her body to the side and let a heavy burst of air escape her nose. "I know. I know you're right." She cleared her throat and scratched between her eyes. "I fucking hate church, though."

"Well, I hate it, too. But it's the easiest way to get everybody off our backs."

Jody groaned and wandered into the living room. She hauled Ricky into her arms, and headed for his room to prep him for bed, leaving Emily sitting at the table, letting the steam subside.

When Jody returned, she rejoined Emily at the table. "How about we go to your mom's prayer circle tomorrow night instead? She has it every Friday, right? It's less painful than church, and I can slip some vodka into the Bloody Mary's."

Less painful for Jody. "Fine. But you text Mom."

"Why can't you do it?"

"I told you. She's mad at me. And I barely get service out here."

"I don't know what you're talking about. I always have service." She sounded like Emily's mom. After she'd punched in a message, she tossed her phone on the table. She held her hair back and stretched. "Jesus, I could use a drink." Her eyes had a spark to them, the promise of something new and different. "Why don't we get outta here tonight? Get a drink, go dancing. I feel like I haven't had fun in forever."

The last time Jody had suggested they go dancing, Jody had disappeared into the dark spaces of a teen dance club. Emily had searched the dance floor, sifting through bobbing and thrusting teenagers. Only when she headed toward the bathroom did she find Jody up against the wall, her yellow panties with blue flowers visible while a boy in a Northside High letterman jacket lifted her skirt.

"I hate dancing," Emily said. "And what about Ricky? We can't take him with us."

Jody sunk into her chair, sullen.

Emily went to the cabinet. She found a bag of marshmallows and riffled through the canned goods until she came to the bottles in the back. She yanked out a half-empty bottle of tequila and placed that and the marshmallows on the table. She grabbed the baby monitor, switched it to high, and said, "Let's get drunk."

A CHORUS OF NIGHT CREATURES—crickets, frogs, owls—called out from the tree line and the tall grass around them in the backyard, mixing with the quiet whirr of the baby monitor on the ground at Jody's side. Not a cloud marked the sky. The fire crackled with the fresh log that Emily had thrown on top. Her fingers were sticky with the remains of charred marshmallow flesh. They'd already stored the lawn chairs in the shed for the winter, so they sat on the bare ground among the leaves and twigs, every move grinding the dirt into their jeans, every swig of tequila lessening their care.

For minutes or hours, Emily wasn't sure how long, they'd sat and watched the fire, talked about classmates who had passed out of their lives, nights spent cruising Grand Avenue in Fort Smith, good times, and the times in between. But there was so much about Jody that Emily felt she kept hidden behind a wall. The more they sat there and talked, the more she wanted to know who had held Jody's heart. How they had found the way in.

"Did you love him?" Emily asked.

Jody took a swig from the second bottle of cheap tequila they had found in the back of a cabinet. "Who?"

August. The boy at the dance. Any number of boys that she'd seen Jody with, whose cars and lives she'd disappeared into. "Ricky's dad?"

Jody kept her eyes on the fire. She seemed to consider another drink but instead handed the bottle back to Emily, who declined. Jody put the bottle on the ground. Just as soon as it hit the dirt, she picked it up again, uncapped it, and took a long pull.

She wiped her mouth and after a while said, "Funny to think of him as having a dad. Dads are guys like your dad, you know? Someone who's around." She picked up a small stick and began to strip off the bark, piece by piece. "Sometimes, I remember that I have a dad. Somewhere. I wonder if he knows about me. I wonder what he's like." She held the stick out to inspect it, broke the ends so that it was smooth, straight, even. "But then I think, no. I don't have a dad. I'm just made up of some guy's sperm." She stabbed the ground with the stick. "If he fucked my mom, he's probably a loser."

"You don't know that."

"It's not hard to imagine. No one ever loved her. I doubt he did. So why would he love me?" A hard look crossed her face. "She never did. No one did."

"I love you." The tequila made her thoughts and tongue flow more easily. As soon as she said the words, she regretted them. "Not like that . . . You know what I mean."

Jody turned to her, eyelids heavy, the sparks from the fire flashing in her eyes. "Yes, like that."

140

Were it not for the tequila, she might have laughed it off and changed the subject. But Jody was right. And she wanted more, more than what they had been.

Jody's leg brushed up against hers when she shifted. Slight and quick as that movement had been, it set off a tremor in Emily's body that centered between her legs and radiated out like some ancient biological response she had no power to control. Ever since that night with Sam, she ached something awful, like she'd awakened something stronger than her willpower. She wanted to hear Jody's breath quicken. To navigate the landscape of her body. To turn over the taste of her with her tongue.

Emily leaned toward her, wondering how close she could get before Jody pulled away, but she didn't. Emily inched closer until their lips almost touched and then did. Jody's lips were stained with the remnants of marshmallow sweetness, and like that honeysuckle from their youth, Emily teased Jody's tongue out and kissed her, gently, testing how far, how long Jody would let her go on like this. But Jody didn't pull away, she moved closer, so close that Jody's leg had become entwined in hers and Emily propped them both up with one free arm, the other arm tight around Jody's waist. When the propped arm began to needle, she drew Jody down onto the ground, hair catching the leaves. Emily's eyes bore into Jody's, asking that question: *stop?* But Jody's eyes and quickened breath told her no, so she cradled her head with both hands, letting the black strands tangle in her fingers, and eased on top of Jody's body, turning her head away, burying it in Jody's neck and hair, which held the trappings of her shampoo, campfire, drops of tequila.

Emily moved her hands under Jody's shirt, roamed her breasts, her sides, the small of her back, down her jeans, past the fabric to the skin that bucked a little each time Emily touched her. She ran her hand along Jody's thigh and yanked it up so that her leg was angled between Jody's. Mouths open and aligned, they exchanged breaths, gasping when Emily moved her leg in between Jody's again and again, close and tight, fully clothed but more vulnerable, more raw, more friction than Emily had ever felt naked. Jody's breath quickened, her back arched, and a small moan escaped her mouth, causing Emily to move faster, harder, to elicit more of those intoxicating sounds until a yank came at her sides, her shirt being pulled. Emily kept going, diving into the curve of Jody's neck, and navigating her leg down slow and hard.

"Stop," Jody whispered. Again, again, Emily thrust. "Stop. Stop it," Jody said, louder this time. She twisted and rolled out from under Emily.

Now that they were separated, a chill spread through Emily from the sweat on her skin and the absence of Jody's body.

Jody's breath fogged the air in quick bursts. The smell of liquor and that primal scent of their bodies was strong in Emily's nose. She ached from their interruption, her jeans damp and too close to all that throbbing.

"What's wrong?" Emily asked.

The moon lit Jody's blank face.

A cloggy sensation inched up Emily's throat. She wasn't the sort of girl who cried, and she loathed the tears that threatened. She sat up and crossed her arms around her knees. The wood in the fire popped and flames folded in on each other.

When she stood to leave, she felt lightheaded, empty. She clenched her jaw so tightly her ears fuzzed with white noise. Not daring to look at Jody, not wanting to see the look that might be on her face, she said, "Don't worry. I won't tell anyone."

CHAPTER NINE

By the time Emily emerged from her bedroom the next morning, head pounding from the tequila and the torment of the aborted tryst by the fire, Jody had already fed herself and Ricky, and she'd cleaned up the general disarray that they had left in their wake the night before. Jody didn't look at Emily once.

Ricky tottered over to Jody, mumbling, "Momma," over and over—his legs still learning how to function—and wrapped his arms around her knees.

"Go on," she said and eased Ricky off her.

His smile faded and his legs gave out. He crashed onto the floor and crawled backward until he hit the top of his head on one of the chair joints. He looked back as if to see if the culprit was a person or a thing.

Jody pulled out the coffee pot, poured cold coffee into a mug, and nuked it, leaving the microwave door open as she plodded into the living room and curled up in the recliner. She blamed the hot coffee when it burned her lips. Ricky followed her and sat against the coffee table, looking at her. A glimmer of sadness grew in Emily when she looked at his little eyes.

Like a kaleidoscope, Jody mesmerized. But just as quickly, a word or a look could shift and scatter the brilliance. And like Ricky, Emily couldn't stand the silence. Silence filled up by an awful feeling. All night long, she'd replayed the way Jody had sounded, how she'd felt under her hands, on her lips. The reminders were maddening.

Emily breathed deeply. "Look," she said. "Last night was no big deal. Let's forget about it."

Jody responded by blowing on her coffee. She sipped and continued to look at some spot ahead of her, away from Emily.

Through lunch and the afternoon, she waited for Jody's mood to brighten, or for some sign, anything to indicate that Jody wasn't freaked out by what had happened. Anything other than silence would have been fine.

After Ricky's snack, Emily had to get out of the house. The tension had wound itself so tight she found it hard to breathe.

"Come on, Ricky." Emily held out her hand. He hesitated and glanced back at Jody to see if she was coming, too. "Let's go outside and play, yeah?" She nudged him on the arm and pulled him up to his feet. Remembering the chill of the previous night, she grabbed a jacket for each of them, opened the door, and shut Jody and that still-raw ache behind them for a while.

In the front yard, Ricky pushed a toy dump truck around in the dirt for a while.

Soon, the underbelly of a rickety kitchen chair she'd pulled off the porch to sit in became a playground where Ricky bashed rocks together. She felt a bump under her seat. She swung her head down between her legs and stared into the baby-sized, upside-down eyes that Ricky had inherited from Jody. Giggles exploded into the air.

"Stop being cute," she said.

He responded by grabbing the long, brown strands of her hair in a Rapunzellian effort to rise from his seated position. She shooed his hands away to stop further damage.

She heard a rumble coming down the road and some time later she watched August walk up the yard toward her.

A shadow fell on the spot where they sat.

"Hey, little man. Whatcha got there?" August dropped into a squat.

Ricky raised a dinosaur in the air and roared.

"You're good with him." August looked at the boy and then at her and smiled that conniving smile that asked, *Are there babies in your future?* He'd fit right in with her mom and Marjorie and the rest of them.

Still, she tingled with pride. All she'd ever heard was how bad she was at babysitting. "Thanks."

"Set any fires today?" he asked.

"Not yet," she said. "Still early, though."

He chuckled.

"You look better when you smile," she said. He glanced over at her like he was weighing an option. She wished that she could think of him the way that maybe he wanted her to, like her mom would've liked. Things would've been a lot easier.

August clasped his hands on top of his knees and made little noises of appreciation when Ricky held up another toy for him to admire.

She narrowed her eyes. "You want something?"

"Just seeing how things are going."

"Boring as hell."

"The gangster life isn't as exciting as they make it out to be, huh?"

KELLY J. FORD

"I'm a little disappointed. You made it sound so dangerous. What about you? Any more mishaps with boy wonder?"

"Not a thing."

August plopped down in the dirt. Ricky launched himself into his lap as if he'd been waiting for the opportunity. August leaned back and lifted Ricky into the air by balancing him on his knees. Finally, August eased the boy down and distracted him from further requests by using the dinosaur to attack a group of dusty farm animals.

"Help me up," he said.

She held out her hand and he pulled her out of the chair and down to the ground with him.

"You asshole," she yelled and tried to release her limbs from his grip, but then Ricky piled on top and crushed her fingers with his shoes. She yelled out, and Ricky laughed even more. Any time she tried to pull herself into a seated position, August launched Ricky on top of her. He landed on her stomach and she groaned.

"Well, aren't you the happy fucking family."

They all lifted their heads and followed the voice. Jody stood at the door. Emily felt like she'd been caught doing something wrong. From the way August held his jaw, she reckoned he felt the same. Ricky laughed and tried to resume their play, but Emily held him back. When he realized playtime was over, he began to cry.

"I best be going," August said. He dusted the dirt off his jeans and wandered back down the hill.

Ricky bellowed into the air. Emily tried to soothe him with his other toys. She brushed herself off, then him, and carried him back to the house, screaming.

"He's filthy," Jody said. She didn't make any move toward Ricky, just scrunched up her nose.

"I'll bathe him."

"There's no time. I still have to feed him dinner and then get him dressed to get to your mom's house."

Emily had forgotten about the prayer circle. "You still want to go?"

"No. But you said we had to, so . . ."

"So, we'll be late. It's not a big deal."

"Your mom will complain the whole fucking time if we show up late."

"If Mom complains, just tell her I had the poor sense to let him play out in the sunshine instead of inside a dark and depressing house."

Emily rushed a still-screaming Ricky into the bathroom and pulled off his clothes. "Come on, Ricky. Let's get you cleaned up." She picked him up and put him in the tub.

Jody followed her into the bathroom. "I never said he couldn't go outside and play. I just didn't want him outside today because I knew that we had to go out later. And if I bring him over like this, they'll for sure think I'm an unfit mother, more than they already do. More ammunition to make me feel like shit, as always."

"Well, why didn't you say something?" Emily kneeled by the tub. Ricky fought her when she tried to wipe him down with the washcloth. "Come on," she pleaded.

"I was halfway asleep. Besides, you should have known."

Emily let go of Ricky and looked back at Jody. "I can't read your mind!"

Emily had only turned away for one second when she heard a thud followed by a whimper that skyrocketed into a wail. Jody knocked Emily aside to get to the tub and lifted Ricky into her arms. A slight trickle of blood wound down his forehead from where he'd slipped and hit it on the faucet. Jody wiped it with a washcloth and rocked him back and forth and shushed him.

147

"Baby, it's okay, it's okay," she repeated. "I know," she told him. "I know."

Emily grabbed a towel from the shelf and wrapped it around Ricky and Jody. "I'm so sorry," she cried. "I'm so sorry."

Jody squeezed her eyes shut and continued to rock until Ricky's cries became a whimper.

"Is he okay? Do we need to get him to the hospital?" Emily asked.

"No."

"Are you sure?"

Jody didn't answer. Emily left the bathroom and returned with a clean set of clothes for Ricky. She set them on the edge of the sink.

"You two stay here. I'll go to Mom's," Emily said. She waited for Jody to say something. "I'll tell her what happened. She'll understand why you're not there. I'll let her know it's all my fault."

Jody inspected Ricky's face. He rubbed at his eyes until the chain she wore around her neck distracted him. She kissed him one last time on the forehead and set him down. "It's worse if you go without me. They'll find some way to make it my fault." She pulled the clothing off the sink and tried to keep Ricky from squirming.

"Let me help," Emily said.

Jody wouldn't look at her. "I've got it."

"I'll get his things ready to go then."

"Forget it. We're not going."

"Let's just go and—"

Jody glared at her. "I said forget it. We're not going. Not you. Not me."

Emily stepped outside the bathroom and eased the door shut behind her.

CHAPTER TEN

As THE DAYS PASSED, RICKY's bump began to recede and the cut looked more like a scratch, one that would leave a small scar. Jody continued to sulk around the house and only talked when Emily asked her a question about Ricky or told her facts: dinner at six, the doctor's office had called to confirm Ricky's appointment, the satellite bill had been paid.

Troy was sprawled on the couch again one morning as Emily fed Ricky and Jody rushed around the house searching for Ricky's lovey and stuffing diapers and snacks into Ricky's diaper bag for a trip into town.

"Are you sure you don't want me to take him?" Emily asked. "I can come along."

Troy mumbled from the couch. The remote control fell to the floor when he shifted.

Jody scanned the contents of a kitchen drawer. Then she grabbed her phone, punched in a text, waited, received a ding, and wrote back. "What?" she asked. "No. I've got it. Doctor stuff. I have to be there."

"Is everything okay with Ricky?" She worried that it had to do with his head. That Jody had called the doctor about a head scan or something and didn't want Emily to know.

"Yeah. Just a regular checkup." Jody paused and returned to her search, leaving Emily once again with a stone in her gut.

Jody grabbed the diaper bag and her purse with one hand and Ricky with the other. On her way to the door, she stopped at the couch and smacked Troy on the head. "Get up," she said.

Troy startled and thrust his hands out to ward off her attack.

Emily hadn't seen Jody lose her temper with him since that day Emily had found him in the chicken house. She wondered if—and hoped that—Jody had finally gotten as fed up with his presence as she had, and he would be leaving soon.

"All right," he said.

She pointed at him. "Get up."

"Okay!" She popped him on the head again and took off out the door, leaving him scratching at the spot where her hand had struck him.

After Jody left, Emily washed the breakfast dishes and straightened the living room. All the while, Troy sat on the couch without a shirt on, the previous night's sheets balled up at one end. The sound of video game gunfire careened off the walls and drilled into her head. She needed a task. An escape. She checked the fridge. They were nearly out of everything.

The grocery store had become a getaway where she could push her cart, smile when women told her what a beautiful baby she had, and pretend that she had a perfect home life. Some days the dream slipped into reality. Jody left for "work" in the morning and came home to a clean house, happy baby, and warm, if not so well-cooked, meal. For an hour or two, the concerns about the drugs and getting caught would slacken like a fishing line in a shallow pond. But since that night by the fire, Jody had clouded over and gripped the house in her ongoing gloom. Emily wondered if the friendship was too broken to fix. She had enough money to leave, but not to survive long without another job. But she couldn't handle things like they were much longer, not with Jody barely talking to her, barely looking at her, her only company the wrecked and wasted teenager on the couch.

"I'm heading to town for groceries," she said. "I'll drop you off at your mom's house."

"Jody said I could stay as long as I want."

Troy's presence was like a poison ivy rash that refused to heal.

Troy flung the Nintendo controller off his lap and onto the couch. He stood up and scratched at the front of his threadbare boxers. "I need to grab some things at the store, too."

She fumbled with her keys to avoid seeing anything more. "I'm not your babysitter or your taxi."

"Well then you're not gonna get paid this week. And I'll have to tell Jody that—"

"Fine," she said, annoyed that he could wield that over her so easily and she had so little power to deny him. "You can come with me as long as you don't talk."

ON THE RIDE TO THE grocery store, Troy propped his head on the window and slept. He disappeared as soon as they walked into the store. All through the aisles of chips, soda, and eggs, she kept looking around her, convinced that he'd show up and plunge her into a bad mood. But by the time she reached the vegetables at the front of the store, the soothing sounds of easy listening music on the overhead speakers and the slow roll of the grocery cart had lulled her into new hopes of things somehow working out with Jody despite their current impasse.

After she checked out, she found Troy sitting on a bench outside the store with a newly purchased red gas can.

"What's that for?" Emily asked, recalling the last time she'd seen one—the boys on the road that day she'd swung her car into Jody's drive.

"Gas. Duh."

He popped off the bench and raced ahead of her on the way back to the car. Every now and then, he'd look behind him and scratch his head or his arm or a hard-to-reach spot on his back, his elbow jutting high above his head. Instead of helping her load the groceries into the backseat, he peered around the lot.

On the ride home, he perched on the edge of his seat, crouching forward. He kept looking in his side mirror. Then he scanned the back window. And he scratched. Red marks appeared where he'd raked his nails across his face. Worst of all were the acne spots he'd scratched. Every time he touched the dashboard or the radio or the seat, Emily gagged quietly and mentally scrubbed the surface with disinfectant.

"What are you on?"

"Nothing," he said.

"Well, then, stop moving so much," she said. "You're bugging the shit out of me."

Troy's eyes focused on her as if she'd appeared out of thin air. He leaned back but wouldn't let his spine touch the seat. He placed his feet flat on the floor and his palms down on the tops of his thighs. Before long, the car shook from the way he bounced his legs up and down. Emily flung a hand across his knees. That solution lasted for about a minute.

"I saw your mom the other day." She hadn't set foot in the Quik-a-Way since that day after church. "She went by the Sonic looking for you. Said she talked to the manager." She waited for a reaction but got none. "She knows you don't work there."

Troy snickered and rocked.

Emily considered her words. "She has it in her head that you're doing drugs."

In response, Troy snarled his upper lip.

"She blames Jody, you know. 'Cause you spend all your time at the house. We can't really afford to have her coming 'round looking for you. Not with what you have going on in the chicken house."

Troy's eyes grew large in disbelief. He shook his head and turned toward the window. "Man, whatever. Fuck you. And fuck Mom."

"The least you could do is call home and tell your mom where you are so she doesn't get suspicious. Let her know Jody is just giving you a place to stay. The more you keep her in the dark, the more she'll believe what she believes. Trust me, I know. I'm not on the best terms with my mom either. But I call her because it's the right thing to do and it keeps her off my back." She hadn't called. Hadn't texted. The longer she waited, the harder it was to do either.

"I'd like to get your mom on her back. She's got a nice rack." He cupped his hands in front of his chest and licked the nipples of his own voluptuous, imaginary set.

She grimaced. "I'm sure she'd be delighted to know your opinion," she said, "but that's not helpful. What would be helpful is if you'd go home once in a while."

"I bet you'd like that," he shot back. Then, he flung his face near Emily's and leered. "I bet you'd love to be all alone with Jody. What makes you think I ain't out there to protect her from you?"

The words so startled Emily that she veered across the lane. Thankfully, they were on a rural route.

"I seen you when Jody's not looking." Troy puckered his lips. "I seen other things."

Had he been there that night around the fire? She raged at the thought of him watching them. "You haven't seen shit."

He laughed and raised his hands in innocence. "I'm just joking. I love lesbians. If y'all wanted to get it on right there in the living room, I wouldn't stop you. Shit, if you asked me real nice, I might even join you."

Emily pushed the gas pedal and then slammed the brakes to jerk him out of his seat. "Get out."

"Come on! I'm kidding. I swear, I'm kidding." He shook his head and laughed. "Shit, you know what it's like to have your mom bitching and complaining all the time. You just said so yourself. That shit wears on you after a while. Come on, you know I don't mean nothing by it." He popped her on the leg. Reflexively, she reared back and punched him on the arm. His smile disappeared and his body shifted toward his door. They sat there silently, each daring the other to speak.

He cracked a grin. "I think maybe I shouldn't have drunk that Monster Energy drink. You ever had one of them? Fuck." He drew out the word. "That shit'll fuck you up for sure. I ought to be like you, stick with Dr Pepper. Though it burns my throat. I don't know how you stand it."

Emily's heart pounded. She felt like she'd stepped into a movie where some woman picks up a friendly hitchhiker only to find out that he's a psychopath. "You keep your mouth shut the rest of the way home, you hear me?" She waited until he nodded to put the car in drive.

"I didn't mean it," he said. "You know me."

"Shut up."

"Okay, I will," he said. "You know I'm joking."

"Troy."

"All right."

He remained quiet until they were five minutes away from Jody's house. Then, he shot a hand out the window.

"Hey, pull in here!" He banged the exterior of the car door with his fist. "Over here." He pointed at the road she had driven past.

"No," Emily said and kept driving.

"Stop! Back up, back up!" He grabbed the steering wheel and she slammed on the brake.

"Are you trying to kill us?"

He stuck his head out the window and motioned for her to put the car in reverse until he held his hand palm up and yelled stop. "My cousin lives down there." He pointed out the window. "I need to grab some things from him. It'll only take a couple of minutes. Jody said you'd give me a ride."

She drilled her fingers on the steering wheel. "Why didn't she ask me?"

"Fuck if I know." Troy held his hands out to make his case. "Jody asked me specifically. Ain't my problem you two are having a lover's quarrel."

Those words rolled off his tongue so easily. "You can walk over here any time from the house."

"I needed a gas can. I can't walk to the Walmart. That's too far."

No way did Jody tell him that Emily would give him a ride. "I'll drop you off, but I've got groceries in the car. You can walk back to the house."

"It'll only take a minute." His shoulders slumped. "Come on. Don't be such a mom."

She thrust her finger in his face. "Don't you ever call me that! You hear me?"

He grabbed the finger she pointed at him and gripped it, tight, then tighter. The animation in his face deadened, his body stilled. "I hear you. Now you hear me." He clenched her finger so tight she thought it might snap. "All them new clothes and that good food you like to eat? That's thanks to me. So if you want to keep living it up, you best head down that road like I asked."

His eyes hooked her and there was a calm that she hadn't seen from him before—so unlike the way he'd been with the girl around the fire, that day he'd tackled her, the way he'd acted at home. Even with all she'd seen from him, she hadn't felt scared to be around him. Not until now. He finally let go of her finger and it throbbed in response. She took the car out of park and made the turn.

"Two minutes," she said without looking at him, not willing to let him have the last say even though she felt like her insides shook.

At a rusted mailbox on the right ten minutes later, Troy told her to stop. His cousin's house was a few miles down the dirt road. Not right down the road.

She rubbed her temples. "Why can't I drive right up to the house?"

"Just stay here." He hopped out of the car before she could move away from the ditch to give him more room. He opened the rear passenger door and pulled out a black duffel bag she hadn't seen him walk out of the house with. He leaned on the window. "If you're not here when I return, that'd be real bad for you."

She flinched. When he walked past the front of the car, he pulled the bag over a shoulder and swung the red gas can. Then he disappeared beyond the brush. Anxiety parked itself square in her gut at his words and the way he'd held her finger.

Still, she yelled out to him, "Two minutes." Then, she muttered, "My milk better not spoil."

Once she switched off the engine, the sounds of songbirds filled the car. The road went straight in either direction without much in the way of trees. Along the road, tangled vines overtook a wooden fence. Weeds and patches of wild brush filled the vacant, fenced-in fields on either side of the drive. A turn-of-the-century plow rusted under a persimmon tree pregnant with fruit near the house. There were limited signs of life around the single-story house, whose clapboards and shutters had also fallen into decay. An empty hummingbird feeder hung from the porch. A box fan engulfed the window. Emily guessed that they weren't relations of Marjorie's.

She rubbed the finger that he'd clutched. Her fright shifted to anger. There was no need to ask what he was on. She'd suspected ever since she'd found him crushing pills. Some days, he'd be fine. Irritating, but fine. Not who she saw today. Or the day he'd tackled her. He'd been using.

She considered all the other things he could forget, ways he could screw up.

She leaned forward, looking for any sign that Troy might be making his way back. Nothing, just an empty, rotting landscape. Something about this didn't sit right with her. Nothing about the day did, especially as she waited for him on the side of a little-used dirt road at the end of a drive for a house set in the middle of an unplowed field.

She started the car. The clock showed that she'd been sitting there for five minutes. She waited a minute more and bumped the horn, barely enough to scatter the birds. She peered down the drive. "Come on," she muttered. This time, she laid on the horn. Again, nothing.

She eased her way down the drive. The fan's blades hung unmoving in the window. No hummingbirds buzzed around the globe. No porch dog investigated her presence or snarled at the intrusion. But the wind caught a rusty set of chimes and set it tinkling into the air.

Shots fired off around her and she ducked her head, tried to locate their origin.

Troy ran down the drive, the gas can hugged to his chest like a football. The front door opened and an old woman in a housedress and kerchief burst onto the steps, hands up and holding a dishtowel, her high Southern vowels scraping the air but not hooking into words. Behind the house, an old man appeared with a shotgun.

Emily couldn't think, couldn't move. Her heart raced as she watched everything play out in front of her like a movie. Troy yelled and ran toward the car. She looked from the woman to the old man and then to Troy, who appeared to have tears streaming down his face.

Another shot rang out. Emily jumped and Troy fell to the ground. Panic sent her pulse surging. What was happening? Her vision felt blurred, her limbs and tongue heavy, as she struggled to understand, to move, to scream.

Fog—fog?—rushed out of the gas can and clouded Troy's face. Emily watched dumbly as he stumbled to his feet and reached for the car like a blind man, the can still clutched to his chest. Finally, her brain caught up and she cried out. She reached for the door handle and the old man fired again.

She ducked and fumbled with the handle but couldn't get it open. Troy scrambled into the back seat. "Go! Go!" His eyes were bloodshot and he coughed.

Emily panicked and punched the gas. The car lurched forward. Her hands shook and slipped off the gear shift. She put the car in reverse and raced backward down the drive until she reached the end and swung the wheel. The tires crunched the rocks, and they sped down the road as shots rang out around her. She feared and expected the shatter of the window. Her skull.

The car filled with a sharp chemical smell. She yanked her shirt over her nose and mouth and forced her burning eyes open just enough to see. In the back seat, Troy gasped for air. She twisted in her seat to see if he'd been shot. There was no blood on him or the seat. He shoved the can between his thighs and the ends of his T-shirt into its opening. Thoughts raced in her mind but she couldn't speak: What was happening? What should she do? Was he shot?

She turned her attention back to the road and stopped at the end. She had no idea if she should turn left or right. She looked back at Troy, dreading the sight of blood. He coughed and gagged, panicked that the car had stopped. No blood.

"Drive!" He opened his mouth wide, his face strained, but his voice came out as no more than a squeak. "Drive!"

"What's wrong with you?" she shouted and coughed at an itch in her throat. "What happened? What is that?"

"*Drive,*" he whispered the word and clutched at his throat.

She scanned the rearview mirror, expecting to see a car behind her, a shotgun out the window. She yanked the steering wheel and made her way down the road, praying that Jody was home.

Emily kept glancing back at him. He scrambled through the bags of groceries, flinging canned food aside and gasping for air. Dry retches and gagging followed. She feared he might be choking on his own vomit.

"Are you okay?" A sensation worked its way into her nose and throat that reminded her of when she had cleaned the toilet at the restaurant and breathed in too much Comet, the fine chemical dust fumigating her. "Are you okay?"

She reached Jody's gate and raced up the drive, past the chicken house. Troy had found the milk, unwound the plastic ring, and dumped it on his head. Emily stepped off the gas pedal and the car started to roll backward. She yanked the emergency brake, turned off the engine, and swiveled around to help Troy.

His hands fell away from the groceries. The gas can dropped from between his legs and his T-shirt slowly pulled away from the opening. Fog seeped out, more slowly now. He leaned back on the seat, vestiges of milk coating his skin. Red and orange splotches mixed with charred black smudges across his forearms and hands. His eyes had grown redder than she'd ever seen anybody's eyes get, like something out of a movie, nothing that looked like real life.

Her nostrils and throat burned. She wanted to get outside the car, to breathe fresh air, but he grasped her hand then and gripped so tightly her fingers screamed in pain. Alarmed at his appearance and how hard it was for her to breathe, she tried to yank herself away from him but he gripped her more tightly. Her scream-filled sobs muffled his gasps. Her tears blurred the sight of Troy's throat puffing out like a frog's, as if all the air left in his lungs was pushing and pushing and pushing against a ceiling at the top of his throat. Through her distorted vision, she watched his eyes bulge and burn red.

His hand tightened around her fingers, now numb from his grip. He yanked her toward him and she crashed her face into her head-rest, unable to release herself. If his voice had not failed him, if his throat had not closed, she was sure his breath would have come out in a howl. Coughing overtook her and her eyes burned like someone had thrown gas in her face. Finally, she released his fingers one by one from her crushed hand.

Fear clutched her: *He's dying. I'm dying.*

She scrabbled at the door handle, desperate for air, and stumbled out of the car, shuffled through the grass, and tripped.

A cold rush of water hit her face. She jerked away from the water, but someone held her head still.

"Shh," the voice said.

She couldn't see anyone. Again, the water came at her, this time all over her body. She felt stripped and frozen, as if she'd been thrown in a winter-chilled lake.

The ground shook and spun, gradually at first and then faster. Vomit stung the inside of her throat and slithered down her chin. Her body rose in the air. Trees rushed by on a canvas of blue. She tried to lift her hand, to reach out and grab a branch to stop the movement, but her body was made of lead.

Then, the world went away.

LIGHT LEAKED INTO JODY'S BEDROOM from the cracks around the doorframe. A fuzzy brown blanket had been thrown on top of Emily. Her lungs and eyes still burned, though not with the same intensity as she recalled feeling . . . when? She struggled to lift her head, to recall what day it was, her last memory. Pain ricocheted around her body and a wave of nausea followed. She propped herself on her elbow and waited for the feelings to pass. Soon, she became aware of the bed sheets and their closeness to her skin. She lifted the sheets; she was naked.

Her hair was damp, her head too foggy to analyze why. She slung her legs off the side of the bed. Her clothing was nowhere to be found. She grabbed a T-shirt and sweatpants from Jody's dresser and padded out of the room.

The TV flickered in the darkened living room. She walked through the kitchen and onto the carpet, past the expanse of TV. Jody lounged on the couch, eyes closed, a hand across her head. She looked up when the floorboards creaked under Emily's feet.

Emily sat in the recliner, her feet up under her. Her body felt unmoored, tossed about. She held the chair arms to steady herself.

"You hungry?" Jody stood. She rooted around in the refrigerator and pulled out a pizza box. Then she flipped on the switch and flooded the conjoined rooms with light. "I grabbed some pizza while I was out."

Emily lifted her sore hand to shield her eyes. Images flashed on the back of her eyelids. Troy in the back seat, eyes red, hands clutching hers until she thought the bones might break. She rubbed her hand in response.

Jody clanged around in the kitchen, opening the silverware drawer, pulling a glass and a plate from the cabinet. She slammed the microwave door shut. The noise reverberated in Emily's head. Jody rushed through the words as she relayed a visit to the park, a store, the pizza place, other words Emily couldn't catch.

"Where's Troy?" Emily asked.

Jody stopped for a moment. The microwave hummed and the pepperoni sizzled as it heated. Jody cracked some ice and poured Dr

Pepper from a two-liter bottle into a glass. Emily swore she could hear the fizz pop and prick the insides of her skull.

"He left a while ago." Jody separated the plastic seams of a chip bag. Emily could hear the chips crunch in Jody's mouth. One, two, three handfuls. "Want some Doritos?"

Emily glanced around the room, as if some piece of evidence would appear and confirm what she'd experienced earlier that day. The microwave beeped. Jody shook some chips onto the plate and brought it and the glass of Dr Pepper over to Emily. The glass shook slightly in Jody's hand.

"Is he okay?" Emily asked.

Jody eased onto the couch and fussed with arranging a blanket around her legs. "Why wouldn't he be?"

Emily's hand was too sore to hold the plate, so she let it warm her legs. "You saw him?"

Jody didn't look at her. "Yeah."

"Did he tell you what happened at his cousin's house?" Even as she said the words, she knew that it hadn't been his cousin's house.

"No." Jody faced her. "What happened?"

Emily placed the plate on the coffee table. She recalled Troy's eyes, how they'd gone red around the rims. "He said he had to get something from his cousin. He came running from behind the house and this guy shot at him." She forced the words out, but they didn't make sense. "Troy had a gas can." But it wasn't gas. "Something came out of the top. Like steam or fog. He passed out in my back seat."

Jody listened, paused, raised an eyebrow and laughed, but not like what she heard was funny. "What are you talking about?"

Emily's body felt empty but heavy and swirling, like the time she took pain pills after having her appendix out. "I think I'm going to be sick." She grasped the arms of the chair again.

Jody picked up the remote control and twirled it in her hands. "All I know is when Ricky and I got back from dinner, you were passed out cold in my bed." Jody flipped through the channels at random.

"Someone dumped water on my head. Was that you? Or August?"

Jody fidgeted with a string that stuck out of the seam of her shirt. She rubbed it between her fingers, twisted, and yanked. All the while, she clenched her jaw. She returned to the TV and lowered the volume.

"Did you dump water on my head?" Emily asked again.

Jody chewed on a nail. "No. I was out all day. So was August." Suspicion or something else lingered behind her eyes. "I figured you took a shower."

The pieces didn't fit. Where was Troy? Why was Jody so calm? And why did she feel like she was going crazy? Like she was being told a story rather than having Jody listen to what had happened. She closed her eyes: Troy came running, a man shot at them, Troy had something in the gas can, he choked and passed out, she choked and passed out. Her eyes still burned. Chemical burns. Chemicals. He'd dumped milk on his head.

She recalled stickers she'd seen on the tractor when her dad had taken her out in the fields as a kid, the warnings, the water tank for emergencies. *Flush the eyes. Flush the body. Wash the burns away.*

The burns on Troy's face. The same burns as Mr. Johnston at church. All the pieces right there in front of her, all the chemicals and the bottles and the questions about what had happened with Troy, clear: He was stealing fertilizer.

Emily lifted her aching body out of the chair to fish around in the pockets of her jacket, which hung from a coat hook behind the front door.

"What are you doing?"

Anger tightened Emily's chest, at Troy for what he'd gotten her into. At Jody for what she suspected was a lie. "Looking for my keys." If she could find her keys, then she would be able to confirm that she was not crazy.

"Why?" Jody stood up. "Why don't you sit down and eat?"

"I don't want to sit down." Emily shoved the sofa pillows aside and checked under the couch. She felt lightheaded when she brought her head back up.

"Where are my keys?" After jerking open cabinet drawers and shuffling through stacks of mail on the side tables and hunting for them in the bathroom and the back room where she slept, she stopped and stood in the middle of the living room. Everything around her spun. "Where are they?"

Jody clutched her hand. Her eyes trained onto Emily's. "Why don't you sit down, have some pizza?"

Emily yanked her hand away. "I don't want any fucking pizza! Where are my goddamn keys?" she screamed.

"I don't know!" Jody stepped back from her. "Stop yelling at me."

A headache throbbed from the center of Emily's skull.

"We'll find your keys," Jody said. "Tomorrow." She placed a hand on Emily's shoulder.

Emily recoiled from her hand and walked back into the kitchen, opened the refrigerator, and peered inside.

Jody followed her. "What are you looking for?"

Emily shoved the mayonnaise and eggs and pickles aside, items she'd bought hours before. All the groceries were there, except one thing. She shut the door and faced Jody. "Milk."

A twitch appeared under Jody's eye.

Emily pushed past her and headed outside.

Jody rushed after her. "Where are you going?"

The car doors were unlocked, something she never did. The inside of the car wasn't any cleaner than before. She knelt down to smell the seat. After that, she smelled the carpet. She didn't smell milk or the chemical smell that had coated her nose, but she did notice another faint chemical and leaned closer to confirm. There was no mistaking the smell of Pine-Sol.

"Did you clean the backseat?" Emily asked.

Jody tugged at her ear. "Why would I do that?"

"You did. You cleaned it." She slammed the door. "There was milk all over the seat. All over Troy. He opened it up and poured it over his head. Why would he do that, Jody? What was he doing out there at that old man's house?"

Emily wanted to shake her. Her whole body, shake her down for the truth, at last. "Don't act like you don't know what I'm talking about. You know exactly what I'm talking about, don't you? What was he doing out there?"

"I don't know."

She pointed at Jody. "You're lying. You always twitch under your eye when you lie."

Jody held a hand to her face, as if she had to touch it to believe it was true.

"That's how I know you're lying about what happened, the same way I know that you're lying about your job. Was he stealing fertilizer?"

Jody stood still as stone.

"Was he? Was he stealing fertilizer for the ammonia? Does he use that for the meth?"

Jody said nothing. Now that she knew about the twitch, it's like she had somehow figured out how to control it.

"I know you're dealing. I knew it from the moment I saw you at the truck stop, even though I didn't want to believe it. I knew it. You did more than let him use the building. There's no other explanation for why you have to leave so often. And if you're dealing, then you know what Troy was up to today. And you had no qualms about lying and making me feel crazy." She waited. "So help me God, I will go inside that house and call 911 and tell them exactly what happened today."

Jody gasped and then thrust her hands to her face. She cried, hard, like that long-ago night, the night before she left for good, her sobs wracking her body the way they had then. Instinctually, Emily wanted to comfort her, but she waited while Jody pulled herself together.

Finally, Emily asked her angrily, "Why are you crying?"

Jody sniffled and wiped her eyes. "You know why."

She wanted Jody to say it. "No, I don't. Is it because you knew what he was doing and didn't tell me? Why did you just pretend this didn't happen?"

Jody's face crumpled into despair. "Because I was scared. I didn't know what happened. But I knew it was bad." Jody sighed and headed back to the house, but then turned toward Emily and motioned. "Would you please come back in the house? Ricky's alone."

With nowhere else to go and no way to get there, especially in a car in which she'd recently fled from gunfire, she followed Jody inside.

Once Ricky's well-being had been confirmed they sat at the kitchen table, not talking, only glancing at one another now and then until Emily couldn't take the silence and the questions ringing inside her head anymore. "Did you know he was stealing ammonia?"

She focused on a spot on the scratched surface of the wooden kitchen table. "No." She looked up at Emily. "But I know he uses it to cook."

"That's why you showed up at church that day." Not because of her. "Is that what happened to Mr. Johnston? Troy messed with his tank, too?"

Jody leaned on the table. "No. I mean, yes. That's why I went that day. I'd heard about it and wanted to see for myself. But I asked Troy if he'd had something to do with Johnston and he swore to me he hadn't. It was an accident, plain and simple. Like you said, it happens all the time."

"But it wasn't an accident. Not today."

Jody collapsed her head onto her palm and rubbed her forehead. "I don't know why it happened today but I know it's never happened before. Not here. I swear to you. I know he uses it, but I didn't know he was stealing it."

"What about Troy? Where is he?"

Jody kept her head down, eyes trained on the table. "I don't know. He was spraying down with the water hose when I got home. He seemed fine."

How could he have been fine after what had happened? "You talked to him?"

"Yeah."

"And his eyes were—"

"Red. He had burns. He was coughing a lot. But he was fine."

How had he been able to get up and walk around when she hadn't? Had he doused her with water? Had he given her something to make her pass out? Nothing made sense. "How did I get in your bed? He didn't tell you what happened? How'd he get home? Where did he go?"

"Oh my God. You're killing me right now." Jody rubbed her face. "I don't know. He didn't tell me. That's all I know."

Emily's senses were overwhelmed with everything she had learned and experienced that day. She burned and ached all over. "Should I be worried about inhaling that ammonia? Do I need to go to the hospital?"

Jody jerked her head up. "Absolutely not." She shook her head as if Emily needed extra confirmation that it was a bad idea. "There's no way you can go in there without them knowing what happened. Owen would be out here in no time."

"He may be out here anyway if that old man talks."

"Did he see you?"

"I don't know. But he saw Troy. He saw my car. Does it make a difference? Is anyone gonna believe that all I was doing was driving back from the grocery store? You think anyone would believe that? 'Cause I don't."

Her chest felt like it'd been afflicted with a multitude of paper cuts. She got up from the table and drank glass after glass of water, trying to lessen the pain and the panic of whether or not the old man had seen her face, where Troy was, and if she might be in the slow process of asphyxiation or going to prison.

After a while, Emily cleared her scratchy throat and sat back down. She tugged her hair behind her ears and wiped her face. "What now?"

Jody checked her watch. "Well," she said, "it's Friday night."

The prayer circle. Emily didn't need to be told. No other night claimed an association in her mind more than that. She massaged her temples. "Why would you be thinking about that?"

"Because today, of all days, we need to be seen in public and together and fine and not like there's this horrible thing that's happened. And we can see if anyone's heard anything."

"Mom's not talking to me. I'm supposed to just show up?"

"She won't say anything while everyone's there."

She didn't say anything when it was just Emily either. "You think it'll help?"

"I don't know. But it's something. And better than any other option we have."

Emily nodded. She didn't want to go. She didn't want to see her mom or her dad, especially today. But then, there were a lot of things she didn't want that had come to pass.

CHAPTER ELEVEN

THE WHOLE RIDE TO THE prayer circle, Emily replayed her memories around what had happened earlier that day. One thing was clear: she could no longer say that she didn't know or suspect something was going on with Troy.

Bugs splattered on the windshield and Jody shifted the radio's volume so loud that the speakers crackled, silencing Ricky's chatter from the backseat along with Emily's questions—questions for which Jody either didn't have answers or didn't want to give any. Emily stared at the passing posts and barbed wire fences and trees, trying to focus on making her mind and her face blank so no one would know she had done something wrong. Something very, very wrong.

By the time they arrived, the sun had dropped below the tree line. The living room lights glowed in the house's frame like watchful eyes. Curtains stirred as the women inside the house did a poor job of spying.

"Let's get this over with," Emily said, and yanked on the door handle. "Show our faces and act normal." Like people who didn't make or deal meth. People who didn't drive like hell from shotgun fire and see teenagers gasp and grab at their throats in the backseats of cars. People who didn't wake up not knowing how they ended up naked and uncertain of what had happened.

Marjorie looked up at their arrival through the kitchen door and made a show of taking in Jody from head to toe. "I thought you all had decided to skip this week, too." Then she took in Emily's appearance. "You look tired." In other words, terrible.

Ricky squealed with glee because he could, and Emily thanked him for the interruption. The wrinkles around Marjorie's eyes deepened with her smile. She held out her hands, and Ricky reached out for her from Jody's arms. Once secure in her embrace, she babytalked and inspected Ricky like she was from Child Services. Her fingers grazed the small pink scar on his forehead from when he had hit the faucet in the tub. "What happened here?"

"Ricky fell in the tub while I was watching him," Emily said before Jody had a chance to answer.

"It was an accident," Jody said.

Marjorie lifted an eyebrow. No doubt she presumed Emily was covering for Jody's poor mothering.

"I do love having a baby around. They're so much sweeter when they're this age. Then they get old and rotten and take up with bad influences." She cast her eyes at Jody and let Ricky stick his fingers into her mouth as she faked biting down on them. Who had been the bad influence? Troy or Jody? At this point, Emily couldn't tell.

Marjorie handed Ricky back over to Jody and resumed her tasks. She busied herself by retrieving glasses from the cupboard. Without turning around she said, "Jody, why don't you go on and join the others in the living room while Emily helps me with these drinks."

"Gladly." Jody slung the diaper bag over her shoulder and made her way out of the kitchen with Ricky.

Marjorie filled two glasses with ice and Bloody Mary mix and capped the bottle.

"I should've figured your mom would invite Jody. Redemption stories stoke her fire. One minute she's complaining about someone, the next she's trying to fix them."

A tension headache worked its way around Emily's jaw and up to the center of her forehead. She didn't have the energy to correct Marjorie's assumption or endure her latest complaint. "Are these drinks ready to go to the living room?" she asked.

In response, Marjorie took two of the glasses and muttered her way out of the kitchen. A swishing sound reverberated against the walls when her khakis scissored against each other.

Emily grabbed the remaining glasses, passed the frames of the disapproving ancestors on the wall, and followed Marjorie out of the hallway and into the light of the living room. Each step pounded out in her head as if her shoes were full of cement, the floor made of wood instead of carpet.

Women chattered around the coffee table. Paper plates left over from Easter held finger food. Besides her mother, Marjorie, Jody, and herself, the group consisted of two others: Misty Wheeler, or Miz T—which she thought distinguished her as a hip and fresh junior high teacher instead of a tired old racehorse—and Sally Druck, their longtime neighbor, who sat solo in a kitchen chair on account of her expressive use of hand gestures in conversation. A stranger might have thought it was a casual gathering of friends on a Friday night. But Emily had always considered them a coven and suspected that at least two of them took advantage of the concealed weapon law and kept a handgun tucked away inside the sparkly purses propped against their legs, along with lipstick and fruity gum.

They had been laughing when Emily entered the room. Her mom stopped at the interruption. "I didn't know you were here, too." She eyed Emily and then turned back to the group. "We don't have enough Bloody Mary mix for all of us to have more than one tonight."

Emily drew a long breath and set the drinks on coasters. Jody rolled her eyes and continued the chore of removing Ricky's jacket. They both knew her mom bought the mix in bulk at Sam's Club in Fort Smith. They didn't even add vodka.

"I'll go check the pantry." No doubt happy for another task, Marjorie headed back into the hallway, away from Jody and Emily's mom.

Heather coughed. Emily hadn't noticed her arrival, or whether she'd been sitting there the whole time. "Oh, hey."

"Good to see you," Heather said, though she barely looked Emily in the eyes. Emily no more believed the words than Heather did, especially after their last exchange at the Quik-a-Way, but she acknowledged them for the social grace they were, thin and nonspecific, and was relieved when Heather returned her attention to a stain on her shirt that Emily couldn't see.

Before anyone else could get a word in, Sally cleared her throat. "I hate to run." She looked to Misty. "But I should really be off." Emily saw her glance at Jody with some kind of look before turning to Emily's mom with a frowny face normally reserved for children.

"Me, too. I've got so much to do before class on Monday," Misty said. Unlike Sally, Misty avoided eye contact with anyone and busied herself with digging through her purse, presumably for her keys.

"But you just got here." Emily's mom looked troubled at the departure.

Sally would hear none of it. She swung her hands out wide. "It was so good to see you." She squeezed Emily's mom and made for the door with Misty at her side in an impressively effective departure that left no room for complaint. "I'll talk to you all soon. Bye!" The door shut on her singsong exit.

Emily's mom stood dumbfounded, looking at the door.

Unperturbed by the sudden departures, Jody settled Ricky on the floor with his toys.

"Well," Emily's mom said. "Come here and give me a hug."

Jody accepted a side-hug but held her body straight and tense and her face expressionless. Emily was left standing there, hugless and headachey.

Marjorie returned with a fresh bottle of Bloody Mary mix and sat next to Heather on the couch after Mom explained Sally and Misty's absence. Marjorie glanced at Jody and clicked her tongue. Jody either didn't hear or pretended not to notice.

"We should continue," Emily's mom said. She dipped her hand into the plastic bowl on the coffee table and pulled out a folded piece of paper. This was new. Before, they would just go around the room and offer up the names of friends and neighbors who likely did not require or desire the women's weekly call for prayers. Apparently, the need was so great now that prayers were on a lottery system. "Mr. Johnston."

At the mention of his name, the noise in the room seemed to drift away and time seemed to slow. Emily turned to Jody, incredulous. Had she slipped his name into the bowl?

Her mom began. "I talked to Mrs. Johnston after church. She said Mr. Johnston may need to go on oxygen if that cough don't clear up."

Emily's own throat itched. She downed her glass of water and wondered how Troy was fairing, given the way he'd looked when she last saw him. She found it impossible to believe that he didn't look like Mr. Johnston had at church. Meanwhile, Jody crossed and uncrossed her legs and scanned the room for something to occupy her attention.

Heather scratched her head.

"What?" Marjorie asked.

"It's probably nothing. Just kids talking."

"Well, don't sit there." Marjorie slapped Heather on the leg when she paused. "Go on."

"There's talk that someone tampered with his fertilizer tank."

Pressure built within Emily and set her nerves on edge. She felt sure that later that night, she would discover long, vertical bruises on her back from where she'd pushed against the chair as much as possible to try to disappear between the bars.

Jody waved a hand in the air. "That's just people making up stories."

Heather straightened her back and turned to Jody. "It's what I heard."

"Why would someone do that?" Mom asked.

"Well," Marjorie interrupted Heather before she could speak. "Times are tough and his farm's still making a profit." Marjorie huffed. "Look at all that land. Most of it, he wrangled off of others who had to foreclose on their own farms. His people have been doing that since they pulled up in their wagons. Probably stole it from the Indians, leaving behind another trail of tears. Wouldn't surprise me a bit if someone fooled with that tank on purpose. Not one bit." She bit into a carrot, as if to make her point. "People get real jealous when others do well for themselves," Marjorie continued. "I should know. You should have heard them talk when I took over the Quik-a-Way from Woodrow. You would've thought I killed the man the way they carried on! Wasn't my fault he didn't have a lick of sense about running a business. Didn't matter to them. I was the devil woman who stole it all away!"

"Should we say a prayer?" Emily asked. She'd never participated, never wanted to be a part of the prayer circle. And here she was, speaking up, but not for the reasons they suspected. And for the first time, she aimed to pray. For Mr. Johnston. For herself. For a way out of the mess that she was in.

"Oh, God," Jody muttered. "I forgot about this part."

Emily wondered how Jody could be so casual, so calm. If she held the same fears as Emily, she didn't let it show.

Mom interlaced her fingers and squeezed them in her lap. "We'll say a quick prayer."

Emily bowed her head along with the others as her mom led them in prayer. Even Jody bowed her head at the request. But she kept her eyes open like Emily, and on her.

"Amen," they all repeated at the end.

Marjorie yanked the bowl toward her before Emily's mom could. "Ricky," she said, and waved the little scrap of paper in the air.

Jody jerked her head up.

"We ought to keep the young and old in our prayers, especially with that cut on his head," Marjorie said.

"What cut on his head?" Emily's mom asked.

"I told you that was an accident," Emily said.

Jody's face reddened. Her jaw clenched tight.

"He see his father much?" Marjorie directed a disapproving eye toward Jody and then Ricky.

Emily inhaled deeply. "Ricky's fine, he just—"

"Does Troy see *his* dad?" Jody launched into Marjorie, ignoring Emily's efforts to redirect the conversation. "Where'd that husband of *yours* get off to? He ever bother to show up after that last time he took off for the casinos in Oklahoma?"

Marjorie sat up straighter, head and nose lifting higher. "Why would you ask that?" Marjorie asked. Emily wondered the same thing. Of all people for Jody to bring up in conversation, why Troy? Why today?

"Can we get back to the prayers?" Emily asked.

"Yes," her mom said. She smiled and nodded at Emily, apparently willing to let go of their feud to defuse the more potent one brewing in the room.

All the talk of Troy got Emily's head spinning around the reminder of him clenching her finger, twice. The first time he'd threatened her. The second time he'd begged her. Both times had scared her. She shut her eyes and tried to shake away the reminder and the question that tormented her: *Where is he?*

"Oh, you can ask about Ricky's dad but I can't ask about Troy's?" Jody asked.

Marjorie jabbed a carrot into some dip. Instead of eating it, she held it out. "We are divorced. And if he did show up at the house, I'd have him arrested." She shoved the carrot into her mouth and chewed with passion.

"For what?" Jody asked.

Carrot bits flying, she said, "For being a no 'count, cheating sonofabitch is what."

Emily startled at the use of the word in her mom's presence—and from Marjorie's mouth. The closest she'd heard her come to cussing was using the word "butt." She wondered what other colors she unleashed when Emily's mom wasn't around. Her mom shut her eyes and said nothing. Heather sat still on the couch, mouth open. Her eyes shifted back and forth between Jody and Marjorie.

"I didn't know that was a crime. I'll be sure to tell Owen to be on the lookout," she said.

Heather's eyes widened. "What about Owen?"

Jody scanned Heather top to bottom as if to help her memory place her. "Oh, Heather." She drew out her name like it had an ill taste. All that was missing was for her to pull the letters off her tongue and flick them from her fingers. "I forgot you were here."

Heather asked, "Are you and Owen dating?"

Emily recalled the conversation about what had happened between Heather and Owen, and thought back to what she had seen at the gas pump.

Jody took a drink and looked Heather square in the eyes. "I wouldn't call it dating."

Heather's head dropped and her chin hit her chest. After a few rare moments of silence in the room, she stood. "I'm gonna get some water," Heather said, barely a whisper. She walked across the room like there were bombs hidden in the carpet and disappeared into the hallway. Emily's heart broke a little at the sight. The poor girl had nothing to do with Marjorie and Jody's antagonism toward one another. But that didn't matter. Jody and Marjorie were more alike than not. Whoever got in their way got knocked down.

Reason wouldn't end the hateful looks or back-and-forth barbs, so Emily tipped her drink until a few red drops made it onto the floor and she could end the night. Or at least the conversation. She tried to remember what had been the point of coming. To act normal. Right. They were certainly on track.

Emily yelled out, "Oh, shoot." She dabbed at the drops with her shoe while the others paused and puzzled at her action.

179

"What are you doing? Stop it." Her mom rushed over to the spill. "You're gonna make it worse." She took a napkin and dipped it in water and proceeded to blot the stain.

The interruption had only paused the conversation, not ended it. If anything, it had given them time to refocus and refuel for the next round.

Marjorie pointed a finger at Jody, ignoring Heather's retreat. "Is that what you call what you're doing with Troy?" Marjorie continued, eyes ablaze. "Dating?"

Emily's mom pursed her lips and let the stain be. Emily waited for the whole thing to be over, not wanting to spend another moment in that room while questions burned her insides—about where Troy was now, and how many ways to Sunday she was fucked.

"Maybe you'd like to fill me in on what's going on over at your house? 'Cause it sure has a hold on Troy."

Emily squeezed her eyes shut and clutched her head. She couldn't take it anymore. "Oh my God. Would you two please stop?"

When she opened her eyes again, her mom, Jody, and Marjorie were all staring at the floor. The room had gone silent. But not for long.

Jody tilted her head and fixed a disinterested gaze on Marjorie. "If you'd like, Dorothy will give you a little slip of paper and you can write your prayer on it. 'Dear Jesus,'" she said and steepled her fingers. "'Please tell Troy to come home to me, even though he hates my guts, so I can suffocate him and he'll probably leave me again like my husband did, amen.'"

Emily let a loud sigh escape. A trail of coughs she couldn't control followed. She downed the nearest glass of Bloody Mary mix.

"Jody," Mom said. "That's enough."

"Dot, there's only one reason for a boy to be holed up with someone like Jody," Marjorie said. "And you know it."

"*Someone like me?*" Jody asked.

Their voices assaulted Emily's ears. Her throat felt scraped dry, but itchy. Her head ached. She wanted to disappear upstairs, back to her old room, her real room, not the spare. She wanted to wash away whatever chemicals lingered on her body, pull the covers over her head, escape into sleep even if it was fitful. No nightmare could compare to her current reality.

"If you lay one dirty finger on my boy, so help me God, I will come after you with a fire and a fury unlike anything you've ever seen."

Jody leaned forward. "You sound like a cartoon character."

Marjorie tilted her head slightly. "I don't care what I sound like to trash like you."

Jody rose from her chair so quickly that Marjorie flinched. Unlike she'd done as a teenager, she couldn't bolt out the door. She slammed every object back into Ricky's diaper bag.

Emily sat upright in her chair. "Wait. What are you doing?"

While Jody stormed around the room, Marjorie slowly inspected carrots and celery sticks before dipping them in ranch dressing. She eased them into her mouth and took her time with the chewing. Every now and then, she shifted her eyes to the side to get a good look at Jody as she gathered her things.

"Jody, stop." Emily stood, hands up, trying to reason. "Please. Calm down." A new round of coughing came over her.

"Get out of my way." The look in her eyes and the growl in her tone shocked Emily, as if she were the one Jody had been battling with instead of Marjorie. Emily took a step back and Jody knocked into her shoulder on her way toward the door. When something didn't go Jody's way, she flared up and shot off like a Roman candle. Like the time Emily's mom insisted she come downstairs and talk to Connie on the phone. After five minutes of screaming, Jody called Connie a bitch and told her to never call her again. Emily had never seen a kid display that kind of grown-up rage. Afterward, Emily had been too scared to say anything to Jody. She waited a whole day to speak to her. When she did, it was like nothing had happened.

"Jody, don't go. You just got here." Emily's mom rested a hand on Jody's shoulder, but it was met with a quick brush-off. Jody swooped Ricky into her arms, rushed to the door, and slammed it behind her. Emily flinched at the sound, stunned at how the conversation had turned and how Jody had reacted. For a moment, she debated whether Jody had intentionally torpedoed the evening. There was no way anyone would forget where they were that night if anyone came knocking and asking where they'd been the day Troy had gotten caught stealing fertilizer.

Marjorie lifted her glass. "Good riddance!"

Emily's mom whirled around to face Marjorie. "Why'd you have to egg her on?"

"Me?" Marjorie's mouth hung open.

"You know better," she said. "You're the adult."

"And she's not? She went and got herself knocked up. Sounds adult to me. And why am I supposed to be nice to her?" Marjorie thrust out her chest. "No matter how hard you try, nothing's gonna change. That girl is trash. Always was, always will be." If they'd been outside instead of in the living room, Emily wouldn't have been surprised if Marjorie had spat on the ground to make her point.

Emily scanned the room for her coat, eager to leave the room and the women behind. She gave up her search and rushed past them to the front door. The effort left her winded.

Outside, Jody latched the buckles on Ricky's car seat.

"What was that? Are you trying to piss her off even more?"

Jody turned around so quickly, Emily jumped back. Jody's hand shook as she held it in the air, pointing an accusatory finger. "I'm not going to sit here and listen to her crap all night. I'm stressed out enough as it is with Troy and you . . ."

Emily dropped her hand from the car door. She knew the stress Jody referred to included what had happened between them the night by the fire, as if the two events rivaled each other in terribleness.

Jody noted the pause but pushed past Emily again. "I'm stressed out, is all. I can't deal with her, too." Jody opened the driver's side door and sunk into the seat. "I need to be alone for a little while."

Emily lifted her head to the night sky to try to force the tears to stay down. The stars looked foggy behind the clouds. She used to be able to look up at the stars and feel calm. Now her eyes were drawn to the gulfs of black between them. "How long is a little while?"

"A few hours or so."

"So you're just gonna leave me here? After everything that happened today?" Emily shook her head and tried to remain calm. "Of course you are."

"It's just for a little while." She gestured toward the house. "Maybe one of them can give you a ride."

"You really want one of them out at the house?"

"Maybe August can pick you up. I think he was planning on coming out later tonight anyway."

"Why? Does he know about Troy?"

Jody shrugged. "I don't know. He just mentioned it is all."

For not knowing what was going on, Jody sure knew a lot—except the details. Except all the things she wasn't saying. "Why do I get the feeling that you're hiding something?"

Emily glanced around the yard and lowered her voice. "You're not just renting to Troy, are you?" Jody dropped her head and gripped the steering wheel. "There's no point in lying to me about it. I'm already up shit creek after what happened today, so you might as well fess up." Emily looked toward the house. The curtains didn't move.

Ricky began to fuss in the backseat. Great timing. For Jody. She twisted around in her seat and tried to distract him with a toy.

Emily reached into the car and grabbed the keys out of the ignition. When Jody faced the front again, Emily continued. "Tell the truth: Are you working with him?" She didn't need to elaborate. Jody hadn't answered the question earlier. Jody would not have forgotten, only delayed.

"Give me my keys."

"Oh, now who's looking for keys? See how irritating that is?"

Jody slammed her back against the seat and stared out the windshield.

Frustrated at Jody's unwillingness to talk, her ability to deflect and move on to another subject, she tried a different tack. "Are you using? Is that how you got involved with him?"

"No." Jody didn't look up, but scrunched her face the way she did when she acted like she didn't know what someone was talking about, and didn't know why they bothered to ask. "I drink. I get high. But no. Not anymore. And only for a little while," she said. "I was depressed at the time."

They lived in an inherited trailer from the eighties in the middle of the woods. An addicted teenager crashed on their couch and was wandering somewhere out there in the unknown with injuries that had to rival Mr. Johnston's. Emily could barely catch her breath, and her eyes stung from being exposed to a chemical used for the meth lab at the bottom of the hill. And she'd finally made out with her best friend but had managed to scare her off instead of seduce her. If ever there was a time to drown oneself in drugs from depression, then it was now.

Exasperated, Jody flung her fingers up on the steering wheel and focused on the windshield instead of Emily. "I'm not asking you to move out. I'm not trying to keep anything from you. I just need some time alone to think about what to do about Troy, okay? I can't tell you what, because I don't know. And besides, you've already been through enough today without adding this on top of it. I can't think while you're asking me all these questions and looking at me like I'm some kind of horrible person." Jody rubbed her face and slumped back against the seat. "God, I fucking hate this town. Nothing good ever happens here. I should've never come back. I should just sell the land and leave."

Jody shouldn't have agreed to the arrangement she had with Troy. She should stick to her original plan and end it. Not in a few months. Now.

"Leaving doesn't solve anything," Emily said.

Leaving Little Rock hadn't. If Emily had left Drear's Bluff and Jody's house and everything that she desired, she might not have anything to solve. But she knew that somehow the town would have pulled her back again.

Jody started to say something, but then bit the inside of her lip. Finally she spoke. "We've had a conversation like this before, haven't we?"

Deflection. Jody's main ammo. "Yeah," Emily said. "In the woods out past the creek." *Don't cry*, she warned herself. Not even if those tears would provide relief to her eyes. *Don't you cry.* "I remember lots

185

of things about Drear's Bluff. I mostly remember you." The words faltered as they left her lips.

Even though it was dark out, Emily could see a flash of empathy or recognition or a question—she couldn't be sure—cross Jody's face. "I know," she said.

Emily fixed her gaze onto the flat fields beyond the house to still her mind.

"I'm sorry about what happened," Jody said. "Had I known what he was doing, I would've never—"

"You didn't bring a gas can full of ammonia into my car. That's on him." She had to get the words out even though she didn't mean them. "And I'm sorry about what happened the other night. I shouldn't have done that." She wasn't sorry. She didn't want Jody to be sorry either. But she didn't want the silence to continue.

Jody's face softened. "Like you said, no big deal. We had a lot to drink."

Emily hesitated, wanting Jody to say something more. She handed over the car keys. "Yeah. That's all I wanted to say."

Jody retrieved a pack of cigarettes from her purse, lit one, and let it dangle from her fingers outside the window. "Maybe you'll catch the spirit tonight and find it in your heart to forgive me for leaving you here."

Time seemed to inch forward while Emily stood there. The car's engine rumbled into life. Jody grabbed Emily's hand and squeezed. Emily winced at the fresh pain and the reminder of Troy's grip.

"Everything's gonna be okay, yeah?" Jody said. "Just give me a few hours to take care of some things."

Emily nodded even though she didn't believe her.

Jody released the brake and put the car into reverse. She sped down the driveway, gravel flying behind her. Bugs and particles of dust danced in the beams of the taillights. Emily's insides twisted into a knot of questions and dread. Was Troy okay? Was she? Would that old man talk? Would Owen show up at their door?

Before heading back inside, Emily texted August, hit send and waited.

Instead of going through the front door, Emily entered through the kitchen. She grabbed a glass and filled it with ice cubes after popping one in her mouth to suck on and ease the itch that persisted. The longer she stood there, the more she replayed the events of the day. Those stickers with their warnings kept flashing in her mind. She rested her head on the freezer door and tried to think of something else. But nothing else could break their hold on her.

No noise came from the living room. It was so quiet she thought maybe they'd all left, but their cars were still outside. She headed upstairs to her old bedroom and shut the door. She sat down at the computer and pushed the power button. While she waited for the dial-up to connect, her fingers hovered over the keyboard. What was she supposed to do? Check WebMD? In the past, she had only looked up stupid things. Weird stomach pains, headaches. The result: cancer, always. But this? How could she describe this thing that had happened to her? Her fingers hovered over the keyboard.

Her phone buzzed with a message. August would head over soon.

Before she could lose her nerve or time, she typed: *Fertilizer. Ammonia. Inhale.* And then, *Hospital?*

She heard rustling noises downstairs. Voices. Someone walking up the stairs. She read through the results quickly. Burning eyes, blindness, throat and respiratory tract irritation. Death. But not if at a lower concentration.

What constituted low amounts versus high amounts? She chewed on another piece of ice and rubbed her throat. It still burned, but more like a normal sore throat. Her eyes burned too, but she could see fine.

The result of her search, the one she accepted because any other result would lead to her fumbling over lies: There was no need to go to the hospital. There was nothing to worry about. She hoped.

She turned off the computer, grabbed her glass, and headed back to the staircase. On the way, her dad called her name. She walked toward her parents' room and peeked in. Her dad lounged on the bed, remote in hand, glasses nudged down.

"Hey." She couldn't bring herself to look at him too long.

"Hay's for horses," he said.

She finished the joke for him. "Too bad I'm a jackass."

He smiled. "Well, if the shoe fits."

She picked at the doorframe. "I guess I deserve that."

"Surprised to see you here."

She wished it had been under different circumstances. She ventured a glance at him. "Thought it might be good to show my face."

"It's a good face. I'm glad to see it."

She wanted to laugh, to cry. To step into a time machine. To return to some previous day where her current trajectory could be reset. Where she didn't wind up as an accessory to a crime against an old farmer. Where her dad hadn't lost respect for her.

"You talk to your mom?"

"Not really. She's busy with prayers." And not talking to Emily. She began picking at the doorframe and a small piece of wood came off and fell to the carpet. She looked up to see if her dad had noticed. If he had, he didn't say. She didn't want to hurt him. She didn't want anyone to hurt him. One day he'd look like that old man with the shotgun, whose face kept assaulting her vision. What if that had been her dad instead of him?

"Penny for your thoughts," he said.

If he knew those, she feared he'd never want to see her again. "It'll cost you more than that," she said. "They said a prayer for Mr. Johnston. Heather said she heard someone had tampered with his tank. That's how he got hurt." Her dad nodded, but didn't say anything. "Has anyone messed with yours?"

He shook his head. "No. Nothing like that."

"But it happens."

"Yeah." He scratched his head and left some hair standing in his wake. "I check them, though. So don't get any more ideas about taking over the farm. I'm not dead yet." He laughed, but she couldn't laugh with him. "Hey. Don't worry, okay?"

"I don't want you to get hurt."

"I won't." He looked up at the TV, and she realized that she was probably interrupting a game. August would be there soon.

"I better get downstairs," she said. "It's good to see you." She wanted to crawl up in bed with him like a child. "I love you."

"I love you too, honey." He smiled before returning to his remote.

As soon as she left the room, the crowd's roar rose from the stadium on the TV.

In the living room, Marjorie was cleaning the paper plates and food off the coffee table, every movement faster than necessary. In the process she flung food all over the carpet. She cursed under her breath and dropped down to her knees to pick up the wreckage.

"Prayers over?" Emily asked. It'd been at least thirty minutes since Jody had left. Emily suspected that they had carried on with prayers despite what had happened. Probably brushed the conflict under the rug, pretending things were fine. The usual.

She looked up at Emily. "Heather left. Your mom's in the kitchen being mad at me." She returned her attention to the floor. "Sometimes I want to strangle her." She slammed bits of food onto a paper plate. "Nothing good ever came from helping Jody. I knew it the first day her momma showed up at church, pretending to be interested in anything other than the free suppers and clothing they started handing out to the poor." She scowled. "Oh, don't look at me like that; we all know it's true. She took about five of your momma's dresses right out of her hands, acting like they were the prettiest things she ever did see and how on earth would she ever be able to wear anything so fine as that and your momma just ate it up like the fool she is. No wonder she dropped Jody off at your momma's door. Connie practically had her eating out of her hand, what with all that crying and carrying on about not wanting to be a mom. Well, who does? It's a thankless job. You spend half your life making sure they do right and then they don't, just to spite you." She puffed air out of her nose, stood, and grimaced when her knees cracked. She pointed at Emily. "Don't you go and tell your mom what I said. I'll deny it."

Nobody ever said what they meant or told the truth, and when they did, they'd swear against it later. Still, Emily wondered if there was some genetic pull that led Jody astray the same as her mom.

"If I asked you what was going on between Jody and Troy, would you tell me?"

Emily nudged the curtain aside and peered through the window to see if August had arrived.

"Don't you go ignoring me. I know you know something," Marjorie said.

She knew something. She knew everything. She knew nothing. "There's nothing going on. He doesn't like living at home is all."

"Well what kid does? What boy wouldn't want to spend all their time out there with two girls doing God knows what instead of working and helping out and going to school?" Marjorie was just like Emily's mom, picking and prying. Never satisfied with the answer given. "What's he doing out there?"

"He's not always there." She almost mentioned that he helped in the chicken house, but she stopped herself. "He hangs out sometimes. I haven't seen him today." The lie burned her throat even more.

Marjorie repeated the words. "Hangs out? That could mean anything. You kids use these words and they don't make any sense."

Emily peeked out the window again and was met with darkness. If Marjorie only knew. She placed her forehead against the windowpane and tried to drown out the sound of Marjorie's voice with the crunch of ice. She peered out into the yard and tried to picture where Troy might be. How he looked. What he would say. Maybe he was home waiting for them. Maybe he had called Jody and that was why she needed to be alone, to protect Emily from the truth. No matter how hard Emily tried, she couldn't get him out of her head. It didn't help that Marjorie kept saying his name behind her, asking questions about when she'd seen him last and what he was doing and who on Earth he thought he was, treating her like that. Emily couldn't stand the sound of her voice anymore or those four letters that plagued her thoughts: Troy.

She took off for the kitchen. Behind her, Marjorie's complaints about Emily walking away while she was asking her a question faded with each step.

She paused at the doorway, breathed in deep for courage, and crossed the threshold. Her mom stood in front of the fridge, peering into it with an assortment of Tupperware on the counter next to her.

Her mom kept her focus on the fridge and her attempt to Tetris all the night's leftovers into it.

Conversation had never been easy between them. Still, Emily had to force herself to say something, anything. "The house looks nice."

Her mom balanced a jar of pickled carrots and a container of Ranch dip in her hand. "I guess it normally looks messy?"

Her mom would not make it easy on her. "No, it always looks nice." She chewed on her lip, trying to locate some sentence that wouldn't raise her mom's ire. She had known the prayer circle would be hard to attend. It was. But it was a familiar type of hard. A normalcy, even if their normal was crazy. The hallway, the carpet, the walls, the smells. All the things that had felt oppressive to her before she'd moved out, today brought comfort. She knew what to expect in that house. A normal trip to town equaled a normal return home. There was nothing normal about her days now. Nothing normal about their lives. She missed her mom, her dad, her simple complaints.

Her mom fussed with jars and cans and a pie pan that was three-quarters full.

Emily leaned against the kitchen island. An untouched meat and pasta casserole sat covered with plastic wrap so tight that a quarter could bounce off it. Emily lifted it. The thing weighed about twenty pounds.

Her mom glanced at the casserole dish. "I don't know what I'm going to do with that thing. Sally brought it. I don't know why. It's not like we needed dinner."

The headlights from August's truck beamed up the drive. Finally. "My ride's here," she said. "I can take the casserole to the Johnstons' if you want, considering everything."

"Have you tasted Sally's cooking?" Her mom laughed in a moment of forgetfulness, as if they were okay again, but then caught herself. "I don't want them thinking I made it."

"I'll take it with me then."

Her mom finally looked at her, but only for a moment. "I suppose that would be fine." She returned her attention to the fridge. "At least then I won't have to lie about throwing it out."

Emily grabbed the casserole and headed toward the door. "I can bring the dish by later this week. If that'd be all right."

Her mom considered. "That'd be fine," she said. But Emily saw a hint of something. Not quite a smile, but something. Something that Emily could take with her as hope that things might be okay, if not good, between them again.

CHAPTER TWELVE

STARS SPOTTED THE SKY, AND the radio played a sad country song. A full moon lit a road devoid of streetlights. Emily propped her head on her arm and let the cold wind from the cracked window rush over her face.

The bottom part of August's face glowed green from the dashboard lights. His eyes were covered by the shadow of his ball cap.

She looked down at the casserole dish between them on the seat, debating what she wanted to do versus what she should do. Her mom had said no. She'd be angry if she found out. "Do you mind making a stop at the Johnstons'? It's on the way to Jody's." The request dredged the memory of a similar one that Troy had made of her.

He looked down at the casserole and then back at the road. "Sure," he said.

The sound of the tires on the road and the country tunes on the radio numbed her mind. The season had stripped the trees of leaves. The whole town looked dunked in the color of drab.

When they neared the Johnstons' farm, she motioned toward the road. "Don't forget to make a stop up here."

He inspected the dish. "What is it?"

"Some sort of pasta with meat and cheese. Probably hamburger."

"Any vegetables?"

"Doubtful."

August gave the pan a once over. "We ought to eat it ourselves," he said. "They won't miss it."

She turned to the window so he couldn't see her lie. "Mom will have my hide if I don't deliver it." She'd have her hide if she did.

"Oh, come on. Live a little." He laughed and smiled at her before turning his attention back to the road.

"Just make the turn."

August headed up the long drive toward the Johnstons' house. A quarter of the way there, they were stopped by a metal gate. Acres of farmland stood between them and the house. The wispy grass clung to the flat ground and barely swayed with the breeze. Even with all that flatness, the house was too far for anyone to notice them.

The gate seemed sturdier, new. A handmade TRESPASSERS WILL BE SHOT! sign had been taped to the gate, a warning that recalled her recent skirmish with a shotgun and her ever-increasing belief that Troy had tampered with Mr. Johnston's tank as well. Though it might not make a difference to anyone but her, she wanted to hear the story from Mr. Johnston himself. A thick lock hung from the post and the handle.

She reached for the door handle.

"Wait." He grabbed her arm and then killed the engine and headlights. "I heard what happened today."

She eased off the handle. "Jody told you?"

"The gist. She called to make sure I'd come pick you up from your parents' house."

At least she'd cared enough to do that. "Are you going to say I told you so? Because it's not necessary."

"No, but this is why I was worried about you being at the house. More people, more problems." He swung his arm along the backseat. "Are you okay? How are you feeling?"

Jody hadn't asked her if she was okay. Not once. Her eyes began to burn with recollection and emotions she didn't want to show him. "Okay. I think."

"What are you really doing? You hoping Mr. Johnston might shed some light on what happened to you?"

She turned toward the window and the darkness. She could see August watching her in the reflection. "No."

"We don't need to draw any attention to ourselves right now."

"We?" she asked. "Were you there today?"

"No. I was at the house with Dad all day." Who had been the one who hosed her off? It couldn't have been Troy. And if not him and not Jody, then who? Someone was lying. "Besides, it's late. They're bound to be in bed at their age. And we ought to get you home so you can rest."

Rest. Like she was a child in need of a nap after a tough day of play. The insinuation riled her temper. She watched the house in the distance while he continued to look at her like he had a question he wanted to ask. She had a question she wanted to ask, too, but neither was willing to go first.

Finally she said, "Did Troy have something to do with Johnston's accident?"

He grabbed a toothpick out of the glove box and worked it around his mouth for a while without speaking.

"Jody said he didn't," she said, looking over at him to see if he had a response. "I think he did."

He focused on her eyes and then her mouth, back and forth like he couldn't trust one over the other. He blinked a few times and paused before answering. "I'm not sure." But his eyes told her different. Something had clicked, but he wasn't saying what. He eased out of Johnston's driveway, and the next words he uttered were just as she was about to close the truck's door and walk into Jody's house. Jody's car was still gone.

"Listen," he said. "Don't tell Jody about going to the Johnstons'. Any of that. If you hear anything that seems out the ordinary, I want you to call me." Nerves shot through his voice, making her own nerves light up in response.

"Everything is out of the ordinary."

"I know," he said. "I'm not trying to keep anything from you, but there are some things I can't explain and it's best if you don't know too many details. I need you to trust me on this one."

"Why should I trust you?"

He tipped his head toward her, eyebrows up. "Far as I can tell, I'm the only friend you've got." The brake lights lit the ground, and August shifted gears. "Try not to worry, okay?"

Impossible. She nodded and watched his truck roll down the driveway.

CHAPTER THIRTEEN

JODY HADN'T COME HOME BEFORE Emily headed to bed. She left the bedroom light on, not wanting or willing to be alone in the dark all the way out in the woods. Emily heard her car come up the drive a little after midnight. She stared at the door and waited to see if Jody might knock. She didn't. After a while, she got up and pressed her ear to the door to see if she could hear anything. A few minutes later, she turned off the light and eased back down onto her bed of blankets on the floor.

The chill in the air had turned to a bone-rattling ache overnight. The crisp days of fall had finally ceded to the cold, strangling darkness of the impending winter. The next morning, Emily rubbed her arms to disperse the goose bumps and placed her fingers between the plastic blinds to peek outside. A drab gray sky cast the day in half darkness. Frost covered the ground. She checked the time on her phone: six o'clock—far too early for Jody to be up, but noise from the kitchen indicated otherwise.

All night, Emily'd tossed on her pallet, unable to adjust either her back or her mind. The thin covers she'd thrown over her head offered little help. For weeks she'd been meaning to buy a bed but had stopped herself, not willing to admit until now that she'd held onto her desires too tightly and ached for a warm spot in Jody's bed.

She pulled on a sweatshirt and a pair of socks. In the hallway, she paused at the thermostat and turned the heat up a few more notches.

"Sorry," Jody said in the kitchen. "Did the TV wake you?"

"No." Emily wandered over to the coffee pot to pour herself a cup. She pushed the salt and pepper and other spices aside to reach for the sugar canister. Inside, a great glob of coffee-hardened sugar sat at the top. Emily had repeatedly asked Troy not to dip his wet spoon into the sugar bowl.

"No word from Troy?" she asked, though she knew the answer.

Jody yawned. "You're worse than a kid asking, 'Are we there yet?' The answer won't change just because you ask. I told you I'd tell you if I heard, but you keep asking." She opened the fridge and then slammed it shut. "We're out of food," she said.

Jody shuffled to her bedroom and closed the door, leaving Emily standing at the counter, staring into the sugar bowl, wondering why Jody didn't seem worried that a boy who had been there for weeks hadn't turned up after what had happened the day before.

Emily's car keys sat on the bar, as if they'd been there all along. When she asked Jody later that day where she had found them, Jody said they'd been in Emily's pockets. Jody had found them when she'd thrown Emily's dirty clothes in the washer.

Jody moved around the rooms in silence, looking shaken and offering no word on what they'd do next. This pattern continued for three more days.

Every day, while Jody hid behind her bedroom door, Emily considered and reconsidered the facts and fragments of memory that loomed in her mind and mixed with everything she thought she'd known about Jody, and what she had seen since she'd come back home. Every phone call Jody took in another room. Every twitch under Jody's eye, every stalled sentence came back to her as a question: *What is Jody hiding?*

Emily hadn't left the house. Wouldn't. The old man with the shotgun might recognize her car, her face. That meant no Quik-a-Way, no trips to town, nothing. Her throat still itched, and she ate ice cubes to try to soothe it. Every crunch reminded her of sitting in front of her parents' computer, reading and fretting about her health and Troy's.

Troy's absence, something Emily had longed for, now tormented her. Despite her terror and the risk of being on the road and recognized, Emily gathered her keys and her grocery list, and steeled herself for her tasks: one that would fill the fridge, one that might let her know where Troy was.

SCATTERED BOUTS OF FREEZING RAIN pattered the window of the Quik-a-Way. Cold radiated from the windowpane, through the thin jacket Emily had pulled over her thin T-shirt. In the process of moving from her parents' house and into Jody's, she'd left the one warm jacket she owned in the closet, thinking that she'd have time and money to buy something new before the weather got cooler.

When she'd entered the grocery store earlier that day, the sun had been out, the chill tempered a bit. All along the ride, she'd searched the road for familiar vehicles and faces. Waited for Owen's lights and siren to buzz behind her. She had wanted to take Jody's car but didn't want to bother her. Their conversations consisted of questions and non-answers. She shifted the rearview mirror so she wouldn't be reminded of what she'd seen reflected back to her from the backseat.

She turned the music up too loud and sung along to distract herself from her paranoia.

In the grocery store she paused in aisle after Thanksgiving-decorated aisle to see if she might catch a glimpse of Troy, or one of the people from the party that first night. Maybe someone had seen him, heard from him. But she saw none of them. Outside the store, she checked the bench where Troy had been waiting for her a week prior. That'd been the last time anything had felt normal.

If he were truly missing, Marjorie would know.

And if not?

Heather handed Emily a menu without a word. She wasn't hungry, but she ordered coffee and a dessert.

She gave the menu back to Heather. "It was good to see you at the prayer circle."

Heather took the menu without looking at Emily. "Sure." She scribbled on her notepad.

"Everything okay?" Emily asked.

Heather shoved her notepad and pen in her apron pocket. "Everything's fine." She walked back to the counter and slammed the door to the countertop pie case after retrieving Emily's order. She came back with the pie, the coffee, and the check without exchanging another word. Emily assumed that she was still mad at Jody for her comments about Owen and not about something else that Emily had done.

The food and coffee didn't appeal to her, but she ate and drank them anyway. Act normal. If she weren't so freaked out, the thought would've made her laugh.

An old man sipped coffee at the counter, and a couple of pimple-faced teenagers hooked school. Emily suspected that Marjorie had already called the high school to complain.

After a while, Marjorie came out from the back of the diner. She noticed Emily, but headed in the opposite direction.

Despite business being slow, Marjorie flew from table to counter to kitchen and back with determination, making it hard for Emily to get her attention. When Emily finally flagged her down, Marjorie didn't offer a greeting other than a lift of the finger to indicate that whatever Emily wanted, it would have to wait. In the meantime, she filled the salt and pepper shakers, married the ketchup bottles, brushed the crumbs off the counter. Tasks dispatched, she strode over to Emily's table. She straightened her back and inhaled as if she were about to belt out a hymn or an admonishment.

"Is there something wrong with Heather's service? Clearly, there's nothing wrong with the pie." Emily glanced at her empty plate. "You got your bill." Heather watched them from behind the counter. "Let Heather know when you're ready to pay."

Emily choked down her hesitation.

Marjorie lifted an eyebrow. "What is it?"

"I was wondering if maybe you've seen Troy." She struggled to find a reason that didn't involve what she knew. "He hasn't been around and I need to talk to him."

Marjorie crossed her arms. "Have *I* seen Troy?" When she spoke, her chin jutted forward.

Emily didn't know what else to say.

"How in the world would I see Troy when he spends all his time out there with you gir—" she said. "Why don't *you* tell *me* where Troy is, 'cause he sure as heck didn't bother coming home last night or any night before that and barely ever does, now that you all've got"—she struggled to find the right word—"whatever you're doing out there at Jody's." Marjorie directed her head toward the window. She raised her upper lip and wrinkled her nose. "Not one of you has lifted a finger to work in I don't know how long, but somehow you manage to get by—"

All she wanted was one person to know something. To give her a slip of reassurance that he was okay, or at least had been seen, so she could crawl down off the panic that held her body on high alert. Just one person. "I know you're mad at Jody—"

"You bet I'm mad. Troy, I can understand. A woman comes along, he's gonna follow." Marjorie crossed her arms and lifted her head. "I tried to raise him right, but he's still a man. And he still has a chance in life, despite the odds given to him by his no-good father and that football injury. But you? Why, I don't even know. Lord knows your mom and I prayed for you. We prayed good and hard. We still do, but it seems to me that none of that praying has done a lick of good. I suppose it's true that some have to work harder than others to beat back their demons."

She lifted her finger to point at Emily, but stalled. Instead she peered behind her in case anyone was listening, and leaned forward to whisper, "That girl is never gonna love you, Emily Skinner. Never. And it's high time you stopped breaking your momma's heart."

Shock and shame, at what Marjorie had dared to say out loud, hit her. Emily focused on the table, unable to look up for fear the tears that had begun to roll down her face would run stronger. She was tired of fighting. Tired of waging this war against her so-called sin when greater sins consumed her. If they only knew how badly she wished that she didn't crave what they all knew she wanted. That she didn't feel antsy and anxious and obsessed. To feel addicted and never able to get enough.

Marjorie placed a hand in the center of the table. "Come now." Her hand, instead of making its way to Emily's face—to wipe the tears, smooth her hair, soften the blow—stayed fixed near Emily's decimated dessert. "People are watching."

Emily shot her hands to her eyes to catch the tears before they dropped onto the table.

Marjorie stood and assumed her natural stance as if to try and normalize the situation. "Tell that son of mine that if he doesn't get home tonight, he's out. This time, I mean it."

EMILY WOUND HER WAY DOWN the soggy red clay road toward Jody's house, the wheel gripped tight to avoid spinning out in the mud.

At the house, she shut off the engine. The windshield wipers came to a halt midsweep. A mixture of sleet and rain pelted the windshield and blurred the world. She dropped her head onto the steering wheel and let the tears come. Her nose clogged so much that she couldn't breathe unless she opened her mouth.

She would've given anything to hear Troy's laugh again, pick his socks up off the living room floor, see the empty milk jug in the fridge. If God would bring him back from wherever he was, she promised, she'd sit through church and her mom's prayer circle and all of Troy's nonsense and not say a word and be grateful for all the grace in her life.

She wiped her face with the bottom of her shirt and stepped out of the car. The wet grass soaked her tennis shoes and colored them gray. She hauled the grocery bags up the steps, the plastic handles cutting into her wrists. She prayed that Troy was inside the house, sitting on the couch in his boxers playing video games. If she could find him, then she could set aside the gnawing fear that things were about to get worse.

But he wasn't inside. Neither was Jody or Ricky, even though Jody's car was in the drive. Emily listened for any sound from Jody's bedroom but heard none.

The pie Emily had consumed in a hurry tore at her stomach. She leaned over the kitchen sink, ready to empty the contents. Dry heaves wracked her body but nothing came. She pushed the curtain away and rubbed out the fog with her fist to stare through the tiny squares of window screen toward the direction of the chicken house, believing that if she looked long enough, Troy would walk up the hill. She stood there until her legs cramped and she had to prop herself against the sink. Finally, she slid down to the floor.

The words that Marjorie had said rushed at her, mixed with her fears about Troy. How far she'd come in such a short amount of time. What a fool she'd been. A fool who had given up a different future for a shot at this one, in the hopes that one day Jody would receive what Emily held out bleeding and beating between them. All she'd wanted was Jody. Instead, she was hanging on to the desperate hope that a boy she'd once babysat was still alive.

She could run. She could grab her things and go. Out of town, out of state. Anywhere but here, practically alone and waiting for her fears to come true. But those worst-case scenario words she'd read on the computer at her parents' house loomed in her mind.

Troy could have died. He could be dead. It was only a matter of time before someone came knocking, asking her the same questions she'd been asking, only they'd be directed at her.

Emily scrambled to her feet and headed for her bedroom. The blinds were smudged from years of collected dust, the carpet a mixture of dark brown to hide the stains.

She tore her clothing out of the milk crates. She combed the floor and picked up single socks and unwashed bras that she'd tossed around the room over the past few weeks. After scanning the room, she went into the bathroom and flung open the medicine cabinet. She grabbed her brush, her toothbrush and toothpaste, hair ties, gel, lotion, everything. Everything had to come out. She didn't want to leave behind one piece of herself. No evidence for anyone to find, not Owen, not Jody. When she got where she was going, wherever that would be, she'd burn it all and never return.

The notion of leaving flooded her with terror, but less than the notion of staying.

Arms loaded, she dropped some clothing and lotion on her way back through the hallway. Her fingers barely reached the dropped items before another batch fell to the floor.

"Goddammit!" Those tears, those hateful tears streamed down her face and she collapsed onto her knees, surrounded by the pile of her meager possessions.

"What are you doing?" Jody appeared in the hallway, looking like she'd just woken from a nap, Ricky still dozing in her arms. Her eyes widened at the sight of her. "Where are you going?"

Every inch of Emily pulled away, yelled at her to run. Run as far away as possible.

"Emily?"

"I can't stay here." She hiccupped the words between her tears and gasps. "I can't stay."

"Shit. Hang on." Jody rushed to Ricky's room and set him down in his crib. She eased the door shut behind her and kneeled on the carpet in front of her. "What's wrong? What's happened?"

"No one's seen him. No one. He's just gone. And you don't seem to care. And Marjorie thinks . . ." And Jody wouldn't talk to her, could barely look at her since the night by the fire. All the fears and worries about what had happened with Jody and with Troy, she'd had to carry on her own. She'd lost her friend. She couldn't bear the weight of all those fears alone.

She couldn't speak, she could only gasp until her body washed all those emotions out. Jody rubbed her back, each circle a stinging pain. She shrugged away and wiped her eyes and nose on her sleeve. No, she couldn't leave, but she couldn't live with this.

"I have to tell Owen what happened." Air eluded her, her heart pounded, and the truth seemed a knife dead set on escape, stabbing and stabbing. "I can't stay here and keep this inside any longer. I can't."

Jody's jaw was set, her body unmoving. "Okay," she whispered. "Okay."

With each utterance of the word, Emily's tension eased.

"Okay," Jody said again and again until she reached for Emily's hands and clasped them in hers. Her mouth opened once more, but this time she didn't speak. Then, slowly and gently, she moved her hands up and cradled Emily's jaw.

Emily squeezed her eyes shut, not wanting to be held in this way in this moment for these reasons, not wanting to see what she couldn't have.

When she opened her eyes again, she looked everywhere but at Jody's face, just inches from hers. Instead, she focused on the hallway light with the dead bugs encased in its bowl of dust. The photos of Ricky that lined the hallway walls, the carpet, the bathroom door, the pile of clothes and bottles of gel and lotion they sat upon.

Then, those brown eyes. The brown eyes she saw when she closed her eyes at night. The dark eyelashes. The arch of Jody's eyebrows. Her nose. Her lips. New details: small lines that had formed along the outside of her eyes. A one-inch scar that ran along her right temple, which Emily had never noticed.

Emily leaned into her, breathed in her scent. Held it, captured it, like the day she had come to see Jody after so many years gone. That day in the driveway, she remembered Jody with her senses. All those years of want rushed at her. She wanted more than what she was given. And she hated Jody for offering it to her now.

"No." Emily held Jody away from her, hurt, wanting Jody to stay, but waiting for her to go, the way she had always done. "Don't do this to me again."

Jody leaned close, closer, until their lips touched for a moment. As if suspended in time, they stayed that way until Jody opened her lips, allowing Emily to tip her tongue against Jody's once again, to test how much Jody would allow. But instead of Jody pulling away, Emily did, gauging the response, expecting Jody's lips to open, her voice to say stop. When they opened, that sweet intake of air said everything that Emily needed to know.

Her anger mixed with want. Emily grabbed the checkered flannel shirt that Jody wore and twisted the fabric at the chest, drawing Jody closer, mouths exploring, arms enclosed around one another. Emily wrapped her arms completely around Jody's thin frame, as if Jody's body had been molded to fit her.

Snaps, unsnapped. Bras, unfastened. No rushing, no shoving. Emily would be so slow, so careful, taking in each inch of skin as it was revealed—unlike that night by the fire.

They collapsed into the pile of clothing around them. Jody's breasts were speckled with goose bumps. Emily warmed them with her hands, her mouth, and thrilled at the convulsions that wracked Jody's body. Each time, Emily waited, silently asking permission, and each time Jody arched her back, pushing her on. She slipped her fingers across the perimeter of Jody's jeans, beyond. Jody gasped at her touch. Urged on by the sound, she sought more skin. First with her hands, then with her mouth. Jody held her knees together and lifted her pelvis to allow Emily to pull her jeans down her thighs.

All that Emily had desired, beneath her, rubbing against her, naked, waiting. Jody might have forgotten their kiss in the woods, but Emily would not let her forget this. Emily would not leave this house, by choice or force, without the one thing she had hoped for. She would make Jody remember this. She would make Jody burn with want for years after, the same way Jody had done to her. Emily kissed the skin of Jody's arms. Her breasts. Her torso, until her mouth was on Jody and Jody's legs were wrapped around her. Jody tangled her fingers within Emily's hair. She gasped again, again, and pressed Emily on. She pushed her hips against Emily's mouth. Everything had to be closer. Jody's fingers pulled at her hair, tugged, faster and faster until she moaned and tried to pull away. But Emily held her tight while Jody's body vibrated underneath her tongue and finally quieted, leaving them warm and quiet on the floor.

Sleet clicked at the windows and the roof. Their bodies were slick with sweat. Emily kissed away the wetness on her mouth with Jody's skin and rested her head on Jody's stomach, listening to the steady slowing of her heartbeat, not daring to look up, not wanting an end, not yet. She shut her eyes and dragged a finger along Jody's outer thigh. She wanted to stay there. Make the moment and all that confidence she'd felt last. But history told her it wouldn't.

Finally, Emily glanced up the plane of Jody's body. Eyes closed, Jody wiggled her fingers out wide as if to bring the blood back into them. Anxiety hovered around Emily, but she raised her body and made her way to Jody's lips. When they kissed, the taste of her own body on Emily's tongue seemed to startle Jody as much as the first bite of foreign food might.

"Are you okay?" Emily asked.

Jody nodded. But Emily couldn't shake the fear that crept in. She had once been the one to run out of a room, away from someone, afraid of what had happened. Unsure what to do with all that guilt mixed with all of that want and not knowing how to reconcile the two.

It was only when Jody smiled, and only when she let Emily run a finger along her lips, that Emily allowed herself to believe that what had happened was real.

CHAPTER FOURTEEN

EMILY SHUT HER EYES AGAINST the morning, let her mind wander to the night before in the hallway. They'd headed to the bedroom and started the night locked in each other's arms. But in the middle of the night, Emily had woken to Jody near the edge of the bed. Now, Emily ran her foot through the sheets behind her, searching for Jody's leg and not finding it.

When Emily emerged from the bedroom, she found Jody rushing around the kitchen. All the lights were on in the living room and the kitchen. Jody was already dressed; Ricky was fed. Jody lifted him out of his high chair and placed him on the floor. In a short amount of time he'd gone from wobbly to sturdy on his legs, and he made a mad dash toward a toy in the living room. Jody wiped the crumbs from his tray into her hand.

Outside, ice hung in heavy spikes along the bare branches of trees and the wooden fence that marked the edge of the property. Sleet glazed the ground. The local news blared on the TV. Overnight, freezing rain had battered the region. Video clips showed ditches strewn with trucks and cars.

Emily placed her hands upon Jody's hips, lips onto hers, a simple hello, a lover's greeting.

Jody froze. "Hey," she said, and shifted away from Emily toward the sink.

The word spoke everything Emily needed to know, and once again Emily's heart skidded at the reminder of how Jody had reacted before. Only now there was a new sort of pain at having captured her heart, but for so brief a moment. Not long enough to sustain Emily, not long enough to keep her from worrying the memory of the previous night.

She prepared her cup for coffee as if it were any other morning, as if she hadn't emerged from Jody's bedroom instead of her own. Once again she noted the sugar clumps and wondered why she hadn't taken the time to remove them.

She reached for the pot but it was empty. She pulled the handle on the faucet, anticipating a cold jolt of water on her hand. A few drops sputtered out and then stopped.

"Pipes froze," Jody said. "Ground's too cold and hard to do much about it right now. I'll grab a few gallons of water while I'm out and deal with it when I get back."

"In the freezing rain? With the roads closed?" *You're running away.*

"Yes." Jody opened two cabinet doors and looked into the space without seeming to notice the contents inside. She slammed one shut but eased the next one closed. "Who knows when the pipes'll thaw. But we can't stay out here without drinking or showering."

"Jody, can you—"

"The roads are fine. People get all worked up for nothing. You'd think we'd never seen an ice storm the way people go on about it.

Every year, it's like they forget how to drive." Jody's tone shifted. She rubbed her fingertips together.

Jody took a deep breath and then took Emily's hands in hers. "I want to talk to you about yesterday."

Every day, Emily straddled the line of fight or flight. Her blood pressure ticked up and down.

"I know you're worried because we haven't heard from Troy. I know you want to leave. And I know you want to tell Owen what happened that day. I know those things seem like a good idea because everything's confusing and scary, but we can't say anything." Her eyes pleaded. "If you do, we're done. All of us."

Don't talk. That's what Jody wanted most. "What if that old man goes to Owen? What if Owen shows up here and starts poking around?"

"He won't—"

"You don't know that. The longer we don't hear from Troy and the longer we have that lab out there, the bigger the risk to us. If we tell him we don't know anything about it, maybe he'll believe us."

"He won't believe us. He's gonna ask questions. They're gonna want to come out here, and then what?"

"So get rid of the lab."

"I can't just get rid of it. I don't know how. Some towns have whole departments of people who do this stuff. I don't want to kill us."

Emily sat in a kitchen chair, dropped her head into her hands, and leaned over, tried to breathe. It'd been stupid to move in. Stupid to stay. She should've run. She could've been in a different state by now.

"Look at me. . ." Jody's finger twirled and tugged at Emily's hair. "Please."

Finally Emily lifted her head and felt the rush of blood, saw the stars speckle her vision. In the living room, Ricky banged on a toy piano and laughed.

"I should never have moved in," she said.

"Don't say that." Jody tightened her grasp around Emily's fingers. That ache would never leave her for as long as she lived. Any grip would remind her of Troy. "Everything had been going fine. We didn't know this would happen."

Emily's heart hadn't stilled since Troy had gone missing. Her mind wouldn't stop racing. Sleep wasn't impossible, but it wasn't restful. Nothing set her at ease. Nothing except thinking about the lab being gone, or Troy showing up, or telling Owen what she knew, relinquishing the weight, giving it to someone else to carry.

"Troy's not okay, is he?"

"I don't know. I think so. I hope so." Then she added, "Nothing's gonna happen in the meantime, okay? I wouldn't leave you and Ricky here if I didn't believe that. And Owen won't show up today anyway. Not with the storm."

Jody's choice of words seemed perfectly timed for when Emily felt the weakest.

Jody reached for her keys. "I have to go."

"Of course you do," Emily said. She began to scrape an old clump of dried glue off the table.

"Don't do this," Jody whispered.

"Tell Owen?" Everything was falling apart.

Jody inched her hand toward Emily's but then let it wander back to her keys. "Give me time."

"To get rid of the lab? Or do you need time for other things?" How she despised those words and wanting more than Jody would give. She felt like a beggar.

Jody stood and collected her purse from the bar. She leaned down, kissed Emily on the cheek, and whispered, "Both."

After Jody left, Emily sat at the kitchen table ruminating on every outcome to their situation—all included prison or death— until she'd picked the glue off, along with a thin sliver of wood. She rubbed at the table to see if she could disguise it, but she couldn't.

She thought she heard a vehicle rumble in the distance. For the days, weeks, months that she'd lived at Jody's, the hours had whiled away with no sign of human life—no cars, no ATVs, no one hanging around the chicken house or knocking on her door day and night as she had anticipated. Instead there had only been the steady sound of wind through the trees and birds chirping. But here was an engine, she thought, growing closer and louder, timed to the pounding in her chest. She couldn't tell if the car was on its way up the hill or if it was her terror hijacking her imagination.

Emily turned to the window and kept her eyes trained on the opening of the drive, waiting for a vehicle to appear. She held her breath and prayed that it wasn't Owen.

Then, rather than waiting for him to show up and knock on the door, Emily turned off the lights and the TV and snatched Ricky off the floor. She ran with him screaming at how she'd ripped him from playtime and his toys, to her room at the back of the house, not thinking about the fact that there was no door back there, no easy way to escape into the woods. She ran back through the dark hallway between the kitchen and Jody's room, her hand on the back door-knob. Ricky's body bobbed against hers as he bawled.

KELLY J. FORD

The vehicle grew louder. Any efforts to remain hidden would have been a failure. She hurried to the window to peer down the drive. No car. No one. Nothing.

Once the adrenaline receded, Emily placed Ricky on the carpet next to his pile of plastic rings. He choked out the last of his cries and looked up at her with those big, teary eyes as if asking, *What is wrong with you?*

Emily buried her face in her hands and tried to rub out her nerves. Jody was right; Owen had no reason to show up on a day like this. No one did. No one would. Troy would turn up and everything would be handled and she would take a temp job for the holidays if she had to. Use what she'd saved to put down a deposit on an apartment. Get a roommate, if necessary. Two. Three. Get away from this madness. She knelt down and wiped Ricky's tears away with promises not to tear him away from his toys again.

Shortly after lunch, Emily paced, searching for something to still her mind and body.

Even though she knew better, every fifteen minutes she tried the bathroom faucet, the shower, and the toilet to see if maybe the pipes had thawed on their own despite the temperature barely needling toward warmth.

Weary of her own thoughts, she decided to focus her energy on the pipes. She called her dad on the house phone. Halfway through his instructions on how to thaw out the pipes with a hair dryer, her mom yelled in the background, "Tell her to bring Ricky over here!"

Emily repeated back everything he'd told her and hung up after his reminder to let the faucet run overnight next time.

After laying Ricky in the crib for his afternoon nap, she shoved the baby monitor in her back pocket, found an orange extension cord, and threaded it out the window of her room. She took a flashlight

216

from the back porch and the hair dryer from under the bathroom sink. At the door, she picked through the pile of coats in search of something warmer than what she owned. A heavy, green army coat hung beneath the layers of sweaters and thin jackets. She remembered Troy talking about how the coat had belonged to his dad. He'd talked about the man as if he'd died in a war instead of disappearing like all the other parents who had left their children. Wearing the jacket felt wrong, like Troy might disappear the way his dad had.

The thought was silly. Troy would show up. And it was too cold, and she didn't have a jacket of her own. She drew her arms through the holes, zipped it up, and stepped outside.

A rush of bitter wind blew through the clearing between the woods and the trailer, knocking shards of ice to the ground. She pulled the hood of the jacket closer around her head. The rubber soles of her tennis shoes were worn smooth from use. She walked slowly so she wouldn't slip the way she had the night of the party. Absent until now, the sun broke free from a cloud. The wind caught glistening ice particles and lifted them in the air for the sun's rays to catch like crystals. Then, as fast as the sun had appeared, it removed itself from the world again.

She circled the trailer and found an opening in the vinyl skirting around the back. She plugged the hair dryer into the extension cord and left it at the opening. First she'd have to figure out where the pipes ran. Before she lost courage, she turned on her flashlight, crouched, and extended her body, head first, down into the cold, dark hole under the trailer.

Mere inches existed between her head and the floorboards of the trailer. She swung the flashlight to gauge her location in proximity to the main water line, which appeared across an expanse of black. She army-crawled around concrete foundation blocks. The whole of the trailer seemed to lean and crack with each lash of wind outside. The smell of earth coated her nose.

Bug casings cast off during molting littered the hard ground. Trails of worms and other creatures had stiffened when the air turned cold. Fear seized her when she thought about other creatures that might have sought shelter from the cold under the trailer. She shined the light into the dark spaces around her and held her breath for another bargain with God. This time she promised a return to church if He would relieve her of the terror of seeing a coiled black body or yellow eyes looking back at her in the dark.

A noise off to the left startled Emily and she whacked her head on the trailer's underside. A car was making its way up the drive. This time she didn't doubt it. Though the siding encased her, she shut off the flashlight and waited for a familiar voice to ring out. The engine stopped, but the car door didn't creak open. Again, she hoped for Jody or August or Troy to yell out and ease her anxiety. She crawled across the ground to a small pinhole of light coming through the front trailer siding to get a better view.

Jody sat in her car in the driveway. The hole was too small for Emily to make out any details and it required her to lift her head slightly to get a better look, but no one else appeared to be in the car. Emily picked at the plastic pieces until she had created a pinky-sized hole.

Cigarette smoke drifted out the car window, and Jody drummed on the doorframe. Her voice rose above the dying wind when she spoke to someone on the phone, the words unclear. A few minutes passed without Jody saying anything more. Or if she did say something, Emily couldn't hear it. She waited and pressed her ear closer.

"I didn't know what else to do!" This time, Jody's voice tore through the confines of the car and past the siding.

The splintered plastic scratched Emily's earlobe. The next words came out muffled. A crick worked its way into Emily's neck. She readjusted and pushed her ear up against the siding again.

"No," Jody said. "I swear to you, August. He was already dead."

CHAPTER FIFTEEN

EMILY DROPPED HER HEAD TO the ground and wriggled a hand toward her mouth. She lay still as adrenaline rushed through her veins. A door slammed. Footsteps pounded out above her through the house. Silence filled the space between the boards and where Emily lay. She told herself that she had to have heard wrong. But she hadn't. There was no way to misinterpret and no way for her to quell her fear. *Troy is—was—already dead.*

Worse: *How does Jody know?*

Ricky's cry penetrated the air around her. The baby monitor. She reached around and turned it off. Above her, Jody paced and called out her name. Emily felt around for the flashlight, clicked it on, and made her way back toward the opening.

The air had grown chillier. She crossed the yard more slowly than before, and this time her insides seemed to pound within her, threatening escape. Jody's car sat next to hers. She dug around in her pockets and Troy's coat for her keys, her hope overtaking her knowledge that they wouldn't be there.

At the door, she clutched her chest. She felt hot, dizzy. Her ragged, quick breaths threatened to overwhelm her. She had to leave. But where, how? She couldn't walk the ice-slick dirt road to the main highway. After one last futile check of her pockets, she held her breath and walked up the steps, focused on one thing: *Get your keys and go.*

Inside, Jody sat in the recliner with Ricky cradled against her, as if she were a model mother. Ricky picked animal crackers out of her hand and shoved them into his mouth. Emily prayed that her body wouldn't betray her and alarm Jody that she was anything but fine.

Jody's eyes fixed on the green jacket that Emily wore. She opened her mouth to speak, but dropped her eyes back to Ricky and cleared her throat. "You left him alone."

Emily pressed her back against the door, wishing that she could disappear into it like some fantasy portal into another time and place.

"I had the baby monitor." She removed it from her pocket and placed it on the couch when she noticed how badly her hands shook. She shoved them into her pockets and scanned the room. She had to find her keys.

Jody brushed hair away from Ricky's eyes. "You look like you've been rolling around on the ground."

Dirt caked the knees of Emily's jeans. "I tried to fix the pipes."

Ricky's body lifted and dipped with the rise and fall of Jody's chest. She clenched her mouth and forced a smile. "I told you I would look at it when I got back."

The heater cranked on. Sweat gathered on her skin under Troy's thick jacket.

"Did you?"

"What?" Emily whispered. She couldn't focus. She couldn't look at Jody too long. She'd never looked at that face and felt anything other than happiness, frustration, desire. Fear: this was new.

"Fix the pipes."

"No. I couldn't get to it." Her keys were on the bar, in the little china bowl, right where she'd left them. She'd specifically placed them there so she wouldn't forget, so no one could tell her she'd lost them. "I heard your car."

"That's too bad." Jody glanced to the side of the couch and chewed her top lip. "About the pipes."

Jody was too calm. She'd raised her voice on the phone. She'd said those words, words that Emily couldn't hook to anyone's name but the one who'd gone missing. There had to be an explanation. She willed herself to ask the question that she'd been asking for over a week now.

"No word from Troy?"

Jody grabbed one of Ricky's animal crackers out of his hand. He grimaced and reached for it. She held it out and then threatened to eat it. Back and forth she went. He giggled at the game. Finally, she looked up. "Nope."

The floor seemed to rumble under her feet and then drop, plunging her stomach with it. She couldn't breathe. Her body ran hot. She yanked at her collar. She shrugged the jacket off and hung it behind the door. She didn't want to move. She had to move.

"Dad called. He needs me home. It's just for the night." She pushed out the words like labor, while her insides clamored to escape the house.

Jody glared at her. "This is your home now."

"You know what I mean." She couldn't bear to look at Jody, but neither could she look away.

"Go on home. I'll take care of the pipes. I'll take care of everything, like always. Ricky and I will be fine right here." Jody finally looked up. Her face appeared hard, like a future Jody, one who had experienced some rough years. "You don't need my permission to leave."

Maybe you heard wrong. Maybe there's an explanation. Stay. Don't leave her. Stay, Emily told her feet but they itched to be back on the path she had come from, beyond the trailer, past the chicken house, toward home. Terror clung to her, clawed at her. Something wasn't right. Jody wasn't acting right. The thought of staying in that house, with Jody, after dark, created a new panic within her, one she couldn't pinpoint. She didn't think that Jody would hurt her. But she knew she couldn't stay. With a seeming will of their own, her hands pushed off the wall. She grabbed her keys and tried not to run out the door.

EMILY PLACED HER HANDS AROUND the coffee cup. She didn't require the coffee, just the warmth. Every time the door dinged and the waitresses yelled out, "Good evening! Welcome to Waffle House!" Emily turned to see if August had arrived, but it was only ever the long-haul truckers who came in for human contact and empty calories.

After she'd left Jody's house, she had called August like he'd asked her to. Hours later, he still hadn't showed.

Then, just as she was ready to take her check up to the counter and pay, the door dinged, the waitresses yelled out their greetings, and August strode inside. He wore his cap low and hunched in his jacket. He threw his keys on the table and eased into the booth without a hello.

He drew the air into his nostrils and then pushed it all out in a huff. "What's up?"

Now was not the time to be polite or pretend that she hadn't seen or done the things that she had. Now was the time for her to come out and say all the words that sat on her tongue. Of all times, this was it. "I heard Jody talking to you on the phone. I was under the trailer. I heard what she said, so don't think about lying."

A pallor came over his face like a ghost had slipped into his skin. He dropped his elbows onto the table, dipped his head, and clutched the bill of his hat. Over and over, he bent the bill into a *v*. It looked liable to snap in half. He lifted his head, cuffed his chin with a hand, and tugged at the skin. His eyes wandered to the window and the view of the parking lot.

"What were you doing under the trailer?" he asked. He tried to sound nonchalant.

"Don't change the subject," she said. "And don't tell me that I didn't hear something, because I did."

Their waitress came over to the table and leaned her hip against the back of August's booth. "Coffee?" She might as well have said, "Sex?" When he nodded, she turned over his coffee cup and filled it. "Anything to eat?"

He shook his head.

As soon as the waitress was out of earshot, Emily leaned across the table. "You told me to call. Remember?" She tried to keep her voice down. "Where's Troy?" When he didn't respond, she asked again.

August rubbed his palms up and down his legs. "Would you give me a moment?"

Why did everyone need a moment? Why didn't anyone say what was going on instead of lying and holding back all that needed to be said?

He didn't meet her eyes. He didn't tease her or nudge her with his leg. Instead, he wet his lips. "What'd you hear?"

She couldn't ask Jody, not like she could ask August. August didn't act like nothing had happened. August didn't pretend like he didn't know something he did. August wouldn't lie to her. She believed that. Emily peered around to see if anyone could hear. "She said he was already dead. Who? Troy?" His name traveled off her tongue and out into the world, her worry turned into a reality.

August scratched at the side of his nose and faced the window. Condensation had formed on the glass. His reflection gave no clue as to what he was thinking. He took off his cap and ran his hands through his hair. "Maybe you could stay at your parents' house for a while."

Though she had every intention of going home, she needed to know why he had suggested it. "Why would you say that? Why won't you answer the question?"

The waitress came back before he could answer. "Can I tempt you with some pie?"

"If we need something, we'll let you know," Emily said, rankled at the woman and her simple life, her simple job with simple math and an easy paycheck, a simplicity that could have been Emily's, had been hers for a few weeks, weeks that now seemed like years ago.

The waitress grimaced and left, but not without tossing her head back to get one more look at August in case he changed his mind about that pie.

"August," Emily repeated, "why should I stay at my parents' house?"

He plucked a sugar packet out of the holder and rolled it up, rolled it out. "Just until things get settled." He rolled the packet again. And again.

"Settled how?"

Sugar granules scattered on the table.

Emily reached over and gripped his hands. They were cold in hers. "August," she said, and tried to catch his eyes. "Tell me what's going on. I deserve that."

He flipped her hands over and traced the lines of her palms with his thumb. The movement was slight, ticklish. She wondered what went through his mind, what solace he was finding there, but she didn't move.

The waitress dropped a glass behind the counter, and they jumped along with everyone else. Amid the other customers' laughter and small talk, August grasped her hands and held them. "There's been an accident."

The words were too ominous. Despite holding onto the hope that Troy would walk through the door any day, she had expected them. But this was Drear's Bluff. Nothing bad happened here. People didn't disappear. People didn't die from anything but boredom or old age.

"What kind of accident?"

She wanted him to tell her that Troy had met with some other accident, something that didn't involve them. A simple and ridiculous explanation. But there wasn't one. There was only what had happened and what would come next.

"Stay away from Jody's," he said. "That's the first place they're going to start asking questions. And the last person who saw Troy was you."

No. She'd heard what Jody had said on the phone but it couldn't be true. It couldn't be Troy she was talking about. Jody had said that she'd seen him. That he had had the garden hose. He was fine. Emily stared at August. Not believing his words, that this was her life. She tried to inch her hands away from him, but he gripped them.

"What are you saying?" She yanked her hands free and pushed them between her legs. She rocked over the tabletop, unable to control the movement. Her eyes darted around the room, looking for something to steady her. Nothing worked. She dropped her forehead onto the table.

"Emily," August said. His hands rested on the back of her head and stroked her hair.

Sugar granules cracked along the skin of her forehead when she moved her head from side to side. "Jody said she saw him. She said he was okay. She said he'd come back."

"Hey." He got up and sat next to her, warming her side. "I'm sorry." His hand stroked her hair, moved it away from her ear, and he spoke low. "I'm sorry you got caught up in this. But I need you to listen. Stay away from Jody's."

She propped her chin on the table and focused on the empty booth across from her, where he'd been sitting, realizing that all along he and so many others—her mom, Marjorie, Heather—had tried to warn her. They'd told her in so many words, and she hadn't listened.

August slung an arm across her shoulders and leaned down onto the table with her, close enough that she could smell his cologne. Hints of grapefruit and cedar. She closed her eyes and considered this new smell of terror.

ALL NIGHT, EMILY TOSSED THE words she'd heard under the trailer around and around in her head to try and work them into some logical meaning that didn't involve her. She told herself that the wind could have distorted the words. But then August had confirmed it, hadn't he? Somehow, from their mouths to Emily's ears, things had twisted. She couldn't trust her eyes or her ears. This was Drear's Bluff, she thought. This was what it did to people.

She hid out in the spare room the next morning and waited to see if her parents would notice her car at the end of the drive. Finally, she snuck out to use the bathroom. When she opened the bathroom door, her mom stood there holding a basket of laundry. She'd already fixed her hair and gotten ready for the day, though it was unlikely she'd take a step off the property or see anyone other than Emily's dad. Or Emily.

"I was wondering when you might come out of hiding," her mom said.

Emily shuffled her feet and tried to come up with some lie, but her brain refused to cooperate. "How long have you known I was here?"

"Since you crept in last night. I figured you might," she said. "Pipes still frozen?"

"Yeah," she said and thought of Jody and Ricky out there alone. "Did I wake you?"

"I haven't been able to get much sleep lately."

She wondered if Marjorie and her mom had made up yet.

"I was hoping that we might be able to talk," her mom continued.

Downstairs, the phone rang.

"Don't you need to get that?" Emily asked.

"Your dad can." The phone stopped. Then, it rang again. She huffed and yelled down the stairs. "John! Would you get the phone, please?"

No answer. The phone kept ringing. Her mom drummed the hard plastic frame of the laundry basket with her fingernails.

"Oh for crying out loud." Her mom set the laundry basket on the floor and marched down the stairs.

Emily went back into her room and sat on the bed to steady herself. The string of events unrolled in her mind and brought her at last to August's words: "*There's been an accident.*"

The way he'd said it made her think that he was speaking of a different accident, one she hadn't witnessed. One that didn't involve her directly. Something worse than what she'd seen. That's what she hoped for, even though deep down she knew that couldn't be the truth.

Every now and then she could hear her mom's voice rise, but she was too far away to hear the words. Finally, her mom reappeared in the doorway, face white, hands at her side.

"What is it?" Emily asked, though she knew that the phone call couldn't be about anything but what she feared.

Her mom moved closer and sat down next to Emily. Her hands trembled in her lap.

"Mom?"

She turned to Emily.

Emily clutched her mom's hand. "Momma, what is it?"

"They found Troy."

Emily tried to look and sound hopeful—enough to disguise that she already knew what her mom had just learned. The thing she had been dreading was finally here. She had to hold it together for a little while longer. She couldn't break down now. Not yet. "That's good news, right?" She didn't answer. "Mom?"

Tears welled and then ran down her face. Emily's eyes responded in kind. "Someone found him in the woods across from the creek." Her mom choked out the words.

The woods where Jody had threatened to run away, the woods where during a short embrace, Jody's heart had become wedged in Emily's like a stone. A place that no one ever went. No one but her—and no one but Jody.

Someone. Who? She shook her head. It didn't matter. He'd been found. One last lure of hope pushed past all the fear. That hope filled her for a moment, and she let herself get swept up in its promise. Everything would be okay. She smiled and chose to believe that good news would finally come. "Thank God. Is he okay?"

Her mom shook her head, and a fresh stream of tears cascaded down her cheeks. "No."

All that time, she'd believed he would turn up. She'd believed he would be okay. She had prayed. This wasn't supposed to happen. He wasn't supposed to die. *He wasn't supposed to die.*

She dropped her chin to her chest and gasped. She couldn't control her mouth, her eyes, her insides quaking and collapsing. She gave in to the grief that had waited for release. She let her mom stroke her hair and soothe her as if she were a child, until the sobs that wracked her body stilled. The flat of her mom's palms rested on her head. Every sensation, every emotion seemed sucked out of her. Her mind, blank. Her body, numb.

CHAPTER SIXTEEN

TROY HAD BEEN A PROMISING young football star. Now he was a dead boy in a box. He'd never have to worry about growing up and growing old within the barbed-wire confines of Drear's Bluff. Now he'd never leave.

Emily sat sandwiched in the pew between her mom and dad. In the time between the discovery of Troy's body and the funeral, her parents had gotten spooked. Her dad had asked her to spend some time at home for the sake of her mom, but she knew that it was for him as well. At night, before bed, her dad would hug her extra long and extra hard. Another night, after not finding NyQuil or some other depressant in the bathroom cabinet, Emily had wandered into the kitchen in search of alcohol—anything to help her sleep and avoid thoughts of Troy, which assaulted her even when she was awake—and found her mom holding a dishtowel tight against her mouth, stifling a mourning cry.

Other than a quick text from Emily about picking up some clothing while Jody was out, there were no phone calls, no babysitting, no visits between either of them. Not after what Emily had

231

heard under the trailer, what August had told her, and where Troy had been found.

During the church service, the pastor did his best to avoid the particulars of Troy's death—suffocated on anhydrous ammonia, discovered dead in the woods—focusing instead on the way Marjorie and Drear's Bluff wanted to remember him. How Troy had caught a Hail Mary pass to score a touchdown and win an important game. And that time when Troy had been a baby, no older than Ricky, sitting on Marjorie's lap in church, transfixed by the stained glass on the wall.

"They all start out as young boys and girls," the pastor said, "and at some point they either shine or shatter."

Marjorie's cry lifted into the church, echoed off the walls, and unnerved Emily.

Before the pastor had everyone stand up row by row and pay their respects at the closed casket, Emily excused herself and headed to the bathroom. If she got close to the casket and the remains of his earthly body, she felt certain Hell would bear down upon her.

Emily could have saved him. She could have taken him to the hospital instead of to Jody's house. But she hadn't. The weight of that one decision plagued her thoughts. They lived at least thirty, forty minutes from a hospital. He might have lived. He might have died anyway. She couldn't know.

Once everyone had returned to their seats and bowed their heads, she slipped back to her dad's side and let him enfold her in the crook of his arm. The pastor lifted them up in prayer one last time before he dismissed them for the graveside service.

Marjorie walked down the aisle first, Heather at her side. Once again, everyone followed, row by row. Emily didn't recognize any of the kids who'd come for the service. None of the people from the party were there, the people who couldn't get enough of Troy's stories and lies. Not Jody. Not August.

These people from his past moved along silently, mourning the Troy they had known, not the Troy he had become. Emily wished that she held those same memories. He'd just wanted to play football. That's all he'd ever wanted, and she'd never even seen him do that.

When it was their pew's turn, they all shuffled out to join the line of people waiting to exit the church. Her dad waited for Emily and her mom to move into the aisle, then he walked behind them, a hand on each of their shoulders. His hand was warm and solid, anchoring her to Earth. With his hand there and her head down, she mustered a thin hope to endure the day.

She lifted her head as they neared the door and noticed August standing off to the side, hovering as close to the wall as he could, confined in what looked like a borrowed black suit, maybe his dad's. When he caught her eye, he waved her over. Every hair on her body felt wired to the touch.

"I'll catch up with you outside," she told her dad. He gave her shoulder a squeeze before navigating toward the door, her mom at his side.

She searched the dwindling crowd to see if anyone might be able to overhear them and struggled to appear as innocent as possible.

"What are you doing here?" she asked.

August shifted and in the light, she saw how his skin had grown sallow, the lines in his face more pronounced. He stared at his feet like he couldn't believe they wouldn't move, then nudged her into the darkened hallway, farther away from the crowd.

"You staying at your parents' house?" he asked.

She glanced behind her. "How did you know that he'd be found?"

August took a few steps back. "I can't tell you anything. Just stay with your parents until things settle down. I'll take care of this. I promise."

He was already dead. Emily couldn't get the words that Jody had said out of her head.

"Why? Because you had something to do with this?" Alarm edged her voice, and she tried to stay in control. That old, hateful urge to cry emerged and threatened. "Did you put him there? Did Jody tell you about the woods?"

"No," he said, surprised and hurt.

"What aren't you telling me?"

Without his trusty, faded ball cap, August had nothing to grip in his hands except the battered program. He cleared his throat. "As soon as I get things cleaned up at Jody's, Pop and I are headed up north." He shifted his eyes to the ground, and she knew that he meant Alaska. Somewhere a person could get lost, he'd told her one random day before Troy had disappeared. His hand touched her finger, slight as a lover's last plea. "You can come with us."

Here it was. The anonymity, the escape that she'd longed for, at last. A perplexing desire to smell his cologne and feel his arms around her for comfort washed over her.

After Jody had left town, Emily had wanted to disappear so that no one could find her, no one could watch her or judge her, to remove the ties that held her to Drear's Bluff. Now, it overwhelmed her to think that she could never return. All she'd ever dreamed about was leaving: being away from her mother, the church, the eternal gossip, the heat, the pain. All of it. Now she had an opportunity to disappear. Start anew, no expectations, no baggage. Free to roam wherever the road, and August, took her. Yet her body shook at the thought. Never seeing her dad again as he withered into old age, becoming less mobile and more dependent on the good graces of her mother, whose only sin was that she wanted too much for Emily and others. All Emily wanted now was to go back to the way it had been. She would've given anything to go back.

With August gone, she'd be alone, without anyone to talk to about this thing that had cleaved Emily's life into a before and after. There was only Jody, whom she wanted to trust but couldn't. Emily couldn't disappear. Not from her parents, not from Jody. No matter how tempting the offer, she knew that half a life was no life at all.

She held her arms out to block him when he moved closer. "I can't do that," she said, and wandered back toward the church doors.

Outside, Heather navigated Marjorie into her car. Owen waited for the pastor to give the go-ahead before leading the procession of cars to the cemetery. Clusters of people spoke in hushed tones, mindful of the solemn occasion that had brought them to the church on a bright, cold Saturday afternoon.

Emily sought the comfort and safety that came from being at her dad's side, but before she could reach him, Jody's familiar voice called out to her.

Her car idled in a lone spot off to the side of the parking lot. Like so many times before, the call of Emily's name from those lips and the desire for Jody pulled at her. Though she'd skipped breakfast, her stomach ached and her skin prickled. The clothing that had once pinched her skin now hung slack. Jody yelled her name again. Then she honked.

Emily's dad turned to see where the noise was coming from. "Jody's trying to get your attention," he said. "Go on. We'll meet you two at the cemetery." He patted her back and disappeared into the crowd.

She'd rather wait there on the church steps alone, thankful not to see the casket or hear Marjorie's sobs anymore that day. But she bit down on her hesitation and walked toward Jody's car.

Heat from the car's side vent warmed Emily's face when Jody rolled down the window. Jody's dress and skin had wilted on her slim frame.

"What do you want?" Emily asked, as coldly as she could muster.

Jody dug into her purse for a cigarette, but threw the bag into the backseat next to Ricky after her search produced no results. "Ride with me to the cemetery."

"You shouldn't be here."

"Act normal. Isn't that what you told me?" she asked. "There's more to this story than you obviously think. Ride with me."

The wind chilled her skin. After what she'd heard under the trailer and from August, every inch of her pulled away, yelled at her to leave. Get as far away as possible. But there was that other side, the side that needed to be proved wrong. This was Jody, after all. Her Jody, the Jody that no one else got to see. Emily clasped her arms around herself and scanned the parking lot before she joined Jody in the car, hoping against all sense and experience that she might learn what had happened, finally.

Jody flicked on the headlights, and they fell in line behind the other cars that swung out of the parking lot.

They sat in silence during the ride to the rural, dirt road cemetery where most of Drear's Bluff's residents were interred at the end of their lives. A radio announcer with a deep voice crackled through the speakers, the volume low. The ride lulled Ricky into sleep.

At the cemetery, they were the last in a long line of cars that snaked from the gate. Jody parked and turned off the ignition but didn't take out the key.

The procession of mourners crunched their way along the gravel path and under the iron gate, past dusty and cracked headstones to a fresh plot near the back, where a line of chairs had been positioned around Troy's casket. Sun-faded flags that had been staked among nearby gravestones for Memorial and Veterans Days past fluttered in the wind.

Jody propped her elbow on the steering wheel and her chin against her fist.

An old pang worked its way into Emily's chest. She gripped the door handle and stared at the floorboard. She leaned her head on the back of the seat.

The sun had come up the same as always on that day she'd gone to the store to get groceries. Only that day, Troy had asked to come along. That one request had changed everything, just like her decision to go to Jody's house instead of her parents' that fateful day she'd seen her at the truck stop. The trail of regrets had become too long, too large.

"I should have taken him to the hospital," Emily said, choking back tears.

"You wouldn't have made it in time. No one could have helped him."

Emily breathed deeply. "What are you saying?"

Jody rubbed her eyes with the back of her hand. She dropped her gaze to the seat and the space between them. Emily waited for an explanation, further reassurance that if she'd done something differently, the results would be the same. That she couldn't have helped him even if she'd made a different choice. That Jody knew why Troy's body had ended up across the creek bed and in the woods where they'd kissed under the tall trees one summer day at sixteen.

A stray piece of hair fell across Jody's forehead. Emily reached up and placed it back behind her ear. Jody moved toward her hand and warmed it with her cheek. If Emily wanted to, she could have drawn Jody's face toward hers, touched those lips once more.

"Tell me what happened," Emily said.

Jody shifted her head to the side, away from Emily's hand. "I don't know what you want to hear."

"The truth," Emily said.

Jody's lips trembled. "I saw Troy." Her voice cracked when she said his name. "I saw him in the backseat of your car." Jody's face seemed to hang from her bones, every curve of skin pulled downward. "I couldn't do anything for him. He was already . . ."

Dead.

The words formed and pushed out of Jody's mouth, but didn't match what she had told Emily before. But they matched what Emily had feared all along, that he had not been fine that day. He had not grabbed a hose. He had not put Emily to bed. He had never left her backseat alive. Yet somehow, he had ended up in the woods, their woods, instead of a hospital. Only one person would have thought to put him there.

She wanted to scream, cry, disappear.

"Why did you say he would show up? All that time we waited, and you knew he was already dead?" Her voice rose as the words and their meaning rushed over her. Ricky grumbled in his car seat. He shifted and she continued, quieter. "You let me believe he would come back when you knew he wouldn't. You said he was fine."

Jody's eyes glossed over. She leaned her head against the window and scratched her neck, leaving red marks. "I thought I was protecting you."

"How? How on earth could you possibly believe that?"

Jody's chest heaved and her eyebrows furrowed. "Why can't you see the best in me instead of the worst?" The words pierced the stale air of the car.

"Because you keep lying to me!" All she'd ever done was believe in Jody. All Jody had ever done was deny her the same. "You're the only one I ever believed. But you keep lying to me and leaving me!" The words came out in gasps.

"When? When did I leave?" Mascara streaked under Jody's bloodshot eyes. "You're the one who left right before they found Troy. Right at the moment when I needed you most, after I took care of you and protected you, you left me. Just like Mom. Just like everybody else." Jody straightened her back and breathed in. "I didn't call for help, and I didn't take him to the hospital because you were with him when it happened. I didn't know how bad you were hurt. I didn't know how much you'd inhaled. You could have ended up just like him if I hadn't gotten you out of there and taken care of you." Jody smacked the seat. "He was already dead. Don't you get it? He couldn't breathe. And then he stopped breathing. And you could have, too. But you didn't."

Emily wiped her eyes with her palms.

Jody transferred the black smears from under her eyes to her dress. "What I did was stupid. I'm so stupid, just like you always said. So you don't have to tell me that again. I already know." She placed a hand at her temple and closed her eyes. "Yes, he was already dead. And telling you the truth wouldn't have done any good. I wasn't lying because I had some sort of plan or something. I was trying to save all of us from his mistake and you from knowing that he died right in front of you. I didn't know what else to do. I panicked."

Jody ran a finger up and down the steering wheel. "When I got home, you were running through the yard with your hands out, screaming about your eyes burning. So I sprayed you with the garden hose. You passed out, but you seemed okay. I didn't know what had happened or what else to do, so I put you to bed.

"Then I went back outside and found Troy in your car. His face and eyes were all red. He wasn't moving. Or breathing. I kept trying to wake him, but nothing happened. He was already gone. I couldn't call the police. Not with everything going on. I panicked. The first thing I thought was, 'I gotta get him out of here.' I took him somewhere I thought maybe no one would find him. But someone did."

Jody dropped her head so low her chin almost hit her chest. "All I did was let him use the chicken house. He screwed up. And if anyone finds out . . ." She choked on the words. "I don't know what will happen to Ricky and me." She paused. "What am I gonna do?"

The question was sent to the heavens, to God, to whomever Jody believed in, not Emily.

Emily rubbed her hands over her face, trying to take in what she'd heard. All those images of Troy swarmed her vision, only now she pieced them together with what Jody had said. The fear and confusion she had felt not knowing what Jody had done, how far she might have gone, shifted to something else, something softer. Everything Jody had done had been for her. A part of her wanted to unlatch her seatbelt and cross the seat that divided them, lean into her and share the small comfort she'd felt the night they'd laid tangled in each other's arms, even if only for a little while.

Jody kept her eyes on the crowd within the cemetery. Everyone stood around the casket and offered their last good-byes.

Emily stretched her hand across the seat toward Jody. Jody glanced down at it, ran her own hand slowly through her hair, and took Emily's hand in hers. She focused on the seat, their hands, nothing.

"Things were fine for so long. I only needed a little more time." A few tears escaped before Jody could wipe them away. "I didn't mean for any of this to happen."

"I know."

"Maybe," Jody said. She struggled to form the words and paused. "Maybe if we lived in another place or another time."

Emily turned away from Jody and shut the tears back. She didn't want to hear those words. Those words killed the small hope she still had. She opened her eyes. Jody looked at her in the way Emily had always hoped someday, somehow, she would.

The muscles tightened at the base of her throat. She lifted her head and swallowed hard. The word sat at the back of her throat and crawled across her tongue in a whisper. "Maybe."

Sadness rushed over her. She tried to breathe slow and deep but the pain wouldn't stop. Why couldn't things be different? Why couldn't she be different? She leaned toward Jody, approached her like a wounded animal caught in a trap. Jody's body shifted toward Emily, but her eyes stayed on the seat. Emily worked her arms under Jody's and moved to fill the space that separated their bodies. In response, Jody wrapped her arms around her, dove her fingertips and face into the thick of Emily's hair. One hand dipped to the small of her back and pressed her close. Jody's lips grazed Emily's neck, her cheek, her temple. Emily gasped and fought the desire to tell her: *Drive. Just drive away from here.*

Lovers would come and go. Maybe there'd be one who would be unafraid and teach Emily how to be brave, brave enough to wake up next to her, to walk hand in hand. Someone with whom she'd have a nice life, without trouble and with love. But in the twilight hours of her life, when her body and memory failed, this above all others would be the buoy she would cling to, the memory she would repeat and repeat until the darkness ripped her away. Because this moment, so small, the smallest, had seared her heart.

Jody pulled away, coughed, and wiped at her eyes. "Service is ending. You should go find your parents. Stay there for a little while longer, okay? Owen's bound to show up any day—" She interrupted her own sentence to answer the question that hung between them. The lab. "August is taking care of it. Today."

"What if Owen comes to the house? What do I tell him?"

"He won't show up. Not today." She dropped her hands and placed them on the wheel, the gearshift. "Go on. I'll call you. Promise."

A loathsome sadness lodged itself in Emily for all that Jody offered—and denied—her. Across the cemetery, people split into separate groups for small talk and condolences. Emily slid across the seat and cracked her door open. The cold wind blew against her legs.

Jody smiled half a smile and switched on the ignition. By the time Emily reached the cemetery gate, Jody was gone.

EMILY MADE HER WAY THROUGH the parting crowd to find her parents. Her dad stood near a trio of headstones. When she reached him, she lifted his arm from behind, ducked under it, and placed it around her shoulders. He pulled her closer to plant a kiss on her head. In that moment, she wanted to be a child again, to let her dad take her up in his arms and carry her away back home.

"What are you doing over here?" she asked.

He tapped his fist against her shoulder. "Nobody should have to bury their kid."

Across the cemetery, Marjorie remained seated in her folding chair on the artificial grass the funeral home had laid out around the casket. A mound of dirt waited off to the side.

Hesitant to return to the present, Emily nodded toward the unfamiliar names on the headstones in front of her dad. "Who's that?"

"Dead ancestors," he said.

"The ones on the wall?"

"Three of them."

Seeing their names and knowing they were there underneath her feet made them more real, less like the ghosts who had antagonized her as a child.

"Come on. We should pay our respects," he said.

They joined her mom and Heather, who talked in hushed tones about the weather. After Marjorie shook all the mourners' hands and received their hugs, she made her way over to them. Emily sank deeper against her dad's body and into the folds of his suit. She closed her eyes and hoped that Marjorie would pass them by.

"Marjorie," her dad said. His voice boomed against her cheek. "I'm so sorry. Troy was a good kid."

Emily's head moved when her dad reached out and placed a hand on Marjorie's shoulder. He nudged Emily with the arm he had thrown around her. She wiped her face and tried to look up at Marjorie. Her eyes made it as far as Marjorie's chest.

"Marjorie," her mom said. She rubbed Marjorie's back. "I don't know what to say. Such a loss." Emily knew that a large part of her mom's mourning had to do with Marjorie's absence since the prayer

KELLY J. FORD

circle. After that initial call about Troy, her mom had waited for Marjorie to call again. She hadn't.

Marjorie nodded, but something rumbled underneath. Her stare landed squarely on Emily. Tears she'd cried during the service had carved streaks through her foundation, but now her cheeks and eyes were dry.

"He's with God now," Emily's mom said, going on with her condolences like she didn't know what else to say.

"With God?" Marjorie asked. "He shouldn't be with God." She pounded her chest. "He should be with me."

Emily's mom stepped back in shock.

"My boy is dead," Marjorie said. "He's dead and he didn't have to die." Marjorie spun in a circle. Her eyes cut to everyone in the group. "And you." Marjorie poked a finger into Emily's arm. "You knew!"

Her mom's mouth gaped wider than her own. Her dad clasped Emily closer to him and nudged her away from Marjorie. Heather held Marjorie by the arm and tried to do the same.

"Marjorie," Emily's mom said. "Calm down."

"I will not calm down," Marjorie said.

The pastor hustled over from where he'd been talking to a group of women, his worn Bible still clutched in his hand.

Marjorie stabbed the air with her finger. "You knew he was taking drugs and you didn't tell anyone! You could've saved him." Her voice came out as a shriek before she burst into a whimpering cry. "Why didn't you tell me?"

Stunned at her rebuke, Emily stepped backward and nearly tripped on her dad's shoes. Though no one could know how accurate Marjorie's words were, that they had been uttered for all to hear sent her head spinning.

244

The pastor navigated Marjorie past gravestones and toward the mound of dirt.

She sobbed straight into the sky. "She could have saved him!"

People huddled in small groups and whispered. Emily shuddered at the scraping sound of Marjorie's cries. Her dad pushed her away from Marjorie and toward their car. He opened the back door and guided her inside. Through the windshield, she saw her mom standing next to Marjorie, trying to pat her on the back only to be pushed away. Heather held out a hand, preventing Emily's mom from coming any closer.

Emily's dad leaned in and rested a hand on her shoulder. "You all right?" he asked.

Emily nodded, but she was far from it.

"I'll be back in a minute." He shut the door and walked over to where her mom stood.

Emily bent over so that her chest rested on her knees. *Breathe,* she willed herself. When she did, she let out all the crying that she'd held in. She hadn't wanted to cry. Not again. But Troy's great gasping search for air, and what might have been had she made a different decision that day, came to Emily again and brought on a fresh round of tears. Marjorie was right. She'd said nothing. Done nothing.

Her mom and dad whispered as they made their way to the car. When they got in, they stopped talking altogether.

Her dad started the engine, and they made their way toward the main road. Emily wiped her face and slumped back against the seat. Dark spots marked her skirt where she had rested her eyes. Her face felt bloated from the tension of keeping the tears in all day and then letting them drown her in one sitting. She propped her head against the car window and let the cold seep through the glass and numb her temple.

"Heather told me you came in to the Quik-a-Way asking if Marjorie had seen Troy," her mom said.

Emily focused on the bare, frostbitten fields that rolled past.

"Is that why she thinks you know something?" When Emily didn't answer, her mom turned around and slapped the seat. "Emily Marie Skinner."

"I don't know what she thinks!"

"Why did you go in there asking about Troy?"

Emily picked at fuzz that had balled up at the edges of her borrowed dress and let it fall through her fingers and drift to the floorboard. "Because he stopped coming around Jody's."

"Did you know he was on drugs?"

Her dad was looking at her in the rearview mirror. She shifted her eyes back to the fuzz balls. "Everyone knew he was on drugs." Prescription drugs. He'd lost his license after his DUI.

"Why on Earth didn't you say something?" her mom asked.

Emily rubbed her forehead with her hand.

"Let her be," her dad said. "It's been a long day."

Her mom continued to glare at her, body and face contorted to confront Emily. The seatbelt cut at the skin of her mom's neck. "I don't understand how something like that could be right under your nose—and Jody's!—and neither of you said a word. What were you thinking?"

"Dot," her dad said.

"I raised you better than that. Somehow, *I'm* responsible for you not telling Marjorie what you knew."

"Dot," her dad repeated.

"Marjorie said it wasn't right." Her mom shook her head. "I should've listened. All of them out there at Jody's in the middle of nowhere. Doing God knows what. And with Ricky right there."

Emily gripped the door handle. They were close to the house, but not close enough. She had to get out of that car. Out of the house, away.

"Dot," her dad said. "Stop it."

"She shouldn't have been there. But, no. She had to run off to Jody's."

The force of Emily's anger was too big, too uncontrolled. She hadn't asked Troy to go for groceries that day. She hadn't forced him to go up to that man's house to steal ammonia. She hadn't known. Troy had made his choice. Whatever they thought about her and Jody, it had nothing to do with Troy. Nothing.

When her dad cut the engine, Emily bolted out of the car and headed toward the house at a clip.

"Don't you walk away from me," her mom yelled behind her.

Her mom kept yelling her name and telling her to stop. But Emily kept walking. She'd grab her keys. Her clothing. She wouldn't stay in that house another day.

Her mom ran up to her and grabbed her by the arm. She stuck a finger in Emily's face, close enough that Emily could have bitten down on it. Every angry feeling that Emily had ever had about her mom came rushing to the surface. She faced her, calm for the first time in years, even in the face of all that rage.

"Everyone knew about Troy, Mom. Everyone. Even you. You knew he was taking pills after his accident and you knew he was in trouble, and you talked about him behind closed doors, and you judged him, but you didn't do a damn thing about it. No one did. So stop blaming me for something he did to himself. And don't you stand there and blame me because you feel bad that Marjorie won't talk to you. That's your own doing."

Her mother's eyes widened in disbelief.

"And you want to talk about me running to Jody? You always run to Marjorie. How's that any different? How does Dad feel about that?"

"Emily," Dad said, and stood in between the two of them. "Stop it right now. Both of you."

"All you do is sit there and judge people and you don't even take the time to find out if they're the ones who did something wrong."

Her mom stepped back. "I most certainly do not."

"You do." The constant tug of war with her mom had drained her. Her eyes felt raw from crying, yet here more came. "I didn't do anything." She shoved her fists to her eyes like a child, trying to stop the sobbing. All she had wanted was to go to the grocery store in peace. She'd wanted a break from all the tension in the house. She wanted to go back to before she'd ever showed up to Jody's house. "I'm so tired. And I don't want to keep doing this." She wiped her eyes on her sleeve. "I screwed up, okay? I shouldn't have dropped out. I shouldn't have lied to you about it. I shouldn't have said those things that I said. But I did. And I'm sorry. I'm so sorry." She gasped trying to get the words out. "I made a mistake. I've made so many mistakes. But I never meant to hurt you."

Her parents stood there, their discomfort at her display of emotion clear from the way they crossed their arms and shifted their eyes from the ground to each other, then to some spot on the horizon.

Time felt like it had reverted back to when she was a teenager and couldn't control or understand why she felt the things she did. And in her mind, Jody was still that teenage girl who had been abandoned by her mom. A few months at Emily's house couldn't remove the stain that years of trying to survive had left on Jody. Emily believed a miracle still existed for Jody. Nothing was irreparable. Emily believed that. She wouldn't let Jody and August clean up the mess alone. It was hers, too. It had become hers the day she accepted money from Jody. For once, she wouldn't run away from her mistake.

"I have to go. I'm sorry," she said again, and headed toward the house, for her keys, for the rest of her things—for the only place where she felt like she belonged.

CHAPTER SEVENTEEN

THE FLOWERING BUSHES ALONG THE side of the house were bereft of color. Most of the trees were bare, leaving the lot empty, the sky shifting between clouds and sun. Emily gripped Jody's doorknob, expecting it to twist in her hand and offer her entry, but it did not. She could have used her key, but with all that had happened, knocking seemed the more appropriate action.

A car came rumbling up the drive behind her. She hoped that, much like the day of the ice storm, her imagination was tricking her. She waited, each breath becoming more difficult to control. But there was no mistaking it. This time the car was real. A door shut behind her. The crunch of shoes across gravel followed, then stopped.

Emily turned.

"Good afternoon," Owen said. "You waiting on something?" Emily returned his greeting with a quick, forced smile. "Can I have a moment of your time?" He moved his jacket so that his badge was visible.

She tried to lock down her emotions, but her awareness made it worse. "Sure." She dug around for her keys and opened the door, and he followed her inside.

The starch on his brown uniform sounded like sandpaper on wood when he walked by. He parked his hands on his hips and turned in a circle, taking in the room. He stopped in front of the TV and ran his hand along the top of it, whistled.

"Some setup you got here." He hiked his pant legs before he sat down in the recliner next to the bar. Finally, he perched on the edge of his seat, elbows on knees, hands clasped, body tilted forward with authority. "How long you been living out here?"

Emily shrugged. "Few months."

Jody walked into the kitchen from her bedroom and, seeing Emily, clutched her chest. "Holy shit. You about gave me a heart attack." All the softness and pain from earlier in the car was gone. "What are you doing here? I told you to stay at your parents' house."

Jody made no indication that she'd seen Owen as well.

This is my home, Emily wanted to say. Especially after they'd seen the most intimate parts of each other. How close they'd been. Emily had seen it in Jody's eyes. Jody couldn't lie about that. But instead she said, "Owen's here."

Jody flinched at the words. Owen leaned forward from where he was sitting behind the bar, where Jody couldn't see him, and waved.

"Did you let him in?"

Emily had a lowdown feeling that this couldn't go any way but wrong.

"He showed up right when I got here."

Owen gestured to the sofa. "Why don't you have a seat?"

Jody glanced at Emily before plopping down next to her. "Mom isn't here, if you're looking to drag her back to your cave." She tilted her head and gave him a pageant smile.

Owen ignored her comment and surveyed the room. "Doing a little follow-up on Troy."

"Today?" Jody asked. Emily tensed. But Jody bounced one leg off the other. Her house shoe dangled from her big toe. "Shame about him."

Owen's eyebrows shot up. "I wasn't sure you cared."

"Why wouldn't I?" She propped her head on her hand and waited.

"Didn't see you inside the church, only in the parking lot. And neither of you got out of your car at the cemetery."

Emily glanced at Jody. A fresh pain loomed at what had passed between them in the car.

"I'm terrible at funerals. I hate all that crying and carrying on."

Emily could have smacked her. She never knew when to shut up.

"Folks said Troy spent a lot of time out here with you two. Marjorie didn't seem too keen on that."

"No surprise there," Jody said. "But Troy's a big boy and he can make his own decisions."

"I think you mean *was* a big boy."

Jody yawned and picked at her cuticles.

"I got a few questions."

"Such as?" Jody asked.

Emily tightened her arms across her chest. She hadn't noticed how small the room was until then. The walls felt like they were closing in, the ceiling coming down, the air slipping through the cracks.

"Mr. Parnell came in to see me a week or so back. Told me he found some kid messing around with his fertilizer tank. Parnell heard about what happened to Johnston and talked to some other folks out this way who'd noticed some tampering on their tanks, too."

Mr. Parnell. The old man. He had come to the house when Emily was little.

"Heather was talking about that at the prayer circle, right?" Jody popped Emily on the leg. Then, to Owen: "You know Heather, right?"

Owen gave her a tight smile.

Emily pulled on the neck of her shirt to try to ease the tightness. She cleared her throat and pushed down any nerves that might rattle her words. "Yeah. I think so."

"What's this have to do with us?" Jody asked.

He held out his hands as if to present a screen on which they could watch the story unfold. "Troy fashions himself smart 'cause he used to run a field and make a touchdown. He finds these old farmers who rarely leave the house, or are too old to run after him if they do catch him. Based on everything I heard, he was pretty good at it, too. Made off with a lot of juice from tanks around the tri-county area."

Lots of juice. So much money. Emily slowly turned to Jody. She must have known what Troy was up to.

"Troy?" Jody asked. "I find that hard to believe. He's lazy and not that smart."

"That's for sure. Something went wrong out there at Parnell's. And instead of hightailing it out of there, he kept at that tank, even as the ammonia started spraying."

Emily adjusted in her seat. She'd begun to sweat. She sniffled and twisted. Jody looked at her. Emily read that look. It said: *Stop acting weird.* But Emily couldn't beat back the itch that arose in her throat and in her body. She wanted it to stop. But her body felt possessed. She thought she heard a car again. She wanted to look outside, see if another patrol car waited but faced forward.

"Is he sure it was Troy?" Jody asked.

"Parnell might be old, but he's still with it. Used to play football himself back in the day. Gets out to at least every home game, every season. He knows about Drear's Bluff football. And he knows the best player we've had in years when he sees him. So when this happened, instead of calling me, Parnell pulls out his shotgun." Owen laughed. "Gotta love living in the country."

Emily sat on her hands to keep from moving. A force knocked her from the inside, as if it were trying to bust out with the truth or break free and run. With every word Owen uttered, she recalled the sight of Troy running down the drive. The sound of gunshots in her ears. Every nerve thrummed in distress at the remembrance of their flight from the house.

"Parnell shot him?" Jody's head shifted from Owen to Emily then back to Owen.

"He got off a few good rounds. Troy ended up running off down the drive and hopping into some car."

Emily cleared her throat a few times. She felt a strong desire to drop her head between her knees to stop the room from spinning, but she forced herself to focus, sit still, and watch them as if she were an innocent bystander instead of the person who had been in the car with Troy that day.

A line formed between Jody's eyes. "Parnell's okay, I hope."

"Oh, sure. Mostly, he's disappointed he missed his target."

"Wow. I'm glad to hear he's all right," Jody said. She ran her hands over the tops of her thighs. "Thank you for letting us know. God, that's crazy, especially since Troy was someone we used to babysit. I have to say, I would've never believed it about him, but I guess it goes to show that you can never really know someone."

Emily turned toward Jody. The scratch in Emily's throat came on so strong she had to cough. Emily willed it to stop, but it didn't. "Excuse me," she said and got up for a glass of water. She filled her glass and gulped it down, trying to drown the panic.

"What happened between then and when he was found, we're not sure."

"I heard he died of ammonia inhalation," Jody said. "Makes sense given what he was stealing."

"Well," Owen said. "That's where the gossip got it wrong. That ammonia sure as hell didn't help. Without that, he might've been able to get up and out of them woods before that ice storm, but . . ." He clicked his tongue to finish the sentence.

"He died in the woods?" Emily asked and avoided the glare coming her way from Jody, which she could see out of the corner of her eye.

"Afraid so. Exposure."

No. Troy was already dead. That's what Jody had said. He was already dead when she took him to the woods.

Dead. Not alive.

Before Emily could fully process what he'd said, Owen turned to Jody. "You know a little bit about why someone would steal fertilizer."

Jody didn't answer him; she clamped down her jaw.

"Your mom told me about that trouble with Rick." Owen turned to Emily and then back to Jody. "I'm guessing she doesn't know about him."

Rick. Ricky's father. "What about him?" Emily asked.

Jody sat still, staring at the floor. Her eyes shifted between patches of carpet. Owen's look told her everything she needed to know.

Emily wished that she'd not let her anger at her mom get the best of her. She wished that she were sitting at the kitchen table with her parents, mourning Troy like everyone else in Drear's Bluff, instead of standing there wondering how she'd ended up in the middle of a nightmare in which new horrors emerged every time she took a breath.

Jody couldn't have known Troy was still alive. She wouldn't have left him out there.

Owen stood and walked over to stand in front of Jody. "You don't mind if I have a look around, do you?"

"Actually, I do." Jody raised her eyes and stood. "I don't know what you're implying, but I don't like it. And I don't know what's going on, but I know my rights. You're gonna need to come back with a warrant."

"Your approval is a nice-to-have, not a requirement. You don't own the property; your mom does. And she already gave me consent."

Confused, Emily looked from Owen to Jody. "You don't own the land?"

"Under the table and without a lease. You're no more than squatting." He rummaged around in his shirt pocket and pulled out an envelope. He handed it to Jody. "Got your mom's signature in writing in case you wanted to see."

Jody ripped the paper out of his hands but took her time opening it. All the color drained from her face. She opened her mouth but didn't speak.

Emily wanted to pummel her with her fists, force her to admit that she was a terrible person, a terrible friend, a terrible lover to hold onto, not worth the trouble of all those years.

"Your cooperation would be smart," he said.

Jody knitted her eyebrows. "I don't know what Troy was up to. I'm not involved in anything and never was. All you've got is hearsay and small town gossip, whispered to you between the sheets." She smirked and crossed her arms. "I have nothing to hide."

Except everything. Emily's head spun with all the things she thought she knew and all the things she might learn before the nightmare was over.

Owen strode through the hallway and into Ricky's, and then Emily's, bedroom. After that, he wandered through the kitchen and toward Jody's bedroom.

"Be quiet," Jody yelled. "Ricky's sleeping in there."

He eased the door open. Jody followed him. He ended his search by hanging his head out the back door. When he shut it, the chain at the top rattled against the frame.

He pointed down the hill. "I'd like a look inside the chicken house."

Jody glanced in the direction of her bedroom. "I don't have a key. August rents it from me."

August. Not Troy. At this point, the truth was a nice-to-have, but not a requirement, apparently.

"Huh," Owen said. "I wasn't aware of that arrangement."

"Cotton and Grandpa used to raise chickens. August took over for them."

Owen stepped out onto the porch and stood on the railing to look down the hill. "Must be my lucky day, 'cause his truck's there." He jumped down and stood in the doorway. "Thought I heard a car."

Jody chewed the inside of her cheek and picked up her phone. "I'll have him come up to the house."

"No need." Owen snapped and unsnapped the button on his holster. "Let's take a little stroll. See what he's got cooking today."

Emily flinched. The rest of her body remained frozen where she stood. *Please*, she prayed, *please let the lab be gone.*

Owen held the door open. "The chicken house, Jody. If you don't mind. If everything's as you say it is, then you all can go back to this hot little fantasy you got going on out here."

"Hang on," she said. "I need to get the baby monitor."

"Make it quick."

Jody huffed, but then headed to the bedroom. She returned holding it in her raised hand. "Don't shoot. It's just a baby monitor."

He rolled his eyes. "Let's go," he said, and pointed at Emily. "You, too."

They headed out the door and down the steps. The cold wind bit Emily's skin even as the sun broke through the thinning clouds and warmed her head. Near Owen's car, Jody stopped.

"Isn't there some other option?" Jody asked. Her demeanor had changed from angry to calm, and willing to do anything to get her way. Emily had seen it happen so many times and hated her for it.

Owen scanned Jody from top to bottom. "I'm afraid not." He rested his hand on his holster and tilted his head toward Jody, almost as if he had heard her plea and was considering letting her slide, like his daddy had done back in the day. "Let's have a look anyway. Just to check it off the list." He unsnapped the holster and left it that way.

"You so certain you're gonna find something, where's your backup?" Jody asked.

"You telling me I need it?"

"I'm telling you I don't know anything about this," Jody said. "I don't know why you're harassing me over something Troy did."

"Don't worry. You're not the only one who's getting harassed today." He pointed to Emily's car. "The last time someone saw Troy alive, he was speeding away in a car with a description that matches hers. A judge is reviewing paperwork for that as we speak." He motioned them forward. "Let's go."

Emily willed her feet to move, though they felt mired in quicksand. She barely registered the walk down the hill.

Trash bags and closed cardboard boxes had been piled into the back of August's truck. Owen leaned into the truck bed to sniff the air. Then he walked toward the building, his hand gripping his still-holstered gun.

He pushed one of the large metal doors of the chicken house and it creaked open. "You got a light in here?"

"I don't know," Jody said, and didn't bother to help him search for one.

Owen ran his hands along the walls but didn't come across a light switch. He pushed both doors open to let the sun light the building's interior. A few chickens squawked at the interruption and ventured out. This time Emily didn't stop them. Though the doors were open, the back end of the house was still bathed in a dimness Emily remembered too well. She let her eyes adjust to the shapes inside and her nose to the smell.

Jody and Emily stayed near the opening while Owen crossed the length of the chicken house. He raked his hand across one of the wooden nests and pulled on the slats. All of them held sturdy under his hand. He kicked at the baseboards as he went. He walked down the right side of the building. When he reached the end, he circled the narrow space between the nesting boxes and the wall of the egg room on the other side. He rapped his knuckles on the wall, held his ear to it to listen.

Jody shuffled her feet and drew up straw dust. "I think I hear August outside," she yelled to him. Nothing but the chickens stirred as they wandered out of the building and into the sun. Jody eased backward, toward them ever so slightly.

Owen reached the corner, turned, and rested his hand on the doorknob to the lab. "I don't suppose you have a key to this, either."

"It's just an egg room." Jody's voice shook and she took a few more steps back toward the door. "I think I heard August." She spoke louder this time. "He's outside." Jody clutched her forehead like she was trying to squeeze out the answer to a life or death puzzle.

Owen spat at the ground and tapped his gun. He shifted his eyes from Jody to the egg room door. Emily pleaded with God, or whoever would listen, that neither Owen nor August would get a chance to open that door.

"Fuck." Jody blinked repeatedly at the space in front of her.

Emily's head pounded and her throat went dry.

Owen eased away from the egg room door, his face so intense that it terrified Emily. "Whatcha got in there, Jody?"

Drugs. Bottles. Emily's fingerprints. In the room, on the door. Emily could explain how they got there, but she couldn't explain why she hadn't said something sooner. Why she hadn't taken Troy to the hospital. Why Jody hadn't. They should've taken him to the hospital.

"I don't know. I told you August was renting it." Jody didn't take her eyes off Owen. Her hands shook so bad she shoved them in her front jean pockets and then moved them to her back pockets.

Had she known Troy was still alive and left him out there anyway?

Had she gone out there the day of the prayer circle? Was that why she needed to be alone?

Why would she lie?

The urge to let all those words out pushed at Emily, like that feeling she got before she had to puke.

"I drove the car," Emily said. She couldn't tell if she whispered or shouted.

"What'd you just say?" Owen shouted over to them.

"What are you doing?" Jody's nostrils flared and her whole body shook. But her feet kept inching toward the door, the sun. "Stop fucking talking."

The egg room door clicked. Then the knob turned slowly from the other side. Owen pulled his gun and pointed it at the door.

"Sheriff Jenkins, here," he yelled. "Come out slowly. And keep them hands where I can see them."

August stepped out of the room. He wore a pair of gloves and held a cardboard box. A bunch of bottles, glass and plastic, tubes, and the top of a propane tank stuck out of the box. His beloved ball cap covered his head and a bandana covered his mouth. He jerked his head from Owen to Jody and then landed on Emily. His face was obscured by shadows, but the outline of his body was clear. His eyes shined, somehow, in all that darkness.

Emily's heart sank at how close they'd come to getting everything out of the chicken house. For once, Jody hadn't lied. If only they'd had one more day.

Beside her, Jody moved back and back, toward the light coming through the metal door. Without thinking why, Emily followed her lead and took a step backwards as well. Then another, until the sun warmed her back. Owen's focus stayed on August.

"Put the box down. Slowly," Owen said. "And move away from the door."

August lowered the box to the ground and lifted his hands in surrender. Owen reached for his handcuffs and moved closer to August, the gun lowered but still aimed.

August held Emily's stare. For a moment, she thought that she'd seen relief cross his face. His whole body seemed to relax.

And she understood: No more hiding. No more wondering whether someone would find out. *We can tell the truth.* She hoped that he would know it in his heart. They could all tell the truth, or the closest thing they knew to the truth. Finally, one choice instead of a multitude. None right, but at least the wondering would be gone.

They could survive this. Maybe not unscathed for their omissions, but at least they—Emily—could let all the dread loose from their shoulders and let it slip down into the tide of memories about this year, this terrible, terrible year.

A sudden movement at Emily's side caught her attention. Jody shifted her arm up and pointed a pistol. *No, no, no.* The words caught in her throat and everything slowed. She stared at the gun, as if it might be fake, instead of the thing that Emily had seen in her purse on a day that seemed far in the past now.

"Oh my God," she whispered.

August yelled over at them, "Whoa! Hold up! Hold up!"

Owen swung his gun toward Emily and Jody where they stood at the door. Jody and Owen locked aim on each other.

"Put the gun down, Jody," Owen yelled. "You're just scared. I understand that." He glanced back at August, who hadn't moved and still had his hands in the air, then returned his attention to Jody. "Let's put the guns down and talk. I'm sure there's an explanation. Why don't you just put the gun down first?"

Emily shifted her eyes toward Owen, August, then Jody, afraid to move for fear that she might set someone off. She felt devoid of a pulse, empty of blood, floating above them all as they waited, guns trained on each other.

Jody's mouth moved. Emily could barely make out the words and wasn't even sure what she heard. But Jody's stance never changed. She never took her eyes off August.

"Don't do anything stupid, Jody," Owen said. "Think about that little boy of yours."

Emily shifted her attention between Jody and Owen, and then glanced at August. Behind the bandana, his eyes came alive and wide at the same moment that Emily caught another movement from the corner of her eye, from Jody, who no longer had the gun pointed at Owen, but toward August. And then down to the box.

August lowered his hands and then waved them in front of him. "No!" he screamed.

CHAPTER EIGHTEEN

A BLAST EXPLODED IN EMILY'S ears and knocked her off her feet and onto her back, far outside the building. Something hard smashed into her eye. Tiny objects pelted her skin, followed by stinging air so hot she thought her skin and muscle would melt off her bones. Her vision blurred and every part of her body needled with pain. A deep ringing stuffed her ears. She coughed to release the swelling itch that rose higher and higher in her lungs. She couldn't see, couldn't breathe. Frantic, she struggled to find something solid to hold onto. She dug her fingers into the dirt to move away from the heat.

Someone's hands grasped at her legs, ran over her jeans, her shirt, her head. They circled her wrists and dragged her over the hard ground, nearly lifting her joints out of their sockets. When the motion stopped, she slumped onto the ground and coughed until she thought she'd see blood. When the fit subsided, she jerked upright.

For a moment she didn't know where she was. Then she remembered. Owen. August. Jody. The sound of gunshot, again. She looked around.

Her vision seemed half what it had been and her eye pulsed. A plume of black smoke rose above the line of trees. Ice dust glittered like raindrops in the crackling light of the fire. The smell that Emily had tried to avoid by covering her face when walking in the chicken house was in her face now, infiltrating her hair. Only, a sting had been added to the mixture. She drew her shirt up over her nose.

She placed a hand to her eye and her senses reported back the feeling of something small, hard, and foreign, the surrounding terrain gooey, wet. Blood ran down her fingers when she pulled them away. She couldn't see out of her right eye. She panicked and turned her head side to side to survey her surroundings.

Jody stood next to her, watching the building burn, mouth wide open. Her face was covered in patches of blood and black smears.

All that time, deep down, in that place that had prevented Emily from seeing Jody with any flaws, she'd known the truth but refused to believe it until now. Until she saw, without question, that Jody was willing to burn down everything and everyone to save her own skin.

The lies Jody told? Those weren't uttered to protect Emily. They protected no one but Jody.

"You blew up the building," Emily said, shocked. Jody didn't move her gaze away from the fire. "Why would you do that? They were in there!" She screamed. "They were right there! And now . . ." Owen. August. Gone. There's no way they could have survived.

Jody's eyes broke their hold on the building. She ran her tongue across her chapped lips. Then she spit to the side and wiped her mouth with her sleeve before she knelt down, placing her head in between her legs and staring at the ground, where patches of winter brown had replaced the summer green. Her shirt pulled tight against her back, the gun gone.

"I had to," Jody said.

Emily could barely hear Jody's voice above the ringing in her ears and the throbbing pain at her eye socket. "No, you didn't. You didn't have to. We could have told him the truth. I would have told him." Her voice rose higher and higher as she spoke.

Jody lifted her head, chin pointed upwards, and pushed out a breath. "You think he would've believed you?" Emily focused on the words as they came out of Jody's mouth. "Our fingerprints were all over it. August. You." She paused. "There was no other way. I didn't have a choice."

There was another way. Telling the truth. Facing the consequences. Not blowing up a building with people inside.

"People are gonna be here soon. If they didn't hear the blast, they'll see the sky." Jody looked up. "Just tell them the truth about that day with Troy, at Parnell's. You didn't know what he was doing. That's the truth." Jody's voice grew quiet but sounded like a plea. "I'll tell them you were sick, and I took care of you. I'll tell them that it was all August and Troy. And that August must have taken Troy to the woods. But don't tell them we knew about the lab. I just rented out the building to August. Everyone knows that."

Owen hadn't known about the rental. He'd said that. "I thought you said you rented to Troy."

"I couldn't say I rented it out to a dead kid."

A dead kid. He no longer had a name. "Owen wasn't going to shoot you."

Jody pointed at her. "Don't mention the fucking lab, okay?" The first part of the sentence came out calm and then crescendoed into hysteria. Jody swiped her hands back and forth across her jeans. "We'll tell them that Owen came over." She pulled her shirt up and wiped her face several times with the inside. "We went to the chicken house and August was in there. We can tell them that he took my

gun from the house. Owen and August shot at each other and everything just exploded. Meth labs explode all the time. They'll believe
that. August and Troy were in on it. Not us. Except you have to tell
them about what happened with Parnell. Tell them you were scared
and that's why you didn't come forward. That's it. That's all you have
to say."

Emily's eye throbbed and the smoke burned her throat. The
words Jody had said jumbled in Emily's mind.

Jody searched the ground and scrambled to get to her gun, which
lay near August's truck. She wiped the gun with the bottom of her
shirt and threw it into the fire. The flames still crackled and burned
behind Jody as she walked closer to Emily.

She squinted up at Jody and swallowed again and again to try to
bring moisture to her raw throat.

She'd been willing to wait and see if Jody's affections took a turn.
She'd been willing to pretend that she didn't know what was going
on in the chicken house. But to disregard two more lives after letting Troy die alone in the woods? All to save herself? There was no
other explanation. There was no other reason why Jody wasn't more
worried. Why she hadn't searched for Troy. Why she didn't get rid
of the lab.

That day in the car, Troy had gotten that look when Emily had
asked what *he* had going on in the chicken house. He'd been incredulous. And now she was.

"It was yours, wasn't it? All of this."

Jody kneeled in front of her and moved Emily's hair out of her
face. "Calm down."

"You lied about that, too."

Jody blinked. "No. It wasn't a lie." The words so measured, so
clear.

KELLY J. FORD

Part of the building collapsed and more smoke roared into the sky. If the neighbors had not heard the first explosion or had thought it was a random event, they would surely hear this one and arrive to find them bloodied and alone with a cop car and Owen nowhere in sight.

"You knew Troy wasn't dead. You could have helped him but you dumped him there anyway. Why? Because he might've told someone who all this really belongs to? Someone who knows a bit about stealing fertilizer? Isn't that what Owen said? It was you, wasn't it?"

"You don't know what you're saying."

The hard ground scraped at Emily's palms when she reached behind her and scooted away from the fire, away from Jody. "I'm not in shock. You can't trick me this time."

In the distance, a siren screamed.

Jody narrowed the space between them and took hold of Emily's jaw. "I know this is hard, and I know you're hurt, but you have to focus. Okay? I need you to focus here or we are going to be in some serious fucking shit. Do you hear me? They're going to ask what happened and you need to tell them that when Owen found the lab, August had a gun. They fired at each other. Then the lab exploded. They started shooting, and it exploded."

No. Emily knew what had happened. She had seen the gun in Jody's hands. Watched her aim at Owen, then August, and then lower it to the ground, toward the box, the propane.

Jody's fingers clenched Emily's jaw tighter. There was no warmth in her eyes. A stranger stood before her, one who would do anything to get her to shut up, the same way she'd shut up the others. Terror flooded Emily.

She turned over onto her stomach and clambered to her knees to get away. She didn't get far. Jody grabbed her ankles and yanked them so hard that Emily's chin hit the ground and she heard and felt a crack. Her teeth rattled from the pain. Jody's knees landed on Emily's calves and then pressed into her back.

Jody's breath pressed hot on her neck, in her ear. "Listen to me."

Emily tried to lift her head, but pain ricocheted through her neck. Pebbles crushed into her cheek. "No." The word escaped as a whimper.

"Listen to me." Jody clutched Emily's arms and twisted her until Emily turned over and Jody straddled her. Her hair hung down in black strings. Some pieces stuck to her damp neck. Her skin, once beautiful, smooth, and soft, was now pocked with red patches along her jaw. Oil shone on her nose and forehead. Emily turned her head to the side. She didn't want to see the face of the person she had loved become the person that she feared.

"Emily, listen to me." Jody ran her hands along Emily's face. She wiped the warm blood that trickled from her swollen eye down her temple and into her ear. "Emily. You're in shock."

"No." Emily tried to shift away from her. Jody's lips landed on her face, her lips. Emily tried to buck Jody off her, but the more she struggled, the harder Jody pressed Emily's shoulders to the ground, her thin body belying its strength.

"It was never Troy's. It was yours." Emily pushed her body up and nearly knocked Jody off. But Jody flattened Emily's shoulders with her knees.

"Stop it," Jody said. "Stop fighting me."

"You knew he wasn't dead!" Emily fought harder and kicked her legs, but her strength collapsed underneath the pressure of Jody's body and the pressure that built inside her. Her breath came out in gasps. "You left him out there to die! And then . . ." She couldn't believe it, even as she said it. "They're dead because of you!"

269

A rumble of car engines joined the siren.

Jody clamped her hand on Emily's jaw. "I thought he was dead. I swear. I thought he was dead! Owen came for you, Emily. Do you understand me? Parnell saw you in the car with Troy." Panic seeped into Jody's voice. "Owen thought you were involved. That's why he came here. You heard him. He was talking to a judge."

"I don't care," Emily cried through her gritted teeth. Pain shot through her head. The cold rocked her core and shook her body. "Get off me."

Jody brushed the hair away from Emily's face. As the roar of vehicles grew closer, her eyes grew wider. "This is the only way. Otherwise, that's it. They'll convict you." She held Emily's face between her hands, moved it so that Emily's eyes were aligned with hers. "Tell them that August shot at Owen. Tell them that it was August's and that we had no idea. I'm trying to protect you! Don't you see?"

Emily moved her head back and forth to try to remove Jody's grip on her face. Rocks banged on the undersides of cars as they raced up the drive. Engines sounded their arrival.

"We can be free of all of this. You can have everything you've ever wanted. I will do anything for you if you do this for me."

It was only ever for Jody, no matter who got hurt, who died. Troy. Owen. August.

Two old women jumped out of their cars and gasped at the building, their hands shielding their eyes from the blaze.

"Please, Emily. Just tell them it was an accident. Please." Jody dropped her forehead onto Emily's so hard that Emily saw stars. She dug her fingers into Emily's hair. Kissed her mouth, her cheeks, her chin, her neck. "I love you," she said as the blood from Emily's face smeared on her lips.

More people appeared. Neighbors came out of the wood-
work at the commotion. Sirens grew louder. People clustered in
groups.

Volunteer firefighters in thick black coats began frantically pulling the fire hose off the truck while others ran over to where Jody
pinned Emily on the ground. People yelled out to them. Someone said something about blood. Jody clenched Emily's arms and
squeezed so hard it burned. Someone clutched Jody and pulled her
off Emily. Jody yanked herself free and grabbed Emily's arms, legs,
whatever body part she could cling to.

"Please," she screamed, even though she was inches away. "Please
don't do this. Please don't leave me. Don't let them take my baby
from me."

A pocket of air finally lifted out of Emily's lungs. She blinked up
at Jody. A man stood over them. He waved someone over, yelled. He
crouched down next to Emily. She turned but couldn't hear any of his
words. His mouth seemed to move in slow motion.

Though it hurt like hell, she managed to get onto her knees. She
shoved Jody's hands away. "You knew what would happen. You killed
August," Emily whispered. "Owen. You did that."

"No!" Jody screamed. The man who'd crouched next to her pulled
Jody off her, but she came back at Emily. Another man came over
and then another. Each time, Jody yanked herself free.

People surrounded them, watching.

"You killed them," Emily said. Someone held her under the arms
and helped her onto her feet. "You killed them."

Jody slammed a fist into her. The knock took Emily's breath away.
Two men held Jody back again. Rage swarmed in her eyes and face.

Emily's head felt heavy, her eye pulsed. "You knew everything."
Emily choked out the words. She couldn't believe them. But they

were true. They were true and she couldn't stop them from coming. "You lied. About everything. The lab. The land. The drugs. About Troy," she screamed. "August. Me. You lied to me. You knew exactly what happened to Troy. What happened to me that day. But you lied. About everything." Screams and tears and snot overtook her. "You only wanted to keep me quiet." And then . . . what she had known. What she had feared. The pain of it sunk her lower than she'd ever been. "You only fucked me to keep me quiet."

Jody dug her heels into the ground. She twisted and turned, trying to release herself from the men's grip, screaming the whole time.

"You fucking liar! Shut your mouth!" Jody yelled. "You shut your mouth!" She kicked and bucked to try to get out of the men's hold. She managed to kick Emily in the shin so hard stars returned to stunt her vision.

But Emily didn't move. She stood there. Ready to take whatever Jody wanted to give her. She could take it. She could take anything now.

They were face to face again. Emily would never forget the face of such rage. Such hurt. Such evil. "I never loved you, you fucking dyke," Jody whispered.

Everything around Emily fell away. The crackle of the fire. Another siren in the distance. Their neighbors' voices, full of alarm and curiosity. Trickles of blood that snaked down her skin. The light and heat, all of it gone, until there was only Emily and Jody, facing each other. Their bodies, so recently vibrating with desire and rage and hurt, had settled. Every sense receded as if they were once again alone in the middle of those quiet, dark woods. For the first time in so long, her body felt still, light. Then an ache no bigger than a marble pulsed inside Emily, an ache born in the woods across the creek. An ache that beat on inside her, steady, steadier, growing until her whole body shook. Jody stood still in front of her, even as Emily shook, even as her tears muddied her vision. As gently as her senses had faded, they came back violently. A cacophony of alarms from vehicles and people, bright hunting jackets amid dull wood and grass, the sting of chemicals and burnt wood in her nose and the pain in her eye. And Jody in front of her, pulsing with rage. What she'd said fresh on her lips, the spit still hanging off her last word.

Jody had never loved her.

"I know," Emily said.

Jody's eyes glossed over. Her mouth opened for speech but nothing came. Then Jody's long black hair slashed Emily's face when she lashed her head side to side and flailed her body wildly, as she tried and failed to release herself from the men's grip.

Jody screamed incoherently as the men dragged her to Owen's patrol car. She placed her feet against the doorframe and resisted being pushed inside. One of them yanked her by the hair. Her body slumped against the back seat, hands in front of her face. Sobs wracked her body until she leaned sideways, slipped down, and disappeared into the seat, leaving the screen that separated the back seat from the front as the only thing visible.

Cars began to jam up the yard, everywhere, with no regard for the grass. More and more of their neighbors appeared like they'd been lured with a song. No one seemed to notice Emily, with everything else there was to see. Her body ached. Her head—her heart— was numb. And everywhere Emily looked, there were feathers. Some had already landed on the ground and been picked up by the bottoms of the shoes of people who had gathered there to see what was going on. In front of her, a feather lingered in the air, held there by the shifting wind that carried fumes across the property and covered the sky like a cloud.

Amid the chaos around her, Emily collapsed to the ground. She stretched her limbs out wide on the grass. Soon the cold, wet ground found its way through her clothing and to her skin. Rocks scratched at her scalp.

Patches of smoke passed above her. One feather fell onto her chest, another onto her cheek. The sun peeked out from behind a cloud. Ash and debris kissed her skin and she waited for whatever would come.

EPILOGUE

THOUGH IT WAS NOT YET six o'clock, night covered the fields along the highway. Frost formations and fog threatened the windshield no matter how high Emily cranked the heater. Nothing appeared in the rearview mirror but the faint glow of her own taillights. She wondered if one day she would feel like a normal person, one who didn't peer over their shoulder to see if today would be the day Owen—no, she told herself, the new sheriff—pulled up to arrest her after all.

It'd been two years since the explosion. Some days she felt that she had recovered from the horror that had been her life. Whenever that happened, she forced herself to remember Troy's eyes as they bled from the inside, the force with which he had gripped her hand. The look on August's face before the explosion.

When she arrived at her parents' house, the kitchen lights were off. Only the living room lights shone. The night birds and the stars held everything in suspension. Instead of heading through the kitchen as usual, she gripped the handle of her overnight bag and veered toward the front door instead. She didn't know if her parents had removed one of the concrete circles on the path to the kitchen.

The stone with Jody's name would be unignorable, whether they had removed it or not. At the front door, she steeled herself and turned the knob.

The warm glow of table lamps lit the room while the hallway and corners remained in shadows and quiet. Like those summer days growing up, when her mom had babysat kids from church, toys littered the carpet. The difference was that these toys belonged to Ricky, who now slept upstairs in Jody's old bedroom. After Connie had declined to take the boy, her parents had petitioned the court. For now, he was a foster. Who knew where he would end up. She hoped that he could stay.

According to her mom's texts, he'd developed into a bright, chattering child full of energy, barely aware of that woman he had called Momma. Not at all aware of Connie, who'd disappeared after the explosion and had yet to return. Now, when Emily's mom texted, Emily learned about dinosaurs and Legos and how exhausting it was to raise a kid at her parents' age, boring life details that had overtaken her mom's old refrains of gossip just like the soiled dirt and weeds had begun to pull down what little remained of the charred chicken house.

Her dad sat in the recliner in front of the muted TV, flipped through the *TV Guide*, and munched on a bowl of potato chips. He lifted his eyes and smiled when she walked in.

"Thought I heard your car." He gripped the armrests of his recliner and pushed the footrest down, groaning when he lifted his sturdy frame out of the recesses of the seat and trudged over to give Emily a hug. "You just here for the night?" he asked.

"Yeah." She avoided looking at him, not wanting to see his disappointment. Though she didn't think she deserved it, her parents tried to shield her from how their lives had changed. They'd found a new church in Fort Smith. They said they preferred the new style. Rock bands and big ceilings. She accepted the lie. It was easier than feeling the weight of all that truth and the burden of her guilt. "I have to get up early and be back in Little Rock for work."

"Maybe next time."

She nodded. "Mom in the kitchen?"

"Yep." He returned to his chair, grabbed the clicker, and pointed it at the TV. Cheers from an audience overwhelmed the room.

Before, the living room had hosted women and party food and prayers on Friday nights. Now: her dad and salt and sadness.

When she turned to leave, he lowered the volume again. "It's good to have you home," he said. The skin around his eyes crinkled when he smiled. "Don't be a stranger, kid."

For so long, she'd sought solace from him. In his eyes and his arms, she'd felt moored. She still did. But now, she noticed the little details that age had wrought on his face. Most of all, she noticed the glimmer of gray that had begun to speckle what was once a thick mass of hair. She didn't like these new details, this growing sense that everyone had aged and that she had been responsible for much of it.

After the sentencing she'd returned to Little Rock, back to being anonymous, with the money she'd saved from babysitting. Blood money, Emily considered it. But she couldn't bear to stay in Drear's Bluff longer than necessary. She didn't want her parents to have the added burden of harboring her. Being associated with cop killers didn't go over well in these parts. But the judge had been right. She had aided; she had abetted—if not in the death, at least in her knowledge of the lab. If she had said something, Troy, Owen, and August would still be alive and she wouldn't be confined to the great state of Arkansas for the foreseeable future.

Emily walked over, leaned down, and kissed him on the top of his head where the gray shimmered in the lamplight. She couldn't remember the last time that she had done that, and she was grateful for the moment, fleeting as it was. She wanted to run her fingers along the gray to be sure that it wasn't some trick of light. He kissed the back of her hand and squeezed it once more before letting it drop. Seemingly satisfied, he let his eyes travel back to the TV.

Only the light above the stove lit the kitchen. Her mom seemed no more than a shadow. When Emily walked closer, her mom placed a bowl in the dishwasher and shut the door.

"I wasn't sure you were coming," she said. "You shouldn't be driving this late in your condition."

That's how her mom referred to Emily's eye. She would let her have that. It seemed easier for her mom to pretend that something else, something internal, had required a glass eye instead of a small shard of metal from the blast that had rendered it useless.

She flashed Emily a quick smile. Then she dropped her gaze and wiped her hands on a dishtowel. She walked over to the coffee pot and poured the morning's coffee into a cup and placed the cup into the microwave. After punching in the time, she watched the cup circle the space until the microwave beeped. She retrieved her coffee and took it to the table, where she turned on the small lamp and sat down.

Emily followed. Cold filtered in from the window's thin pane of glass and chilled Emily's side. She crossed her arms and hugged herself close in an attempt to stay warm. Outside, only shades of darkness separated the fields from the grass, even though the moon hung high that night. No city lights diffused the dark. Around them only nature and whatever wild things Emily's imagination had conjured in times past. Now, when Emily's mind wandered, as it often did, it was to August. All those stages of grief came and went, sure as the tides. She would settle into forgetfulness, and then an unbidden memory would plunge her into a depressive state.

Her mom looked out the window as well. Her head rested on her chin, a position more relaxed than Emily was used to seeing. She looked almost dreamy, as if she were now contemplating more than her immediate surroundings. Maybe she always had and Emily had never noticed, had never asked. Her eyes drifted off into the distance. She sipped her coffee and Emily ached at the absence of words between them when once it was the thing she had longed for.

When her mom paused, she knew it was her place in the conversation to say something nice. All she could do was sit there. She watched her mother's reflection in the glass, not wanting to look at her directly. Lines ran along the side of her mom's hands, lines Emily hadn't noticed before. No matter how hard she tried, her mom's shoulders eased up toward her ears. The fabric between the buttons on her shirt gaped open when she forgot her posture and allowed herself to slump.

"You look good," her mom said, and tried to smile. "How's work going?"

In the past Emily had braced herself for such questions, wondering at their intention. But since the explosion, there was no longer a reason. She'd already done everything she could to break her mom's heart and soil her reputation in town. A lack of jail time in exchange for testifying against Jody hadn't erased the outcome. And even though Emily felt more trapped now than she ever had living in Drear's Bluff, she worked at gratitude as if she were a piece of wood that would one day be whittled into the shape of something better than she had been. "It's fine. They might let me work the register soon."

Her mom looked pained, but she smiled and nodded. "That's wonderful." Her eyes drifted out the window and off into the distance again. "It's good to have somewhere to go every day. Keeps your mind from wandering."

While her mom examined the darkness outside, Emily ran a fingernail up and down a crack in the table from beginning to end. She'd cried too many times in the past couple of years for anything to come now. The well of sorrow was dry, but she still felt raw. No amount of church could fix her sin. No one could come along to erase her memory. Not even the sweet girl who waited for her text to let her know that she'd gotten home safe.

Emily recalled the way her new girlfriend's hand had draped over the curve between her rib and hip that morning. They'd been seeing each other for a few weeks now and had settled into a routine of phone calls, nervous dates, tentative kisses, and more—a routine Emily enjoyed. A routine she feared. A routine that kept her cautious, waiting for the thing that could destroy it, or her.

All that she could hope for was to be happy, in the moment.

"I made the bed in the spare room. What time are visiting hours tomorrow?"

"It's about an hour and a half drive, so I'll probably leave here around seven." She didn't need to be there until eleven. "Thanks for letting me stay."

"Of course. It's a long drive from Little Rock," her mom said. "Shame you won't be able to see Ricky, though." Emily had only visited twice before. When she did, she came after his bedtime and left before he awakened. She didn't want to see any similarities or mannerisms. She didn't want any reminders of the past.

Her mom reached across the table but stopped short of placing her hands on Emily's. In the past, she would have—not to comfort but to still Emily's hands from creating a wider crack in the table. Change wasn't a once-in-a-lifetime event. Change happened every day. But here she was in the thick of it. And she was grateful in that moment and stopped picking at the crevice.

Her mom stood up and placed her empty cup into the sink, turned off the stove light, and walked over to where Emily sat contemplating the crack in the table. Her mom drew her hand across Emily's hair. "Be careful tomorrow."

Anyone watching them from the shadows might have believed the words were meant for the drive ahead of her. But Emily knew that the words were directed at her heart.

EMILY HAD LOST WEIGHT AND had to hike her pants after the officer patted her down. She hadn't worn a belt because of the metal detectors. But she still had to walk through several times before she got every piece of change and metal off her body. After she had successfully navigated that barrier, a green light flicked on and a buzzer signaled the opening of a door. The sound jolted her with its reminder of the months she'd spent in county waiting for her testimony, and the trial, to end.

Through the crisscrossed wire plated over with glass, Emily could see down the long white hallway. Other visitors walked beside her. Emily felt the edges of the envelope in her pocket. She rubbed her fingers along the corners like it was a talisman. Errant children pushed past Emily in a foot race toward a door at the end. A smaller girl fell behind two older boys. For a moment, Emily allowed her thoughts to drift to who they'd come to see and why that person was here.

Her therapist said it might help with forgiveness, if not forgetting. She could never forget. She didn't deserve that. And though forgiveness sounded good, that wasn't something she could grant herself, or Jody either, and that wasn't why she had come.

She had not seen Jody since the trial. In the courtroom she'd avoided looking at her. She refused to say her name except when compelled by the court. In her mind, she had buried her.

But like a drug, the cravings returned. Those old fantasies she'd entertained haunted her, left her crying on the floor, her eyes puffy with exertion. Even with all that had passed between them, her mind wandered to Jody and what might have been. How one event could have changed things. If she'd done this instead of that, people would be alive. Jody would be free. Emily would be with her. Slowly, and with the right people and prescriptions, the longing that had consumed her began to lift and life normalized in a way that she hadn't thought possible the day she was put in the back of a cruiser. She eased into each new day, willing herself not to fall into despair, not to let her depression strangle her again. Things were not great, and she wasn't sure they ever could be. But they were good. Good enough that she could balance her gratitude at having been saved too much pain and guilt, at having not felt enough pain. Then Jody's letter had arrived.

She had ignored the first one and the ones that followed. She had thrown them out. But one day, she opened a new letter that had come. The pages shook in her hand.

Emily had thought she was fine. She needed to know she was.

She waited outside the visiting room, sheltered behind a window. In there, the kids continued to chase each other and knock the metal chairs on the ground, scraping the floor. Emily glanced around the room and made a game of deciding relationships. Most of the visitors were women. Some were mothers, others were sisters. Some were friends. Many might be lovers. She wondered what the lovers might think of their girlfriends being surrounded by other women all day long, stuck in a small cell or a hallway or an exercise yard. If they worried about fidelity, even if the infidelity might be the only thing that kept their lovers from tying a shoestring around their necks and hanging themselves from the window bars.

She wondered if Jody had taken a lover.

Then: Perhaps it was too soon. Perhaps she wasn't ready to see her.

Another buzzer sounded and then a lock clicked. Behind the door, women in orange jumpsuits blended into the visiting room. Some stood on their tiptoes to see past the crowd of other inmates and then hurried over into waiting arms when they were spotted.

Jody was the last to enter the room. She wore her hair pulled back. The natural curves of her body had returned, the softness, the blush in her skin. Jody had always looked best without makeup, in plain clothes, with her eyes, her hair, that devastating smile. Prison had done none of the other women the same favor. Prison, if possible, had made her lovely again.

Jody glanced around the room, not seeing Emily at the window, and sat down as if her bones ached. She folded her hands on the table. Moved her hands to her lap. Chewed on her bottom lip, picked at her nails, and dropped them back into her lap. It had to be hard for her to sit still, to be caged.

There was a time, after Jody's sentencing and Emily's release, when all the local cameras and headlines and people with their opinions and hatred and all the gossip had slipped away. Emily had daydreamed about what Jody might be enduring while she ate a supper of her own choosing or licked an ice cream cone or watched a movie. Then guilt at her own freedom would set in, leaving her ashamed.

Jody shifted and made invisible circles with her finger on the tabletop. She looked up and finally noticed Emily standing outside the visiting room in the hallway, staring at her through the window.

For two years, she had waited. Two long years, she had wondered if a night would come without Jody in her thoughts. If she could handle the sight of her nearby without wanting to rush toward her, to weasel her way under her skin and into her heart. Even with all that she knew about Jody now—all the lies, the ugly truths—she didn't know if she could ever truly let go.

But as they stared at one another the stranglehold of desire, once so tight that she'd discarded all reason, lessened. Desire, her constant companion, slept.

Even from the short distance and with only one good eye, Emily saw the rims of Jody's eyes grow glassy. She thought she detected a lone tear making its way down the line of Jody's jaw. That's what she chose to believe as she walked away from the window, away from Jody.

The soles of her shoes squeaked along the hallway. One last time, she brushed the edges of the envelope in her pocket. The envelope held a picture. The picture held a moment of her and Jody from the state fair, the photo she'd always loved, their arms slung around each other's shoulders, their grins wide and sticky from cotton candy. Much like the photograph, over time Emily would come to appreciate the moment outside the visiting room, when their hearts were not hard and guarded, but safely partitioned from the world that awaited them, from each other. As she left the prison, she pulled the collar up on her coat and inhaled the crisp morning air before stealing one last look at the photo and dropping it to the ground.

ACKNOWLEDGMENTS

THIS BOOK WOULDN'T BE WHAT it is without the support and enthusiasm of two amazing women. Thank you to my incredible agent Patricia Nelson, who believed in my book and me—especially through my rough patches—and whose wit, guidance, and humor are a true gift. And I am indebted to my editor Chelsey Emmelhainz for her intelligence, insight, and the continual push to make the characters and the story stronger. You have made me a better, more thoughtful writer. Thanks also to the entire team working behind the scenes at Skyhorse Publishing, especially Matt Lehman, Jessica Moss, Jordan Koluch, and Bri Scharfenberg.

My gratitude to Eve Bridburg and everyone at GrubStreet for cultivating a supportive and welcoming space for writers in Boston. Thank you to everyone in the Novel Incubator community, especially my classmates: Belle Brett, Amber Elias, Jack Ferris, Marc Foster, E.B. Moore, R.J. Taylor, and Rob Wilstein, with extended and heartfelt thanks to Emily Ross for the debut author support you've shown me and for several sanity reads, and to my dear friend Jennie Wood for being hardcore and encouraging me to be and do more.

285

My affection and appreciation go out to Michelle Hoover and Lisa Borders for their instruction, the friendship that formed from the class, and for their continual attagirls and consultations on life and writing.

Thanks also to the following people for their generous feedback on drafts along the way: John Boveri, Louise Miller, Kelly Robertson, and Elizabeth Shelburne.

For kind words and encouragement at important stages in the development of this book and my confidence as a writer: my first GrubStreet instructors, James Scott and Adam Stumacher; my Sewanee instructors and fellows, Steve Yarbrough, Diane Johnson, Joanna Rakoff, and Jamie Quatro; my Sewanee confidants, Kimberly Elkins and Kerri Quinn. I hope to be as gracious and supportive to unpublished writers as you all were to me.

To Jay and Boog Welsh for the long conversations in Conway that you didn't realize helped bring this story to life. To my aunt Judy Smith for the same.

To my longtime friends for all the laughs, love, and food fests after all these years: Greg Adams, Janet Reindl Edgar, Jenna Mayo-McAuley, Cindy Nguyen, Brian Olson, Christel Shea, the aforementioned Jay Welsh, and Barbara Kyriakidis Zeppieri.

To my dad, Glen Ford: my first and favorite storyteller. I love you, old man.

No one deserves more thanks than my first and final reader, who never falters in her belief in me and my stories, and who has read more drafts than any person should. My deepest gratitude and the highest of fives to my best friend and beloved wife, Sarah Pruski.